DEPRAVED
TRUTHS

EMMY WADE

Book Cover by Artscandare Design

Editor: Samantha Swart

Proofreader: Jan Hurst

Paperback ISBN: 979-8-9986002-03

Contents

This one is for the good girls still waiting
for someone to embrace their dark side.
Here's hoping you find your very own Eli.

DEPRAVED
TRUTHS

Trigger Warnings

Serial/vigilante killing

Graphic language

Graphic sexual situations

Death of a child (not on page)

Arson

Sodomy (not involving main characters)

Traumatic water events

Rape (not on page)

Interactions with rapist

Child assault (not on page)

Drug paraphernalia

Drug and Alcohol use

Medical supplies/needles/hospital setting

Overdose

Domestic abusive relationship

miscarriage

Psychological and physical torture

Narcissistic manipulation

Torture of a child (revealed during a news broadcast)

Human trafficking

Genital mutilation

DEPRAVED
TRUTHS
PLAYLIST

Inside by Chris Avantgarde, Red Rosamond

Animal by AG, MOONZz

Don't Fear the Reaper by The Spiritual Machines

Crazy by 2WEI, Marvin Brooks

Somewhere I Belong by Linkin Park

I See Red by Everybody Loves an Outlaw

Driven Under by Seether

Water's Edge by Seven Mary Three

In the Air Tonight by Natalie Taylor

Beautiful Things by Benson Boone

I Need You by Jelly Roll

Simple Man by Lynyrd Skynyrd

The Devil Wears Lace by Steven Rodriguez

Trouble by Camylio

History of Violence by Theory of a Deadman

Pretty Little Poison by Warren Zeiders

Scars by Papa Roach

Send the Pain Below by Chevelle

Enter Sandman by Metallica

Down the River by Chris Knight

Send the Pain Below by Stone Sour

Sin So Sweet by Warren Zeiders

Wicked Games by Stone Sour

Cold by Crossfade

45 by Shinedown

Always by Saliva

Face Down by the Red Jumpsuit Apparatus

My Hero by Foo Fighters

AND AS IS WITH WHITE ROSES, YOU
CAN SEE THE PURITY THEY
REPRESENT, EVEN WHEN THEY
HAVE THORNS TO SHOW FOR IT.
YOU KNOW THERE'S SOME KIND OF
INNOCENCE WORTH PROTECTING.

-AUTHOR UNKNOWN

PROLOGUE

He will never see it coming.

But then again, they never do. They believe they can get away with the most depraved acts imaginable, without any consequences. From the moment we're born, we're gifted with an innate sense of morality. A moral compass, designed to ensure we adhere to basic standards of decency. But there are those who choose not to follow that righteous compass. They stray down paths that, as a society, we cannot and should not accept. And when the legal system fails to deliver justice, I am here to make sure that innocent victims are vindicated.

One monster at a time.

The monster I'm hunting resides in a grand mansion sitting at the top of the hill surrounded by a sprawling fifty-acres. Its sharp, angular design is a statement of power and wealth. The stone facade, a flawless blend of polished limestone and dark granite, shines brightly under the setting sun—too pristine, too perfect. The mansion's immaculate appearance hides the rot beneath the surface, its cold opulence a mask for the evil it harbors within its gleaming walls. Everyone believes he's one of the good guys, highly respected for his charitable contributions to the community and his picture-perfect family. A family that has no idea of the sick, vile things he does behind closed doors.

But, I know.

And soon, the world will too.

The fury inside me burns with the damning knowledge of his twisted acts, fueling my rage at their blissful ignorance.

I wonder if he'd still recognize me. A smirk tugs at the corners of my lips. It's been almost sixteen years since he last saw me. The night my soul was shattered and broken.

Stepping out of the car, anticipation bubbles within, and a cold smile spreads across my face as I head up the driveway toward the estate. The time has come for this monster's depraved truths to be exposed.

Chapter 1

Tessa

Present Day

"**N**o, stop!"

I jolt awake, my body trembling as the same nightmare that haunts me nearly every night since I was twelve fades into the shadows of my mind. A soft whimper escapes my lips, and I press a shaky hand to my forehead, damp with sweat. Reaching under my pillow, my fingers brush against the reassuring cold steel of the knife I keep close, just in case.

The clock blinks 4:15 a.m. I reach for my phone on the nightstand, already knowing what I'll find, yet I scroll through the security footage anyway—empty, as always. But the habit lingers, the need to check, to reassure myself that I'm truly alone. The cameras are the only eyes watching me in the dark.

I take a deep breath, forcing the remnants of the nightmare to slip away. I remind myself that, despite the shadows that seem to lurk in every corner of my mind, I'm safe here. Safe in Lake Falls, in my bedroom overlooking the tranquil shores of Lake Lucia. Safe from the hell I left behind in Atlanta.

Sighing, I push the last threads of the nightmare further from my mind. It's futile to try and sleep now. Instead, I scroll aimlessly through my phone before tapping the app that triggers my coffee maker. I may as well channel my restless energy into the one thing that consistently controls my thoughts—work. I pull up the file on my next target. There is so much evil in the world, so many people who don't deserve to walk the earth. That's where I come in. To eradicate the monsters who commit unimaginable heinous acts toward the innocent. I don't hunt randomly; I'm very particular about my targets.

One hour and two cups of coffee later, I change into running gear. Tight leggings, a sports bra, and my favorite sneakers. Running is another activity that helps to clear my mind. The pounding of my heartbeat, the steady rhythm of my feet hitting the pavement, remind me I'm alive, that I'm still in control. I pull my blonde hair into a high ponytail and study my reflection in the mirror. The shadows under my steel-gray eyes are more than just exhaustion—they're reminders of a past I can't shake.

My eyes—the only feature I share with my father—stare back at me, cold and haunted. But that's a story for another time. I break my gaze, bend down to tie my shoes, and head out the door.

Normally, I run three to five miles a day, taking different routes around the lake. But today, I have a specific path in mind.

I head down the stairs and out the front door, making a left at the end of my driveway. As always, my gaze is drawn to the lake. This morning, tiny ripples dance across its surface, and the gentle breeze cools the dampness in the air. Spring is drawing to a close, and with it, the promise of summer. Soon, the tourists will begin to pour into Lake Falls, and with them, the influx of money. Even during the busiest times of the year, I find peace living in a rural area compared to the hustle and bustle of the large city I grew up in.

Two miles down the road, I reach Conrad Johnson's home—a stunning two-story red-brick house. The front lawn is perfectly manicured, flowers in full bloom, giving no hint of the unspeakable darkness that unfolded within its walls.

Conrad Johnson's family was found brutally murdered almost a year ago. His wife, strangled to death in the kitchen. His two-year-old daughter, suffocated in her own bedroom upstairs. The authorities ruled the cause of death as asphyxiation—his daughter's pillow the weapon used to end her life.

Conrad vehemently denied any involvement, portraying himself as a grief-stricken father, heartbroken and helpless. He had no alibi, though. He claimed to have been out of town on a business trip. The police found solid evidence, including Conrad's DNA, on both victims, and the case appeared to be airtight. I followed the story, just like everyone else. The public believed he was guilty, yet he got off on a technicality.

A few weeks ago, the authorities released him from holding, letting him walk free as though nothing had happened. How could they just let him go like that? It's infuriating that after everything, he's back to his normal routine, working for a company that either believes his story or doesn't care about his morality. It's hard to shake the deep disappointment that comes with realizing just how little accountability seems to matter in the world. I've heard Conrad is expected to return this afternoon and if he sticks to his normal routine, he'll likely head straight to the dive bar he's always frequented— the one where he's known to drink himself into oblivion.

I do a final scan of the perimeter of his property. No new security cameras, nothing out of the ordinary. I plan on paying him a visit, but for now, I have to wait. My shift is about to begin.

CHAPTER 2

Tessa

At twenty minutes to seven, I walk through the Emergency Room entrance at Lakeside Memorial Hospital and use my badge to clock in. This place is like a sanctuary for me. I feel oddly comfortable here. Ever since I was eight years old, when I fell off the monkey bars at school and broke my left arm, I've known that I wanted to go into the nursing field. The nurses had been kind to me that day—something I wasn't used to receiving at home. From that moment on, I knew what my future held. I wanted to help people.

After leaving the hospital that day, I was certain I would become a nurse. It was all I ever talked about. My parents, absent both physically and emotionally, made up for it by throwing money at me. The following Christmas, it was no surprise to find neatly wrapped gifts under the tree—a stethoscope, the Operation board game, and a doll dressed as a nurse. It's interesting how the little things bring us the most joy. Back then, I assumed I had a normal life as an only child.

That is, until *he* happened.

Shaking myself out of the past, I head over to the doctor's lounge to get a report from the night shift staff. After completing my nursing degree, I took it a step further, earning both my graduate and doctorate degrees in the field, and now I work as a nurse practitioner. I've always loved the emergency department. It's fast-paced, and there's never a dull moment. You never know what's coming through the door. It could be an infant with a cold, someone in a life-threatening situation like a heart attack or pneumonia, or a car accident victim.

Saving lives and improving the well-being of others is a gratifying experience, but there are days that weigh heavily on my soul. Losing patients, particularly children, tears at me in ways I can't put into words. Watching innocent lives end so tragically feels personal. It's not a profession for the faint of heart; it demands everything, especially when the darkest moments come knocking.

In the doctor's lounge, I find the night shift nurse practitioner flipping through a chart. "Good morning, Marsha. How are you doing?" I ask with an easy smile. Marsha is in her early forties and a mom to four hellions. She has a strong work ethic, and I enjoy coming to work after her shift because I know she has everything under control. "It wasn't so bad last night, but I'm ready to be home, resting in my bed."

She fills me in on the patients still waiting for blood work and other test results. The most excitement they had overnight was a patient who came in experiencing hallucinations of purple elephants chasing him. Crack is wack, for real.

"And now I'm handing the reins over to you," she says with a light laugh. It's Friday morning, so I know she'll be off for the weekend to be with her kids. "I've got this covered. Go. Enjoy your time off."

I glance over the four charts in the rack, deciding which one to tackle first. There's a sixty-year-old male with chest pain who is waiting for lab results. His initial cardiac enzymes were normal, and the GI cocktail administered on arrival after the EKG eased his chest pain. This likely means he has undiagnosed gastroesophageal reflux disease. Then, there's a six-year-old boy with flu-like symptoms, a twenty-one-year-old with abdominal pain, and one of our frequent flyers, Scotty, who is here for the third time this month for IV hydration. Scotty is a fifty-five-year-old chronic alcoholic who doesn't know when to quit. He usually presents after a fight at a local bar or passing out in the alley behind it.

Lucy, a spunky nurse who has worked here as long as I have, sticks her head into the doctor's lounge. "Dr. Sparks, we have three coming in via ambulance—a two-car motor vehicle collision. The medics just called it in."

Holding back a sigh, I place the charts back into the rack and head to the ambulance bay.

CHAPTER 3

Tessa

"I'm calling it. Time of death, 9:01 a.m.," I say solemnly.

For the last forty-five minutes, we've been trying to resuscitate the driver responsible for the accident, but to no avail. An autopsy will be performed, but it seems probable that the elderly man suffered a massive cardiac arrest and ran a red light, resulting in a head-on collision with the other vehicle.

The man had no pulse on arrival, and despite chest compressions, respirations, and multiple rounds of epinephrine, we were unable to sustain a cardiac rhythm. The occupants of the other vehicle walked away with minimal injuries.

"We need to move the family into the quiet room. Please notify the on-call social worker to meet us so we can deliver the news," I instruct Lucy. I glance around at my colleagues, noting their responses. Losing a patient is never easy, and there are times when the staff needs counseling too.

I silently hope that Allie is scheduled to work today. She's one of four social workers at the hospital and one of my closest friends. She's someone I can always count on, no matter what, and we've been friends since we met at summer camp when we were thirteen. My parents sent me there after the incident, and it was the best decision they ever made—because otherwise I might never have met Allie.

We were roommates, and we instantly bonded. Allie is the extrovert to my introvert. Where I'm serious and quiet, she's outgoing and radiates energy, effortlessly striking up conversations with anyone. I had no choice but to be her friend.

Unlike me, Allie was born and raised in this town. We spent six summers together at camp here at Lake Lucia. When I returned home after the summer, we stayed in touch through letters and texts.

At eighteen, I moved out of my parents' house and haven't spoken to them since. I didn't need their money—my paternal grandparents had set up a trust fund for me when I was born. The only condition was that I had to complete my college degree, to prove I could live independently. After graduation, the lawyer representing my late grandparents contacted me and granted me access to the fund.

With financial freedom, I moved to Lake Falls and applied for a nurse practitioner position at Lakeside Memorial Hospital. This town had been my refuge during those summers— a place where I could breathe, where I felt both safe and at peace. There was never a question in my mind that I would eventually settle and build my life here.

"Dr. Sparks, Allie's here. The patient's wife and daughter are waiting in the quiet room," Lucy says, pulling me from my thoughts.

Relief washes over me. Having Allie here will make this process a little easier.

"Okay, let's talk with the family," I reply.

Breaking the news of a patient's death is never easy. Their loved one's eyes—desperate, hopeful—search yours, but soon, you see that hope drain, leaving only despair. Allie has a special way with words that soothes families in their darkest moments, so I leave them in her capable hands and move on to the next patient.

After an uneventful remainder of the workday, and a report to the nurse practitioner covering the next shift, I head to the doctor's lounge to grab my things. On the way, I pass Allie's desk and see her documenting her notes for the day. As I walk by, she lightly grabs my arm, and my body tenses involuntarily. Allie is very touchy-feely, and I'm not. I prefer to keep people out of my personal space, and being touched makes me deeply uncomfortable. I accepted this about her long ago, but every now and then, it still catches me off guard.

"Are we still on for coffee at The Donut Hole tomorrow morning?" Allie asks, her hopeful blue eyes shining with excitement.

Inwardly I groan. I had forgotten all about our plans for Saturday. It's been weeks since we both had a Saturday off. The Donut Hole is a cute little coffee shop next to the hardware store. They serve everything from basic black coffee to fancy specialty espresso and cappuccinos.

I had hoped to relax on my back deck tomorrow and dive into the stalker romance novel gathering dust on my bookshelf, but I know the time with Allie will do me good, and I need to check in on how things are going with her douchebag boyfriend. For months, I've been hinting that she should break up with him, but she refuses to listen.

"Of course, girl," I reply. "Ten tomorrow morning?"

Allie nods with a grin, and we wish each other a good night. After gathering my things from the doctor's lounge, I climb into my car, and head home. There's a lot to get done before meeting Allie tomorrow.

CHAPTER 4

Allie

"Again, please reach out if you need anything," I say softly to Mr. Smith's wife and daughter. Larry Smith was a loving husband, father, and grandfather who tragically lost his life in a car accident today while traveling to visit a sick friend. Though grief overwhelms them, they seem to be holding together as best they can. Still, the pain in their eyes is unmistakable, and the days ahead will be difficult. Losing a loved one is never easy, no matter how much time passes. Moments like these are the hardest, and no one should have to endure them.

Being a social worker and therapist can be fulfilling, but it's not a career for everyone. My work often involves gut-wrenching cases that burden my heart with their weight.

I'm looking forward to unwinding with my best friend tomorrow. Tessa and I rarely have days off together. I don't know how she does it—she's incredibly dedicated to her work, but I could never handle dealing with blood and bodily fluids like she does. The thought alone makes me shudder.

Getting away from the hospital for the day will be a much-needed break for both of us. Usually, I have to drag her out of the house after a long week of work. Tessa isn't the most outgoing person, but she loves me, and we both share a passion for books, although her taste leans toward darker genres than mine. Back in the day, we were both obsessed with *The Twilight Series*—she was all about Edward, and I was Team Jacob.

Though I have many friends in this town, Tess is the one I feel most comfortable with. She's the one I turn to when I have troubling cases—child abuse, domestic violence, and sexual assault. It's something I can talk to her about because she understands the healthcare system and, more importantly, knows that mental health is just as crucial as physical health. Sometimes, we meet for coffee at The Donut Hole, and other times it's girls' night with margaritas at her place. We talk nearly every day, even if it's just to share a funny video one of us found while scrolling through social media.

Stepping out of the quiet room I hear a familiar voice in the hallway. "Hey, Hannah." I greet her with a smile. Growing up in Lake Falls, Hannah and I have known each other since childhood. I've lived in this town my whole life and never dreamed of living anywhere else, not even after what happened that summer.

I grew up with my mom and dad and have twin brothers who are five years younger than me. My parents met as teenagers, fell in love, and got married right after high school, giving us kids a picture-perfect childhood. Though I've always felt loved by my family, there was always a sense that something was missing, and I wanted to find my true love, the kind my parents had, and I believe I've found that in Dalton.

Dalton took me by surprise, seemingly appearing out of nowhere. He grew up not far from here, in Stillwater, and had just moved to Lake Falls after accepting a manager position at the local bank. The first time I saw him, I was at the bank depositing a check, and I remember feeling an odd sense of déjà vu, something I still don't quite understand. Then, it seemed like he was everywhere I went—at the gas station, the grocery store, and the mall. I ran into him one evening after being stood up on a blind date. I remember feeling so upset, vulnerable, and insecure. Dalton approached me and offered to buy me a drink, and we ended up chatting, flirting, and having a few glasses of wine. He was so sweet, walking me to my car and then asking me out.

About two years into our relationship, we moved in together. Dalton had been persistent about it, pointing out that we'd already waited a long time. At first, I hesitated. Despite his usual caring and affectionate nature, he's very particular about his privacy and doesn't like people coming over.

A few months ago, I tried to start a book club with some friends. Dalton came home furious and made everyone leave, completely embarrassing me. The next day, he showed up with flowers and my favorite chocolates, apologizing profusely. He knew how much his behavior had hurt me and kept apologizing for days. Eventually, I dismissed it as him being overwhelmed by work. I know his job is demanding, so I try not to make things harder for him.

Glancing at the clock, I see it's almost eight p.m. On-call days often stretch into late hours, and today is one of those days. Normally, I finish work at five, go home to cook dinner, and clean the house before Dalton gets home. But today has completely drained me, and I'm crossing my fingers that he'll be okay with pizza tonight. Not only have I had to navigate the heartbreaking situation with the Smiths, but I also met a new client—a seven-year-old girl named Ansley, living with her drug-addicted mother. Ansley's trapped in a tough situation, and it's clear from her behavior the strain is starting to take its toll on her. The school reported the case to Child Protective Services for a thorough investigation, and I've been told their inquiries could drag on for weeks, maybe even months. I'm hoping Candice, Ansley's mother, can pull herself together for her daughter's sake and keep bringing her to our sessions. But deep down, I fear for Ansley's future if things don't change soon.

With a heavy heart, I end my shift and head home, knowing that talking to Tess tomorrow will help.

CHAPTER 5

Tessa

Deep into the midnight hour, I stand in the shadows outside my target's home, dressed in black leggings, a thin, long-sleeved black tee, and a black ski mask. There are times when I'll conceal my face with a mask or alter my appearance with wigs and contacts. It depends on the situation, and how much trouble I expect.

Conrad isn't the type to give me trouble. He's probably returning home from the bar soon, likely shitfaced. I can only hope he decided to Uber instead of risking lives by driving intoxicated.

That hope fades as I see headlights coming down the road, weaving into the driveway. His black BMW knocks over a potted plant at the edge of the house. Miraculously, he parks in his garage without causing further damage.

Good Lord.

I shake my head in disgust as he staggers out of the car and walks toward the open garage door, struggling with his keys, and I slip in behind him, soundless. The moment he gets a foot inside the door, I pull the syringe from my pocket and jab it into his neck. He teeters forward to land face down on the hardwood floor.

With a smirk, I shut the door and lock it behind us. I drag his unconscious body to the living room, where he usually crashes in his recliner, often with a lit cigarette. It's truly a miracle he hasn't burned his house down yet. But that's about to change. I undress him, haul him closer to the recliner, and secure his wrists and ankles together with the zip ties from my trusty duffel bag. Once I double-lock the restraints, I grab a few other items from the bag and drop his clothes in various spots across the living area.

A few minutes later, he stirs. I didn't inject him with much of the sedative—just enough to move him into position. Eager to get this started, I pull out a fresh syringe and shoot pure adrenaline into his arm.

He startles awake. "What the hell?"

I always enjoy this part. It's always the same questions: "*Who are you? Why are you doing this? Please, let me go.*"

"Hi, Conrad." I smile sinisterly at my prey as he looks around wildly. "Welcome to your own personal hell."

"What's going on here?" He fights against his restraints.

"Did you really think you could get away unscathed? You brutally murdered your wife and two-year-old child. And you got off on a fucking 'technicality'?" I stare at him, disgusted. "I'm sure it had nothing to do with your uncle owning Hudson Oil in Texas. It must've been nothing for him to drop hundreds of thousands to pay off a few people to make the evidence disappear."

His face pales. "I didn't do it. I swear."

"That's what they all say," I taunt. "It wasn't me. I wasn't there. I'd never do anything like that."

"No, really, I wasn't even here!"

Plugging in the curling wand, I turn it to the highest setting, eyeing the pathetic excuse for a man. I never thought of a curling wand as a torture device, but after a few accidental burns while curling my hair, I had an "ah-ha" moment. *Pretty genius, I think.* I grab the wand and press it against his hand, and he screams out.

"Uh-uh. Hush, or I'll tape your mouth shut. Do I really need to do that, Conrad?"

"N-no, no, please stop."

"I'll stop when you tell me the truth," I retort. I'm lying, but he doesn't need to know that.

I move closer, placing the wand against his abdomen, slowly drawing a smiley face as he tenses, tears running down his cheeks. "Are you ready to talk?" I smirk down at him.

"I-I swear, I didn't do it," he whimpers, sticking to the same story he's had for months.

My eyes harden. I really didn't think he would be this stubborn. Is this guy kidding? Or is he legitimately crazy?

"I don't believe you."

I retrieve another item from my bag—lubricant. As I pour it onto the wand, I hear the satisfying sizzle and catch a whiff of the burning scent in the air. I was wrong if I thought his eyes couldn't get any bigger. They look like they're about to pop out of his head, and immediately he begins spouting out a platitude of denials.

A photo of Conrad and his family catches my eye, and all I can envision is him suffocating his daughter with a pillow. Rage courses through me as I roughly roll him over, exposing his backside. My grip tightens around handle of the scalding 450-degree curling wand as I forcefully press it against the entrance of his anus. Instinctively, he recoils, attempting to escape, but there's nowhere for him to go. Rotating the wand, I slowly inch the device deep into his rectum.

He lets out a piercing scream, his cries echoing through the room as his body convulses uncontrollably. Thankfully, the nearest neighbors aren't home. They're renovating their house, which made tonight the perfect time for me to set my plan in motion. The only other neighbor nearby is legally deaf.

Conrad continues to writhe in pain, his voice hoarse from screaming. "Please, for the love of God, stop it."

"What, are you not enjoying this?" Chuckling darkly, I withdraw the wand before shoving it back in. "It's a bit different when you're the one feeling helpless isn't it?"

"Alright! I did it!" he yells, his hands struggling against the restraints. "The bitch wouldn't shut up, and the kid wouldn't stop screaming. Are you happy now? Go away. Leave me alone. I'll never tell anyone you were here. I don't even know who you are," he begs.

Really? Is that all he could handle? *Amateur.* I remove the wand and unplug it from the wall, tossing it aside.

"See?" I wave my hand out. "Don't you feel better now that you've owned the truth?"

I allow him to drag himself into the recliner, whining the whole time. I grab his pack of cigarettes, pull one out, and offer it to him. He takes the cigarette; his hands tremble violently as I light it for him. He inhales deeply and blows out a thick stream of smoke.

"Be right back, buddy," I say gleefully as I walk out to the garage, grabbing the two gasoline canisters I'd stored earlier, and bringing them inside. He becomes panicked again, his face contorted as he screams, "You said you'd stop if I told you the truth!"

"Did I? Oops, I lied."

I pour gasoline onto the carpet around his chair before drenching his body; the liquid splashes around him, and the potent smell fills my nostrils. He howls loudly. I'm over him now. I pull out the bowie knife strapped to my back and run it across his jugular artery, effectively slicing the skin open, and blood pours out. Savoring every moment, I watch as his life drains away. The cigarette falls from his mouth, starting a small blaze beside the recliner. I cut off the zip ties and gather my belongings, careful not to leave anything behind.

Casting one last glance at the photo of his innocent wife and daughter, I head toward the door. Before I leave, I turn around and light a match to ignite the growing blaze, watching the flames swallow the pathetic excuse for a human being in front of me—*another monster who can't hurt anyone else.*

CHAPTER 6

Elijah

It's six in the morning when I pull my truck into the parking lot of my office. I started Huntington's Construction Company a little under two years ago after getting out of the military.

From a young age, I always had a passion for building things. Pair that with the values instilled in me by my family; it was inevitable that I would open my own business in the construction trade once my military career as a Navy SEAL was over.

Mom loved the idea. She was relieved I came home from overseas unharmed and having me back in Lake Falls made her incredibly happy. As a kid, some of my fondest memories are of the times I spent with only her and my grandparents. In his own way, my dad is proud of me too, although he doesn't say it much. It's so hard to gauge someone who's so damn formidable and commanding in their personality. I've never felt adequate in his eyes.

Especially after my sister disappeared.

Keeping Paisley safe had been my responsibility, and I failed her. We had been a semi-normal family before that fateful night, but the pain of losing her consumed me. A couple of months after her disappearance, I forfeited my football scholarship to the University of Georgia.

When my best friend Jace enlisted in the Navy, it played a major role in influencing my decision to join as well. Jace came from a family of naval officers, so there was always an expectation for him to pursue that same path. However, I joined so I could do everything in my power to battle the inner demons that were threatening to overpower me.

It wasn't until years later that I realized my efforts had been completely useless. I gave everything to my country and like to think I brought some peace into the world. I realize it may sound narcissistic, but it's simply the truth. However, saving innocent lives couldn't take away the painful reality of losing my sister. I don't have the answers I desperately need about the person responsible for her murder, and it weighs heavily on my mind. Eventually I realized I wasn't going to find those answers in a scorching desert in the Middle East. You can only run from your past for so long.

Friends since kindergarten, Jace and I were always causing trouble. During our time in high school, if you were searching for one of us, chances were high that you would find the other. When we weren't out partying or getting laid, we spent our time duck hunting by the lake or deer hunting at his dad's cabin. Going through basic training and being recruited to join the SEALs strengthened our bond.

The two of us have been through some tough shit together, and I know he's got my back like I've got his.

The bond between members of a SEAL team is so strong they become like family. Every mission poses life-threatening situations that demand complete trust and unity. Out of the other four soldiers in our sector, Jonah, became like a brother to me, and saved my ass too many times to count. I've shared things with him that I've never told Jace. We rode the highest of highs and sank to the lowest of lows, because for every victory we celebrated, there were also deep, heartbreaking losses. When the three of us retired, Jonah left to join the FBI, and Jace and I started our own construction business in our hometown of Lake Falls.

Jace should be here any minute. Typically, we begin our workdays bright and early. Our current project involves renovating a home on Cherry Lane. The owners, Richard Cunningham III and his wife Lorna, are obnoxious motherfuckers who have too much money and too much time on their hands. The house on the lake makes this their third vacation home. They also own a beach house in Florida and a cabin in Colorado. Their primary home is in Atlanta. Richard is from old money, and that wife of his is the typical trophy wife. Lorna Cunningham has sent us ten different *Pinterest* ideas for the kitchen remodel.

Pinterest is a bitch for those of us in this business.

"Hey, Jace, you ready, man?" I call out to him after he parks next to me. He climbs into the truck with a soda and a bag of candy in hand.

"Let's head over to the Cunninghams and see what we need to do today, then we'll head over to the job in Blakely and measure it."

"Let's do it," Jace replies. On the drive over, we bullshit about his current flavor of the week. Unlike myself, Jace is a notorious player, and without fail, there's always a woman texting him.

As we pull onto Cherry Lane, I hit the brakes hard and Jace slaps a hand on the dashboard before exclaiming, "What the fuck?"

Police officers and firefighters surround the home next to the Cunningham's. The whole place is a goner. Conrad Johnson—an absolute piece of shit—owns the house and has recently gotten away with murdering his wife and daughter. As we pass by, I see the coroner's van is also there. *Good*, maybe the sorry motherfucker burnt up inside the house. The community would be better off without scum like him.

We pull into the Cunningham's driveway, park the truck, and as we head inside, I spot something—or someone—out of the corner of my eye. It's a jogger who has stopped to observe the scene. She's speaking with an officer when her steel-gray eyes drift over to my blue ones, and I freeze, unable to look away. *Fuck.* This woman is the most beautiful creature I have ever seen. She's wearing black capri leggings, a hot pink sports bra, and her blonde hair is in a high ponytail. She has a perfect rack and long, tanned legs despite her short stature.

"Hey, Earth to Eli!" Jace punches me in the shoulder, pulling my attention back to him.

I glance back at the blonde goddess, but she has resumed her run. How have I never encountered this beauty before? Lake Falls isn't a large community, but it's not tiny either. Curiosity stirs within me, and I can't help but find myself hoping I'll cross paths with her again, and sooner rather than later. For now, I inhale deeply and force my attention back to the job at hand.

The Cunningham's home is a complete remodel, and I've been measuring and talking with the subcontractors I hired about the multiple renovations that are being planned. A little after nine, I hear a knock at the door downstairs. At the door is Marshall Randall, one of the deputies at the sheriff's office, and another skinny guy who looks like he just graduated high school. I've known Marshall all my life, even though he was a couple of grades ahead of me. He's always been a good guy, and we've never had any issues with one another. His father, Bob, is the local sheriff. I ran into the man a few times in my youth. Nothing too serious—once I accidentally broke a neighbor's window with a baseball, and in my teens, I was caught spraying graffiti on the walls of the high school locker room. Not my best decision ever, I was young and reckless back then, but I've never been one to back down from a dare.

Marshall gives me a wide smile. "Eli, I thought that was you I saw pulling in this morning."

"Hey man, it has been a while. How are the wife and kids?" I ask.

"They're doing good. Our son Billy just began kindergarten, and our baby is just starting to take her first steps," he says, pride gleaming in his eyes. "Claire and I can barely keep up with Lucy these days."

"I'm glad they're doing well," I reply. "How can I help you, Marshall?"

"I need to ask you a few questions about the Johnson place next door. We were called out late last night to the fire, and it was already blazing when we arrived. Have you seen anything unusual the last couple of days?"

"We've been working here for a few days, but I hadn't seen anything unusual until we drove up this morning. I know from the Cunninghams that Conrad Johnson has been out of town for a few days," I state. "In the time we've been working here, I haven't seen anyone else at the house."

I turn to Jace, "Can you think of anything important I might have missed?"

He shrugs and shakes his head no.

"Do you have any idea what happened?" I ask.

Marshall's gaze turns grim. "It appears that Conrad fell asleep in his recliner with a lit cigarette and a bottle of Scotch, and the liquor ignited the blaze. We'll have to wait until the DNA comes back, but I have no doubt it's him."

"I'm sorry I couldn't be of more help," I say, the words leaving my mouth with a practiced tone. But I'm not at all sorry. Every part of me knows that bastard got what he deserved, and I feel no regret for it.

"This is most likely an open-and-shut case. It's not a secret that Conrad had a drinking problem. If you think of anything, let us know. Good to see you," Marshall replies.

"Yeah, you too, man," I say, shaking his hand.

The truth is, Conrad was never meant to last in a town like this. We hunt, we fish, we help our neighbors—we look out for each other like family, because that's what we are, and we damn sure don't harm our own. Nobody is going to miss the sick bastard anyway.

Giving him no more thought, I head back into the house with my mind already running back to thoughts of the strange blonde goddess with killer legs that would look fantastic wrapped around my waist while she rides on my cock. I need to find out who she is.

This is going to get interesting.

CHAPTER 7

Tessa

The shrill of my alarm slices through the quiet morning, pulling me from sleep. I reach for my phone, slapping the stop button, and stretch. My body feels light and rejuvenated. It's always like this after I take down a target.

I take a moment to bask in the memories, a deep satisfaction filling every inch of me. It's the same feeling I get when I save a life. Isn't that ironic? Whether it's the adrenaline rush of taking some sick bastard's life or the gratification of saving one, both bring me equal pleasure. But the satisfaction of eradicating a monster from this world is the only thing that lets me sleep at night without nightmares. And I never know how long those nightmares will stay at bay, so I take advantage of the peace while I can.

My thoughts drift to my morning run yesterday by Conrad's burned house. It's true what they say about killers returning to the scene of the crime. You can't make this stuff up. Part of me wanted to scope out the scene, but also, I had to maintain my routine. I strategically switch between several routes to keep things unpredictable. Most of them have a view of Lake Lucia, because there's nothing more peaceful than a lake. The vibrant colors, the soothing sounds of nature—it's calming.

As of now, the investigators have ruled the incident an accident. Multiple surveillance cameras caught Conrad's reckless drive home from the bar. Everyone believes what I want them to—that he was drunk, passed out in his recliner with a cigarette. If there's any suspicion of foul play, I haven't heard about it. But then again, the local police might not care. Despite their best efforts, the justice system failed the first time around. *Fucking politicians.*

I've always loved this town, ever since that first summer camp when I got away. The summer I met Allie. The summer after everything changed. Lake Lucia has a mysterious past. They say there've been mysterious deaths and drownings over the years. Locals call it 'Devil's Lake,' adding to the mystique. I remember sitting around the campfire, listening to the stories. Back then, they used the legends to keep us from sneaking out or going off alone at night. As I got older, I did my own research. It only intrigued me more and is another reason I chose to make Lake Falls my home. I don't know where I'd be now if that camp hadn't saved me.

Once again, I feel an unnatural pull, a need to retrace my steps, to return to Cherry Lane. I can't help but wonder if someone might've been working late at the Cunningham's place that night. I knew they were starting renovations soon, but I didn't realize they'd already begun. Thankfully, no one was around when I scouted Conrad's house—otherwise, that could have been a problem. And who was that guy working at the house next door?

The guy with the eyes I could drown in.

I've lived here for a year now, and I've never seen him before. Though our encounter was brief, I remember the flip-flop in my chest. That never happens. I don't feel intense lust at first sight. But that morning, something was different. Between working in the emergency room and spending time with Allie, I thought I knew everyone who lived here year-round.

Oh shit, Allie!

We're meeting at The Donut Hole at ten. I need to hurry if I want to squeeze in a shower and look halfway decent before heading into town.

Just before ten, I slip out the door and into my silver Lexus. I glance down at my outfit. The yellow sundress clings just enough to accentuate my legs, and the cute sandals complete the look. My blonde hair falls in soft waves down my back and I kept the makeup subtle—just mascara, a light dusting of bronzer, and my favorite lip shade, Lovedust. I check my reflection in the rearview mirror, popping my lips in approval.

As I pull out of the driveway, I smile at the sight of the sun bouncing off the glistening lake. I love the variety of homes here—some have that rustic cabin feel, others are sleek and modern, and some are more traditional. My own place is a contemporary two-story, with an open floor plan and large picture windows overlooking the lake.

Arriving at *The Donut Hole*, I pull into the parking lot. Allie's already inside, chatting with the barista and likely everyone else in the café. She's one of those people who doesn't meet a stranger, and I've never seen anyone who hasn't fallen for her charm.

The door jingles as I step inside. Allie's head snaps in my direction, her blue eyes lighting up as they meet mine. She's wearing Capri pants and a blue blouse that complement her eyes. Her shoulder-length brown hair falls in a sleek, straight line, gently framing her face. There's a natural beauty about her, the kind that radiates from within, and draws people to her effortlessly. She grabs two drinks from the counter and walks toward me as I plop down at our usual table by the window. From this vantage point, I can easily see anyone entering or leaving the cafe.

"I'm so excited to see you!" she exclaims, handing me my iced caramel macchiato with an extra shot of espresso before sitting down. "It's been forever since we've done this! We have so much to catch up on! OH MY GOD, did you hear about Conrad Johnson?"

"Take a breath, girl," I laugh. "It's great to see you, too. Especially away from the hospital."

Is discussing Conrad something I want to do? Not at all. But I know we'll circle back to it. Allie has a heart of gold, but she loves a good gossip session. She doesn't always know when to keep her mouth shut, but she's the only one in Lake Falls who knows what happened in Atlanta. And as far as I know, she's kept it to herself.

"What do you think happened to Conrad? I can't believe he's dead," Allie leans in, lowering her voice as she glances around before speaking again. "I bet his uncle hired a hitman to take him out. Everyone knows he did it."

"You've been watching too many crime shows, Alls," I state casually, glancing down at my light pink nail polish. "I'm sure it was just an accident, like the police said." It's a logical theory; I'll give her that.

"So, how's everything with you and Dalton?" I ask, desperate to change the topic as I sip my drink, the sweet aroma of coffee swirling around me. The buttery caramel floods my mouth, leaving a warm sweetness behind. Something about Dalton, Allie's boyfriend of two years, doesn't sit right with me. He's good-looking, but his unpredictable mood swings often leave her in tears, and there's a darkness about him that sets me on edge. She deserves better.

"Oh, everything's great. I think Dalton may propose soon. I overheard him talking to his mom about his grandmother's wedding set," she whispers, practically glowing.

She fills me in on the latest happenings in her life and around town. Allie's always involved in something, volunteering for this or that. She has a heart that won't quit, and I love her like the sister I never had. There's never a dull moment when she's around, and no matter what's happening, she manages to make everything feel brighter. I've always envied her bubbly, extroverted personality, the way she can walk into a room and instantly light it up. It's something I've never been able to do.

She pauses for a beat, her face falling into something more serious. "This week was tough at work. There's this little girl I'm worried about. Her mother brought her in after the school reported that she had been acting out in class, showing up unkempt and without money for lunch. While her mother insisted that everything was fine at home, I have a gut feeling that there is more to the story. I think the mother is on drugs."

"God, that's horrible. I know those cases are so hard to prove. Did you reach out to Child Protective Services?" I ask, concern threading my voice.

"Oh, definitely. The problem is, those cases take time. Sure, they have to respond within twenty-four hours, but I'm worried something will happen to her in the meantime." Her eyes fill with unshed tears. She has the biggest heart.

"It's going to be okay. I know that little girl is in good hands with you. You'll help her. You were born to be a therapist," I reassure her, patting her hand briefly.

I make a mental note to investigate the woman and her daughter later. Allie's always careful about breaking confidentiality, but figuring out who she's talking about won't be difficult. We both work at the same hospital, and I have my connections.

We're chatting about going to the lake when the front doorbell jingles. Allie looks up and freezes, her smile faltering. Turning my head, I meet a pair of vaguely familiar blue eyes—eyes that mirror the deep tumultuous blue of a stormy ocean.

He stares at me, and for a moment, I can't tear my gaze away. Then I regain my composure enough to avert it. He walks toward us, flashing a casual grin at Allie as he stops to speak.

"Hi, Allie. How's it going?"

Allie musters a smile. "I'm good, Eli. How're you doing?"

"Doing good. Who's your friend?" His gaze slides over me, lingering on my lips for a heartbeat before lifting back to meet my eyes. "I don't believe we've met before."

"Oh, this is Tessa. She moved here about a year ago. We've been friends since we were kids. We met at summer camp—" she pauses abruptly and clears her throat. "Tess, this is Elijah Huntington. Eli's from a long line of families that have lived in Lake Falls for decades. He's also my cousin."

Cousin? When the hell did Allie get a cousin? Has she been hiding this guy from me?

After composing myself, I extend my hand. "Nice to meet you, Elijah." His grip is firm, an electric shock tingling my skin. Startled, I glance down at our joined hands before meeting his gaze again.

"You can call me Eli." A slow smile spreads across his face, making his eyes sparkle with warmth. His expression only enhances his already stunning features. He stands nearly six-foot-four, towering over me, his lean, sculpted frame highlighting well-defined muscles. Elijah Huntington is the epitome of rugged charm. His disheveled caramel-brown hair and chiseled jawline blend effortlessly with the deep blue hue of his eyes, and I could spend days memorizing every inch of him. His full lips, with a hint of a sly smile, pull my attention.

"It's a pleasure to meet you, Tessa," he replies, his voice low and lazy. "Maybe I'll see you around sometime."

A flush spreads across my cheeks, and a pleasant warmth blooms in my stomach. My gaze follows him as he walks to the counter to collect his order. His eyes dart toward me as he hands over his money, the burning intensity of his stare making it clear that he's interested.

Allie raises an eyebrow, sarcasm thick in her voice. "You're drooling."

I dart my eyes back to her. "No, I'm not." Jesus. What's wrong with me today? I've never felt an immediate connection like this with anyone before—if at all. Something deeper than attraction alone.

Just as we're about to resume our conversation, Eli interrupts with a final, "Have a great day, ladies."

As he exits the café, he shoots me a flirtatious wink and a lingering glance.

After he's gone, I hiss at Allie, "What was that about?"

"What do you mean?"

"You looked at him like you'd seen a ghost—or like you were afraid of him. Is there something I need to know?" I demand, suspicion rising.

"Eli's a good guy. We've never been very close. My dad and his mom are siblings. I was a couple of years behind him in high school. He was always busy with one sport or another. I was closer in age to his sister—" She stops suddenly, her voice trailing off. Now I know she's hiding something. But what?

Allie quickly changes the subject, trying to deflect. "Shall we go to the lake and soak up some sun?"

"That sounds good to me." I reply, more distracted than I want to admit. "I'll need to swing by my house and grab a few things. Meet me there in an hour?"

"I can do that. See you soon." Allie hurries out, the door chiming behind her.

What was that about?

CHAPTER 8

Allie

Every time I see Eli, I'm jolted back to that horrible night at camp so many years ago. If Tess had been there, things might have played out much differently.

It was a dark summer night. I was seventeen, and it was my first time at camp without my level-headed best friend. Just a few weeks earlier, Tessa had graduated high school and wasted no time escaping Atlanta, moving to Athens to begin her first semester of college. I couldn't blame her, given her strained relationship with her parents. And while I missed her, I was determined to have a good time.

That night, I had snuck out to drink in the woods with my bunkmates, Brittany and Ashley. We'd paid one of the custodial workers to smuggle in some Boone's Farm, and he'd left it hidden under a rock near the big oak by the lake.

We found a quiet spot by the water's edge. The night was still, except for the party raging across the lake. Even from a distance, I recognized the house—it belonged to my aunt and uncle. I hadn't realized it at the time, but they were out of town, and my cousin Eli was throwing a birthday blowout.

Brittany giggled at something, pulling my attention back to my bunkmates as we worked on getting drunk. I remembered stumbling away from them to find a small patch of bushes where I could relieve myself.

What happened next would stay with me until the day I died.

As I'm walking back to my friends, a sharp cry cut through the night, and I freeze. Several hundred feet away, a white van is parked by a small boat ramp. Squinting, I see two figures forcing a young brown-haired girl into the van. Her screams pierce the air. Is that... PAISLEY?

I step forward to get a better look but trip over a fallen tree branch. The two figures turn and stare in my direction, and one of them looks... familiar.

I scramble to hide behind a tree, my heart pounding in my throat. They're still looking at me, and I feel a surge of panic. Oh God, I need to run, but my body is frozen.

After what feels like an eternity, I think I hear the van pulling away. What should I do? I need to return to my friends and call for help. As I turn to hurry back, a hand suddenly grips my shoulder, jerking me around. My heart stops as another hand clamps over my mouth, silencing me. I try to scream, but no sound escapes. A cold, harsh voice whispers in my ear.

"You didn't see anything. Understand?" A shiver runs down my spine as the sharp edge of a blade presses against my throat. "I know who you are, and I know all about your family. If you say a word, I'll kill them. Then you'll be next. Do you want that for your mom, dad, and twin brothers?"

Tears spring into my eyes. I can't make a sound, but I weep silently as the words sink in.

He removes his hand from my mouth and I manage to croak out, "I won't tell anyone, I swear."

"You better not," he hisses coldly. "We've got eyes everywhere in this town. I'll be watching you, Allie."

With that, he shoves me to the ground and disappears into the trees. I stay kneeling, shaking, trying to steady my breathing. My heart is racing. I feel dizzy, my body cold and numb and suddenly, everything goes dark.

I wake up to find Brittany and Ashley staring down at me, and a camp counselor, checking me over. She looks upset, obviously not impressed that we snuck out when we were supposed to be asleep.

"You girls are in a lot of trouble. But first, let's get Allie checked out by the nurse." She gives us a sharp look. "Then we'll call your parents."

My parents arrive less than an hour later. The disappointment in their eyes is palpable, only making me feel worse. The silence on the car ride home is deafening and I know my life will never be the same.

I've never told anyone about what happened that night. The fear of losing my family kept me silent, and I regret it every day. Two days later, a body was discovered in a creek that ran off the lake, about four miles away, in the neighboring town of Stillwater. The remains were identified as my cousin, Paisley—a fourteen-year-old girl with long, brown hair.

I can't forgive myself for what happened that summer night. If I'd spoken up, maybe I could have saved her. Maybe she'd still be here, living her best life. She could have grown into adulthood, found love, started a family. But instead, she's gone, and I'm haunted by what I failed to do.

Paisley's death is the reason I became a therapist. I dedicated my life to helping others because I couldn't bear the thought of someone else being hurt because of my inaction.

A heavy sigh slips from my lips as I drive home, the weight of guilt pressing down on me yet again. I long for solace, but I know it won't be found at the lake.

Despite the darkness that often creeps into my thoughts, I force myself to look for something good in each day. I have to. I'll put on my happy face and try to enjoy the afternoon.

As I turn onto our street, I distract myself by taking in the scenery and the modest homes that line our neighborhood. When I pull into the driveway, Dalton's truck is parked there and I frown, thinking it's odd that he's home early.

Inside, I find him in the recliner with a beer in hand. It's barely noon.

I force a smile. "Hey, honey, I thought you were going fishing with your brother today."

"Nothing was biting, so we called it quits. He glances up from the TV, a flicker of irritation and impatience shining in his eyes. "Where've you been?"

"Do you ever listen to what I say?" I joke, trying to keep things light. "I met up with Tessa at the coffee shop."

Dalton reaches out and grabs my left wrist, his fingers tightening.

"Ouch, you're hurting me," I gasp, feeling a sharp pain shoot through my arm.

He doesn't let go, his grip tightens even more. "We've talked about this. You're my girlfriend, and I always want to know where you are."

"I... I'm s–sorry, but I had my phone, so you could've called," I stammer.

Tears prick at the corners of my eyes, threatening to spill over. Dalton suddenly seems to realize what he's doing. He releases me, and I massage my wrist, trying to ease the pain.

"Allie, I'm sorry. I didn't mean to hurt you. I overreacted." He draws in a deep, audible breath. "Let me make it up to you. What are your plans for today?"

Letting out a shaky breath, I try to hide the lingering pain. I know he didn't mean to hurt me—he never has before.

"Tessa and I are going to hang out at the lake and get some sun," I answer, my voice uncertain.

A bright smile lights up his face. "That sounds nice. Enjoy yourself. I'll go into town and pick up some steaks and a bottle of your favorite wine. When you come back, we can spend the evening together."

"That sounds lovely, honey." Hoping he doesn't notice my discomfort, I swallow the lump in my throat and steady my trembling hands. Pushing aside the thoughts of what just happened with Dalton, I quickly change, grab up my tote bag, and leave for the lake.

CHAPTER 9

Elijah

Jace and I work for several hours, meeting with Mrs. Cunningham and reviewing blueprints for the ongoing construction project. Even though I have multiple subcontractors, I still prefer to be hands-on and involved in every project we take on. By early afternoon, we're making no progress, so I decide to call it a day. Being the boss has its perks, and since the weather's perfect—clear skies and a gentle breeze—it's a great opportunity to go fishing.

"Hey, man, let's give up for now and hit the lake," I suggest.

"Hell yeah, let's do it," Jace agrees.

I text my buddy Trevor, who does framing work for the company, to see if he wants to join. He replies almost immediately that he's in, so we make plans for him to meet us at my house in an hour.

After dropping Jace off at the office to get his truck, I stop to pick up a few bags of ice before heading home. My place is a two-story modern house with an expansive view of the lake and a large boat dock.

Inside, I change out of my work clothes, fill the cooler with bottled water and beer, and head outside to load up the boat with fishing gear. I'm almost done when Jace and Trevor pull up. Aero, Jace's dog, trots over to me, tail wagging and I crouch down to scratch his head. "Hey, bud."

With the fishing poles and tackle boxes on board, we head out on the bass boat with me at the helm. This boat's my baby, second only to my truck. I love the feel of the engine roaring to life beneath me. Lake Lucia is a vast body of water that spans forty thousand acres with nearly seven hundred miles of shoreline. Eight towns surround the lake, most with beaches where locals and tourists gather on warm summer days. The water's stunningly blue, making it famous and perfect for all kinds of water sports. Older residents call it "Devil's Lake," fueled by the cautionary tales of mysterious drownings, yet despite the stories, swimming remains a popular activity on hot summer days.

My sister, Paisley, loved swimming. The familiar flash of pain hits me as images of the two of us splashing in the water when we were kids flood my mind.

As I drive toward our favorite fishing spot, my thoughts drift back to that fateful night, so many years ago.

It was a warm summer evening in late July, just after my eighteenth birthday. My parents were out of town for the weekend, and I had planned a huge party they knew nothing about. They had only one request: I had to look after my little sister, Paisley, and keep her safe.

My birthday bash had been in the works for months. I'd invited all my classmates, especially my buddies from the football team. It would be my last hurrah before heading to the University of Georgia, where both my father and grandfather had studied. I couldn't wait to leave Lake Falls, eager to move on to bigger and better things.

Jace and my girlfriend, Molly, were busy putting up last-minute decorations when the keg arrived. Inside, Paisley spent most of the day sulking in her room. She had wanted to go to her friend Sasha's house, but I wouldn't allow it. I didn't trust Sasha. She was two years older than my sister and had a reputation—she had hooked up with half the football team, myself excluded, and had even been arrested for shoplifting a few weeks earlier. I didn't want Paisley falling under her influence. Though my sister could be a spoiled brat at times, I was still protective of her. Instead, I offered to let her invite other friends over—on the condition that no one drank.

By ten that night, the party was in full swing. The guys played beer pong, laughing and trash-talking, while the girls danced. I kept an eye on Paisley, making sure she wasn't sneaking drinks or doing anything stupid. But as the night went on, one beer turned into ten, everything blurred together, and I lost track of time. Molly had been all over me, dragging me into the pool house to hook up. The last thing I remembered was glancing at the back porch and seeing Paisley talking with one of her friends.

Little did I know, that would be the last time I saw my sister alive.

The next morning, I woke up on the couch in the pool house, surrounded by my friends, who were either passed out on the furniture or sprawled across the floor. Empty red Solo cups littered the ground. Groggy, I immediately went in search of Paisley, expecting to find her asleep in her bed. But she was nowhere to be found. Panic set in. I woke everyone up, and we frantically searched the property, calling her friends and checking with our neighbors, but there was no sign of her.

It wasn't long before the news broke—another girl, around Paisley's age, had gone missing that same night in a neighboring town. Paisley's phone was never recovered, but text records showed she had planned to meet up with Sasha. She never made it to her house.

I still check with the sheriff several times a year for updates, but there's never anything new. To this day, the case remains unsolved. No leads, no evidence—just an empty hole in my heart and the crushing guilt of having failed her.

I snap back to the present as we reach our fishing spot, drop the anchor, and grab our poles. The faint sound of Lynyrd Skynyrd's *Simple Man* hums from the radio as I crack open a beer and toss one to the guys. Just as I'm about to take a sip, something—or someone—nearby grabs my attention. I spot my blonde goddess, Tessa, and my cousin Allie walking along the lake's edge, each with a tote bag and a lounge chair and I can't help but gawk at Tessa as she gracefully removes her black swimsuit cover-up, revealing sun-kissed skin. The shimmering gray bikini fits her body like it was tailor-made for her.

"Hot damn, the view's amazing today," Trevor drawls.

Jace turns his head, his gaze flicking over to land on the girls. "Is that Allie? I wonder if she's still with that douchebag, Dalton," he mutters, clearly disgusted. "She could do so much better."

"Last I heard, she was," I say.

"Forget Allie, look at Tessa. I'd tap that ass," Trevor leers.

"Be respectful, man," I say, reaching over and sucker-punching him in the stomach. An inexplicable anger roars to life inside me, along with a feeling of possessiveness.

Trevor grabs his stomach and laughs. "Don't tell me you wouldn't. I saw you checking her out. Beauty and brains, too."

I shoot him a sharp look. "How do you know her?"

"Remember when I nearly cut my finger off with that table saw? She was working in the ER and sewed me up. She's like a doctor or nurse practitioner or something."

I frown. "Why have I never seen her before?"

"I think she moved here a few months ago," Jace says. "I heard her dad's some bigwig in Atlanta, and she spent a few summers at Camp Lanier when she was younger."

"You're wasting your time, Eli." Trevor smirks. " My buddy Shane says she's turned down every guy who's asked her out since she moved here. Guess small-town boys aren't good enough for her."

We'll see about that.

I feel a tug on my fishing line and grin as I start reeling in, eager for more than just a bass today.

I've barely finished putting the eight-pound bass in the live well when a boat approaches loudly, coming in way too fast. My eyes scan the surroundings. Out of the corner of my eye, I catch a flash of blonde hair. Tessa breaks the surface of the water, unaware of the approaching boat.

"What the fuck?" I yell, diving in, adrenaline surging through me as I plunge into the water.

CHAPTER 10

Tessa

I t's such a beautiful day to be on the beach. Although it's not a *real* beach, the beauty of this man-made creation is undeniable. This spot is my favorite on the lake, nicknamed Laguna Beach because it resembles a lagoon, and with its clean sand and sparkling, crystal-clear blue water; the lake offers a picturesque sight.

I thought we'd never get here. Being her typical self, Allie was almost an hour late but brought gifts that made her tardiness forgivable: a half gallon of wine slushy from the nearby winery and a charcuterie tray with various cheeses and salami. *That's my girl.* Hopefully, the warm embrace of alcohol will soothe the whirlwind of thoughts in my head. While waiting for Allie to arrive, I did a deep dive into Candice Smith, mother of seven-year-old Ansley. They live in a low-income neighborhood on the outskirts of town, and Candice has a history of multiple arrests for public intoxication, possession of methamphetamines, engaging in prostitution, and shoplifting. She's been investigated by the Department of Family and Child Services a staggering four times for child neglect. It's unfortunate that the woman couldn't utilize her Oscar-winning acting skills to benefit her child. Several neighbors have stated that Ansley is frequently left home alone or under the care of strangers Candice invites into her house, and teachers have also reported that Ansley shows up in dirty clothes with unwashed hair.

The little girl recently started acting out at school, likely due to her home situation and bullying by other students. I make a mental note to contact Bryce, my college best friend, a hacking expert, and someone I can always rely on. Aside from Allie, Bryce is the only person in the world I completely trust, and he lives in North Carolina with his partner.

"I'm really happy we decided to do this," Allie exclaims, pulling out two cups and filling them with wine slushy. The dark red marks on her wrist immediately grab my attention.

"Allie, what the hell happened to your arm?" I demand, anger boiling inside of me.

Her eyes dart away. "Oh, it's nothing," she says dismissively. "I snagged my bracelet on the door handle at work."

I narrow my eyes suspiciously, my attention drawn to the distinct fingerprints. "Huh," I mutter under my breath, barely audible.

I've never seen her wear jewelry on her left wrist. I let it go for now, but if Dalton is hurting her, I will fucking kill him.

Frustrated, I look over at the lake. The gentle lapping of water against the shore is accompanied by the distant chirping of birds. It's quiet and peaceful, with only a few boats scattered around. Firmly resolved to embrace the day, I push aside my dark fantasies of torturing Dalton.

Taking a leisurely sip of my drink, I lean back into my lounge chair, and the sun's caress lulls me into a state of pure relaxation.

I must've dozed off for a few minutes because I suddenly jolt awake, my heart pounding and my lungs gasping for air as my recurring nightmare slowly dissipates. *Why do these nightmares persist, refusing to release their grip on my mind?* And what caused them to come back so soon? After eliminating a monster, I usually feel a sense of relief that lasts for weeks or even months.

I steal a quick glance at Allie, who remains engrossed in her phone, seemingly oblivious to my current state. She must have noticed me drifting off and decided to give me a chance to catch some much-needed sleep.

I hastily gulp down the remainder of my drink, anticipating the warm sensation of the alcohol coursing through me.

"Do you want to join me for a quick swim?" I ask.

I catch her gaze as she rolls her eyes in my direction. "Eww, no." She grimaces. "I'll stick to swimming pools, thank you very much."

"You do know you're more likely to catch a disease in the community pool, right?" I retort with sarcasm, strolling to the edge of the water. The sun glistens on the surface as I wade in until the water reaches my waist. Then I dive forward, feeling the cold slap of it against my skin. Despite the chill, I can't help but love it. It provides a cathartic experience for me. In the water, I can disconnect from my thoughts and the outside world, simply reveling in the serene sensation of effortlessly gliding through it.

As I resurface for air, urgent shouting to my right reaches my ears. In an instant, I feel two powerful hands gripping me tightly, guiding me toward the safety of land. My instincts kick in, and I fight back with all my might. With a sudden burst of strength, I push away from the thick, muscular arms restraining me. Just as I'm about to deliver a powerful punch to his face, I stop in my tracks when I hear someone calling my name.

Out of nowhere, the deafening roar of a motorboat fills the air, zooming dangerously close to us, missing by a mere fraction of an inch.

Once the boat passes, I start thrashing again, and the person holding me instinctively retreats. His voice laced with amusement and caution, he says, "Easy there, Little Killer. You need to calm down."

Slowly, I become keenly aware of the warm, muscular arms holding me close, and I raise my head to look up at the man who seemingly just saved my life.

The moment our eyes meet, I instantly recognize the intense, dark blue of his gaze—one that radiates both anger and concern. It's clear the anger isn't directed at me as his piercing gaze surveys my body, searching for any sign of harm.

"Tessa," he rasps. "Are you okay?"

I nod slowly, the gravity of the situation making it difficult to find the right words. With a shaky hand, I brush a strand of wet hair behind my ear.

"Oh my god, Tessa!" Allie's screams pierce through the air, reaching my ears.

The motorboat comes to a halt and reverses its direction.

"Yo, I'm sorry. I didn't see you swimming out there," the driver of the boat calls, a guy with red hair wearing a wife-beater and cutoff jeans.

"Wilson, what in the actual fuck?!" Eli yells at the boater. "You could've killed her!"

"Take it easy, man. I can assure you that she looks completely fine to me," the driver says, his gaze shifting to me as he offers me a lecherous smile, openly ogling my breasts. "Sorry, sweetcakes."

"My eyes are up here," I state coldly, glaring at him.

He meets my gaze and smirks. His pupils are wide and dilated—a clear sign he's under the influence of something. Behind the haze, there's a disturbing, almost sinister quality to him. A sense of unease washes over me, a deep darkness I can't explain, and my gut tells me he's dangerous.

"Just get the fuck out of here asshole," Eli growls, his voice dripping with rage.

Another boat approaches with two familiar-looking men on board, both staring down Wilson, who starts his boat again and speeds away.

It doesn't escape my attention that Eli's still right beside me in the icy water. My body is tingling in response to his presence.

"You sure you're okay?" he asks, the worry still evident on his face.

Only then do I realize he's without a shirt. I take my time to admire the sculpted perfection of his abs. *Jesus, how long has it been since I had my last orgasm?* Or, more accurately, since I had one without relying on my vibrator. There's something about this guy that ignites all my senses. A smirk lights his face, as if he could hear what I was thinking.

"I'm alright. Where did you even come from?" I ask, perplexed.

"We were fishing when I saw that idiot speeding toward you at ninety miles an hour."

He points to the men in the boat idling up beside us, a golden retriever happily wagging its tail.

"This is Jace and Trevor."

"Good to meet you. Mr. Long, how's that finger doing?" I call out, remembering the moment I had to stitch up his right index finger after a near-severing incident with a table saw.

With a grin, he says, "You can call me Trevor, and my finger's healing well, thanks to you, Doc."

I catch Eli's intense glare directed at Trevor from the corner of my eye.

"Tessa, are you okay?" Allie's voice trembles as she reaches my side. "You scared the life out of me."

"I'm fine," I respond, steadying my tone. "Eli saw what was happening and pushed me out of the way."

Turning to Eli, I add, "Thank you for saving me. I didn't see that guy coming. Who is he?"

"Wilson Randall," Eli snaps with disdain.

"Randall... is he related to Sheriff Randall?"

"Yeah, he's Sheriff Randall's youngest son. He's constantly causing trouble, and his father always bails him out. I'll let Bob know what went down, but I doubt he'll do anything. In his eyes, Wilson does no wrong," he says with a severe expression.

Eli's gaze flickers to Jace for a moment, who is busy watching Allie, then returns to me.

"You should check out the local band performing tonight at The Blue Lagoon—they're really good. We're planning to meet up with some friends, and you two should join us," he says as he wades toward the boat.

In one fluid move, Eli hoists himself out of the water, his glistening, toned body reflecting the sunlight and water around him.

I fidget uncomfortably. When it comes to socializing, I tend to shy away from large crowds. As his eyes implore mine, I can feel the intensity of his gaze, like a burning flame. Is it really that terrible to go out and enjoy ourselves? I quickly look at Allie and notice a hint of uncertainty in her eyes.

"Um, I will have to see what Dalton wants to do tonight," she replies meekly, her eyes downcast, her voice lacking confidence. I can't help but notice Jace's eyes narrowing, his gaze becoming sharp and focused on Allie's statement. It piques my curiosity, and I wonder if the two have a past connection.

"You two should come along and don't worry about bringing that asshole," Jace says.

Glancing away, Allie fidgets with the bracelet on her right wrist. The bruise on her left wrist is already turning a darker shade, the shape of the imprint now looking more like fingers.

I confront her with a determined look, ready to challenge her. "I'll only go if you go."

She's constantly pushing me to be more social, and now she's got her shot.

Allie merely shrugs in response.

I face the boys and casually brush my wet hair off my shoulder. "We'll try to make it. I owe you a drink, after all. Bye, boys."

As Allie and I make our way back to shore, I toss a wink at Eli, feeling his lingering gaze on my ass.

CHAPTER 11

Tessa

After wading back to shore and pushing the near-death experience to the back of my mind, I pause to steady myself, exhaling slowly as I turn to my best friend.

"Okay, I've been waiting for you to tell me what's going on." My voice is sharp, but Allie's behavior is driving me insane. "You've been acting so strange ever since we saw Eli at the coffee shop this morning," I say to her while we dry off and gather our things. My eyes never leave her, my frustration simmering beneath the surface.

Sadness clouds her face, her expression turning distant. Finally, she meets my gaze, and I catch the shimmer of unshed tears.

Damn, am I being too harsh?

"Allie, you're scaring me. You know you can talk to me about anything. We've been best friends since we were kids. You were the one I turned to when I first came to summer camp, and you're the one I trusted with my past. But I can't help if I don't know what's going on."

She takes a deep breath before responding. "Alright. I've been keeping something from you for a while. I just didn't want to burden you, and I don't know where to start," she says, her voice trembling.

"Start wherever you're comfortable."

"I've lived here my entire life. In this town, everyone knows everyone—or at least knows about them. Eli and his friends were two grades above me in school. After graduation, they threw a big party one weekend while I was at camp. It was the summer you didn't come. I missed having you around, but I wanted to go one last time. It was always the best part of my summer."

I nod, urging her to continue.

"One night, my roommates and I snuck out to the woods near the lake to get drunk. I bribed the janitor to let us sneak in some Boone's Farm. We were just planning to relax and have fun. I never thought anything bad would happen."

"I had to pee, and I didn't want to walk all the way back to the cabin, so I went behind some bushes by the lake—and that's when I saw it. Something terrible."

"What did you see, Allie?" I ask, my heart racing in my chest.

She meets my gaze, her face pale. "I saw someone being taken."

"Taken?" I frown, confused. "Taken where?"

"I saw a girl being forced into a van by two men. She was fighting them off, but all I could do was stand there. My legs froze, Tess. I was going to call for help." Her voice cracks, and tears spill from her eyes. "I swear I was going to call for help! But I couldn't."

"What happened?" A thousand scenarios swirl in my mind, none of them good.

"I guess one of the guys saw me. His face was hidden behind a terrifying mask. He grabbed me, held a knife to my throat, and threatened to kill me—and my family—if I told anyone."

"Oh my God, Allie!" My heart clenches. "You should've told me! Why didn't you come to me?"

"I was terrified. I didn't know what to do. You were already in college, and I didn't want to risk talking on the phone. This town... it has eyes and ears everywhere."

"You must've been so scared, Allie. You've kept this to yourself all this time?"

"Yes," she whispers, broken. "And I've regretted it for years." She swallows hard, her voice faltering. "I haven't even told you the worst part. The girl... was my cousin, Paisley. Eli's little sister. Just a few miles from here, they found her—raped and murdered. She was only fourteen. And I did nothing. I'll never forgive myself."

I hold her tightly, offering what comfort I can as she sobs quietly. How could she have carried this burden alone for so long? I can almost sense the terror she must have experienced in that moment, and the isolation that comes with facing a difficult situation alone. If anyone can truly understand that, it's me.

"Every time I see Eli, I remember how I failed his sister. And his family." She swipes the tears from her cheeks. "That's why I became a therapist. It probably sounds stupid, but I thought if I could help others, I could somehow make up for what I didn't do."

A frown creases my brow. "Allie, you were only seventeen. You're not to blame for what happened. I can understand why you kept quiet, especially with how scared you were. Did you recognize either of the men?"

Her eyes flicker away, uncertainty clouding her face.

Before I can press her, her phone rings. She grabs it quickly, visibly relieved by the interruption.

"It's probably Dalton, wondering where I am," she mutters, answering the call.

My eyes narrow as I patiently wait for her to finish talking to the asshole. I wrestle with the guilt that surges through me. How had I missed this? I knew Allie was hiding something, I should have pushed her harder to open up. She hangs up, dropping the phone into her tote bag.

"What's the plan here?" I ask, my voice steady but urgent.

"What do you mean?" She stares at me, her eyes widening in fear as the realization hits. "You can't tell anyone. How would that even help now? The damage is already done."

"Okay, fine. But what do you know about the investigation? Was the killer ever caught?"

She shakes her head slowly, her face still streaked with dried tears. "She wasn't the only one. Another girl went missing that night—close by. Victoria. She and Paisley didn't know each other, even though they were the same age. Victoria was never found. It's like she disappeared into thin air."

I try to process everything, the weight of what Allie's just told me settling in like a stone in my stomach. I can't help but think about Eli— what he must have gone through, losing his sister like that. The grief he must have felt, the helplessness. And Allie, having carried the weight of this secret for so many years, pretending like everything was fine when it clearly wasn't.

I scan her face, a puzzled look crossing my own. "What was Paisley doing out there alone that night?"

"Their parents were out of town. She was supposed to stay at home with Eli, but I guess she snuck out to meet a friend. The moment I heard Paisley was missing, I knew it was her I'd seen.

And then they found her body..." Her voice cracks again as fresh tears well in her eyes.

I decide not to push further. For now.

"Alright," I concede. "My lips are sealed. Let's get out of here. A night out is exactly what we need, don't you think? Let's go to that bar, listen to some music, and get fucked up."

"I'll have to check with Dalton. He mentioned doing something special for me tonight to make up for—" She hesitates, tucking a strand of hair behind her ear. "Well, he was in a mood earlier. It's nothing."

I force a smile, clenching my teeth. "I have an idea. Let's invite him out with us." It's something I wouldn't normally suggest, but Dalton's a dickhead, and she needs this as badly as I do. If I have to deal with him for a few hours, I will, for Allie's sake.

Her face lights up, a genuine smile spreading across her features as she picks up on my change in tone. "Okay, I'll ask him and call you in a little while."

CHAPTER 12

Elijah

After arriving home and unloading the boat, Jace and Trevor head out with plans to meet up at the bar later. I can't shake the thoughts of Paisley. I'm tired of the police fucking around. It's been almost ten years, and I need to know what happened to my sister. At the time of her murder, investigators were also looking into a separate case they believed might be linked to Paisley's disappearance. The last fifteen years have been marked by a disturbing pattern of unexplained disappearances. Every time, it's the same story—two girls from various counties around Lake Lucia disappear without a trace. Paisley is the only missing girl whose body was ever found. They couldn't establish a link between the cases and stubbornly refused to seek help from federal authorities. I'm glad I have a connection on that end now. Jonah. It'll make things easier. I'm going to hunt down every lead—no matter the cost, no matter how long it takes—until I find the person responsible for her death. I'll never be able to bring her back, and that pain will haunt me forever. But maybe, just maybe, I can find some semblance of closure for my mom, and perhaps ease a fraction of the guilt and regret that weighs on me every single day.

I also can't stop thinking about what happened with Tessa earlier, and my anger only grows the more I replay it in my mind. I've always known Wilson wasn't the sharpest tool in the shed, but his behavior today? Just fucking stupid. I make a mental note to speak with the sheriff about that as well.

I quickly shower, the hot water washing away the day's grime, and get ready for the night. Around nine, I arrive at *The Blue Lagoon*. This bar's been a local fixture for ages and is usually packed on weekends, especially on nights when bands are performing live. Tonight is no exception, and the bar is filled with patrons of all ages. Jace and I are the only ones flying solo tonight. One by one our friends arrive with their significant others, including Trevor, who shows up with a girl he's been seeing.

The worn leather cushions welcome us as we settle into our favorite booth, and we order a round of draft beers. I catch the scent of sizzling appetizers coming from the kitchen, my stomach grumbling in response. Conversations with the guys are always effortless, and soon enough, we're deep into a discussion about baseball, all while digging into plates of crispy chicken wings and loaded fries. I'm halfway through my second beer, eyes glued to the big screen where the Braves are up 9-3 over the Phillies in the seventh inning when Tessa and Allie walk through the door. All thoughts of the game vanish from my mind.

God damn. The short, skin-tight black dress clings to Tessa, highlighting her exquisite figure. Her sun-kissed blonde hair falls in loose, cascading waves around her toned shoulders. She's stunning, and I'm completely mesmerized. My dick hardens at the sight of her. *Down, boy.*

Her gaze sweeps the room before landing on mine, a smirk playing at her lush, coral painted lips as her gray eyes seek out mine. They head to the bar to order drinks. Moments later, Dalton arrives and joins the girls at the bar. The bartender places a martini in front of Tessa, and I assume Allie's waiting for Dalton's permission to order. Tessa's eyes flash with anger, but she quickly covers it, forcing a smile. Allie eventually gets a daiquiri when the bartender arrives with Dalton's drink.

They choose the booth next to ours, and the girls quickly down their drinks. After a second round, Allie grabs Tessa's hand, tugging her toward the dance floor with a grin, leaving Dalton behind in the booth, his brow furrowed in silent disapproval as he watches them go. Tessa and Allie dance together, their movements perfectly synchronized to the beat. They're clearly enjoying themselves, and Allie's infectious laughter echoes across the room. The longer they dance, the more visibly agitated Dalton becomes. He meets Allie's tentative glances with a scornful stare. Allie hesitates for a moment before slowly heading back to Dalton.

With her eyes shut, Tessa dances, her dress clinging tightly as she moves, revealing more of her thighs. The dress is modest, but I can't help but imagine running my fingers under it, feeling her silky skin. I'm mesmerized.

Until I see the other men in the room eye-fucking her.

Wilson's creeping up on her from behind, and my blood boils when he whispers in her ear. *What the fuck?* I'm halfway out of the booth when her body stills. Her gaze turns cold as ice. She spins suddenly, shoving Wilson away as he says something I can't quite make out. *I guess she can take care of herself*—good to know. Wilson doesn't fight back as she pushes past him, but the angry gleam in his eyes tells me he's more than a little pissed at the rejection. Only when he steps away from her do I realize my fists were clenched, and I slowly loosen them. Tessa returns to the table where Allie and Dalton are sitting. She grabs her drink, but instead of sitting with them, she tosses back the martini and comes to stand in front of me.

"Hey, hero," she whispers, leaning in close to my ear, her breath warm against my skin. "Dance with me."

The room seems to hold its breath; all eyes fixed on us.

A playful grin spreads across my face. "I'd love nothing more."

Grabbing my arm, she pulls me toward the dance floor. The band is playing a rendition of The Devil Wears Lace. I follow her. Fucking hell, I may have only just met her, but I already know I'd follow her to the ends of the earth. At the lake, Tess had come off as the quiet and controlled type, but tonight, she looks ready to cut loose, and I'm here for it. A wild, fiery look burns in her eyes—one that, while surprising, seems more natural than the facade she usually keeps on a tight leash.

She gives me an appraising look, her gaze lingering in places. "You clean up nicely."

I smirk and toss a wink at her. "Well, you've only ever seen me in work clothes... or half-naked."

A flush spreads across her cheeks, the pink deepening as she laughs softly. The sound is like music to my ears. "I guess that's true."

As I pull her into my arms, she tenses briefly and just as I'm about to step back, her body relaxes against mine. The scent of jasmine—sweet and heady—fills my senses. She smells like heaven on earth.

I lower my lips close to her ear, my voice soft, "You look beautiful tonight."

Her blush deepens, her eyes flicking nervously around the room. She clears her throat and quickly changes the subject. "Thanks. So, did you guys catch a lot of fish today?"

Okay, we're going to talk about fishing. Whatever makes the lady happy.

"I did, but Jace and Trevor weren't as lucky." I shrug innocently, a teasing glint in my eyes. "Fishing is just one of my many talents. But what I love most is being on the water, feeling the power of the engine beneath me, the way it hums and pushes us forward."

"Is that so?" she breathes. "Maybe I should come along sometime."

Her lips are just mere inches from mine. She's truly beautiful—more than just the softness of her features or the way the light dances in her eyes. There's something deeper, something magnetic about her that draws me in. The music pulses in my ears as she dances against me, her body moving with intoxicating energy.

I notice Wilson standing by the bar, his arms crossed tightly over his chest. His eyes are fixed on us, and there's no mistaking the jealousy carved into every tense muscle of his face.

Flashing him a smug smirk, I watch with satisfaction as he slams his empty glass onto the bar and storms off, before returning my full attention back to the enchanting woman in my arms.

Her arm snakes around my shoulders, her fingers grazing the nape of my neck, sending goosebumps down my skin as she pulls me closer, and we move together in perfect sync. With her toned body pressed against mine, soft curves teasing my chest, I resist the urge to grab her ass. The rhythm of the music wraps itself around us, and we sway as if our bodies had always known this dance.

For a moment it feels as if the rest of the world has faded away, leaving only the two of us, but the spell shatters far too soon.

Allie's raised voice cuts through the music, yanking us back to reality. A flicker of concern crosses Tessa's face, her brow furrowing as she pulls out of my embrace. She offers me a lingering, wistful smile and without another word, she turns and walks toward my cock-blocking cousin.

Jesus fucking Christ. This woman is going to *kill me slowly*.

CHAPTER 13

Tessa

S tepping out of Eli's hold, I head toward our table, clenching my thighs together. With a little liquid courage, I'd felt confident enough to grab Eli and pull him onto the dance floor. There's something about Eli that draws me in—his intense stare has been burning into me all night. It's startling how natural it felt to be in his arms, how he looked at me as if I were the only woman in the room. He called me beautiful. Sure, I've heard that countless times before, but never has it felt so sincere, so genuine.

If Wilson dares to come near me again, I'll make sure he regrets it. That sleazy bastard thought he could rub up on me, and it took everything in me to stop myself from doing something rash, like stabbing him in the eye.

As I approach our table, I find Allie and Dalton in the midst of a heated argument, with Allie sounding visibly upset.

"I was just dancing with Tess, that's all," she insists, her voice trembling.

"You were acting like a fucking idiot," Dalton snaps. "It was embarrassing watching you out there, and that behavior makes me look like a fool for putting up with it."

Allie's eyes widen with shock, her cheeks burning bright red as if she'd been slapped.

"Wha—? Why are you being this way?" she stammers, her voice barely a whisper.

Dalton yanks her out of the booth, his fingers digging into her arm.

I take a step forward, positioning myself directly in front of him.

"What the fuck, Dalton?" I hiss, anger consuming me. "Get your hands off her!"

"Stay out of our business." He sneers down at me. "Go back to dry-humping Huntington."

I sense Eli's presence behind me before I actually hear him.

"What the fuck did you just say?" Eli growls.

From across the room, Jace glares at Dalton. His gaze is sharp and hostile as he comes over to back Eli up. "Are you alright, Allie?" Concern is written on his face as he positions himself closer to her.

"I said—" Dalton sputters, as Eli grabs him up by his polo shirt. "Get your hands off me!"

Dalton's face contorts with rage, and Allie's eyes dart around frantically, landing on me as if she expects me to intervene, but I only shrug.

"Show these women the respect they deserve, asshat," Eli snaps.

"Fuck this, I'm out of here. Let's go, Allie," Dalton orders, his voice laced with venom as he throws some cash on the table and storms out without a second glance.

Allie crosses her arms over her chest, blue eyes glistening with unshed tears.

"You don't have to go home with him," I plead with my friend. "Come back to my place for the night."

Allie looks conflicted, biting her lip nervously, avoiding my gaze. After a moment, she says, "I'm sorry, I really have to go." She grabs her purse and bolts out the door.

I stare after her in stunned silence as a wave of emotion washes over me.

"Dalton's a real piece of work," I sigh as I glance back toward Jace and Eli. "I honestly don't know what she sees in him."

"He's an asshole. She deserves better." Eli's troubled gaze meets mine.

I'm so livid I don't trust myself to say anything else right now. What is Allie doing? Why is she letting him treat her that way? Needing a moment to compose myself, I march off to the bar, requesting two tequila shots. I slam the drinks back, throw a few bills on the counter, and head toward the restroom, the sound of laughter and chatter fading as I move away from the crowd.

Rounding the corner to the hallway, I feel a presence behind me, and my pulse quickens. A shiver runs down my spine, the hairs on the back of my neck stand on end. I feel a hand clamp down on my arm, and I react instinctively. With a swift twist, I turn and drive my attacker backwards against the wall. The Damascus pocketknife I never leave home without presses against his throat, aimed just over the exposed artery pulsing beneath his skin. Eyes like a stormy sea, heated with a hint of wariness, meet mine. Before I can react further, he flips the script, spins me around, and I'm the one with my back against the wall. The knife clatters to the floor, a hollow, metallic sound that echoes in the silence, and his hand clamps around my throat.

"Woah, there, Little Killer. A knife? Are you flirting with me?" Eli smirks.

Shit. I can't believe he managed to catch me off guard and overpower me! I stand frozen, my gaze fixed on his, the intensity of his stare making my heart pound in my chest. I didn't know who was following me, and now I realize I probably overreacted. Then again, a girl can never be too careful these days.

And *Little Killer?* If he only knew how accurate that was. But there's no need to fill him in on my extracurricular activities.

His grip eases, but he doesn't remove his hand from my throat.

"I– I'm so sorry. You startled me," I gasp.

Only then do I realize his body is pressed against mine, every ridge of his hard physique brushing against my curves. His other hand rests on my hip.

"Why are you carrying a knife, Tessa?" He leans in, his voice a hushed command, and I instinctively bite my lip. His heated gaze follows the movement, his eyes filled with a lust that both thrills and unsettles me.

"Self-protection?"

I'm not sure if it's the alcohol clouding my judgment or my inexplicable attraction, but I'm finding it harder and harder to resist him, and I'm no longer sure I want to.

I shove him with a force that sends him sprawling against the wall, and our lips crash together in a searing kiss. His tongue slips into my mouth, warm and desperate, meeting mine with the same fervor. Rough hands grip my hips and pull me against him, sending a jolt of electricity through me.

A soft moan escapes my lips, and he takes it as an invitation. One hand slides around the back of my neck, pulling me closer, while the other roams to cup my ass, sending shivers down my spine. The heat of his skin touching mine makes me gasp. I can feel him hardening against me, and I grind against him shamelessly as my fingers trace the smooth curve of his biceps, gliding up to his neck. He tastes of a potent blend—the sharp burn of whiskey mixed with the subtle sweetness of mint gum.

I've never felt such a strong pull toward anyone before, but this feels deeper, more profound than a simple attraction. Every inch of my body is begging for this, pleading with my brain to let this happen, to give myself to him.

He knows how to use his tongue, and it has me imagining other uses for it as well. His mouth pulls away from mine and he gasps, drawing in a rush of air. His breath tickles my skin as his lips wander down the side of my neck, softly biting and sucking the sensitive skin. My taut nipples strain against my dress, my pussy soaking wet for him. I'm reaching down to rub his cock when we are suddenly interrupted by a couple of loud voices coming from two guys stumbling down the hallway in our direction.

I leap away from Eli, my cheeks flushed with crimson. I avert my gaze, unable to meet the eyes of any of them.

"I can't do this, I'm sorry, but I have to go." Slowly, I back away.

As I burst through the side door and out onto the street, I hear my name being called, but I don't look back.

CHAPTER 14

Tessa

I wake with a start, gasping for air, my heart hammering in my chest. Another nightmare, another night of reliving it. Oh God, will it ever stop? How do I make it stop? I glance at the clock: 2:05 AM. My limbs feel heavy as I throw off the covers, my chest tight with a wave of emotion. I bite my lip, desperate to hold back the tears threatening to spill. The memories assault me with no mercy.

At twelve, my life had been perfect. My parents and I lived in a beautiful house. My mom had let me paint my room bright pink just last month. They were always gone, but that meant I had the freedom to do whatever I wanted. Nina, our housekeeper, made my breakfast and packed my lunch for school. Tonight, though, I was excited—my parents were taking me to a dinner party at their friends' house. They were leaving me to babysit their two sons, and I was being paid for it. My mom and Mrs. Tammy had been best friends for years. I adored Mrs. Tammy—she was so kind. Their children, Phillip and Chad, were six and four, and were like little brothers I never had.

My dad and Mr. William were also good friends, often spending Sundays on the golf course. William was fine, I guess, but I didn't always like the way he looked at me after a few too many drinks. Still, he always had my favorite candy ready for me.

I couldn't wait to wear my favorite pink dress. I was definitely a girly girl, not yet old enough for makeup, but my mom let me wear clear lip gloss. With a bag of snacks in hand, I raced down the stairs when my mom called my name. She didn't like tardiness, and I could feel her approving gaze sweep over me when she saw me.

About thirty minutes later, we arrived at their house. It was much larger than ours—and ours was big. The driveway was full of fancy cars, parked by a man my mother referred to as a valet. Whatever that meant. A stranger opened the door to greet us. Mrs. Tammy was right behind him, and she smiled brightly at me before leading me upstairs to the "kids' living area." My parents headed toward the large ballroom to join the other guests.

The boys dragged me to their playroom. They had so many toys, and the TV was playing an old Disney movie. The couch was comfy, and they fought over who would sit next to me. I giggled, telling them I'd sit in the middle.

Two hours later, Chad was asleep in the crook of my arm, and Phillip was fighting to keep his eyes open. I picked up Chad and carried him to his room, placing him gently in his toddler bed. Then I took Phillip to his room and began reading him a bedtime story. He drifted off almost instantly.

When I returned to the playroom, I turned off the movie and found a Nickelodeon show I liked. Settling onto the couch, I snacked on chips and sipped a Capri Sun.

A few hours later, I woke to something brushing against my leg. My eyes fluttered open, groggy, and I saw a familiar man sitting next to me.

"Look at you, Sleeping Beauty," he slurred, his breath thick with the smell of liquor. His eyes were glazed over.

This didn't feel right.

"Where's my daddy?" I asked, my voice shaking.

"Don't worry about that right now," he said, his voice low and grating. "It's just you and me, Sleeping Beauty."

I squeezed my eyes shut, wishing I could be anywhere else as my life irrevocably changed.

I don't know how long I lay there after, curled in a ball, numb both inside and out. Tammy and my mom came to find me when the party ended, and I remember seeing my favorite cinnamon candy resting on the couch next to me. I was too stunned to speak on the drive home.

The next day, I tried to tell my parents what had happened—what William had done to me—but they didn't believe me. They stared at me in horror, insisting it must have been a dream, telling me I shouldn't read such disturbing books.

That night changed everything. I was silenced and told never to speak of it again. They couldn't risk a scandal—couldn't let anything stain their perfect image or ruin their impeccable relationships.

A month later, I was shipped off to summer camp in Lake Falls. It was there I met Allie. She welcomed me with open arms, helping me break free of my shell, even if only for a little while. One night, she found me crying in bed, and I opened up about what had happened. She believed me and promised to keep my secret safe.

I learned how to be self-sufficient, gaining new skills with each passing summer: fire-making, fishing, and archery. By the end of my last summer there, I was ready for the next chapter in my life.

The summer I turned eighteen, I packed up my things, leaving my parents behind to start over. I haven't had any contact with them since, not even when my mom has occasionally tried to reach out. I won't let anyone hurt me like that again. And I'll protect those who've suffered as I have.

CHAPTER 15

Tessa

A few days later, as I'm leaving work, my phone vibrates with a text from Bryce telling me to check my email. Bryce has some unique skills that are beyond anything I've ever learned, and while he's been involved in some nefarious shit, my friend wouldn't hurt a soul. He's careful with my secrets, just as I am with his. We don't judge each other. He's been digging deeper into Candice Smith's life, and I've been eager to hear from him.

I open the email on my phone while getting into my car.

"Son of a bitch," I mutter under my breath, my voice low, full of frustration.

I know his number by heart, so I grab my burner phone from the console and dial him.

He answers immediately. "I knew you wouldn't be pleased with what I found."

"That's putting it mildly. A sexual predator and drug addict moved into their home weeks ago, and nobody's raised an eyebrow?" My frustration over the lack of follow up with this case seriously makes me want to throw my fucking phone.

"We need to move faster. I'll contact you as soon as I have a plan."

"Okay, talk to you soon," Bryce says, ending the call. I toss my burner back into the console.

Shifting into drive, I punch the gas and speed out of the parking lot.

The following morning, I hack into the Lake Falls Elementary School records and confirm that Ansley's at school. She doesn't need to see what's about to happen. I throw on black jeans, a tank top, and grab a hoodie as I walk out the door.

I pull into the parking lot of the local dollar store, a few blocks from Candice's apartment. Once inside, I grab a cart and begin shopping. There's a working security camera at the front of the store but none in the back. I throw some paper towels and dish detergent into the cart, pushing it to the corner of the building. Only two employees are working: one at the register, the other assisting a customer. I discreetly check if anyone's watching before slipping into the back room, bypassing the restrooms, and exiting through the rear door. With my hoodie pulled up, I walk toward the apartment.

The apartment building is in a dilapidated state that suggests minimal upkeep, just enough to meet basic state regulations. Several months ago, a gang shooting destroyed the security cameras, and they've never been repaired. Candice usually has a john or two around this time of day. Her neighbors are well aware of her activities and tend to avoid her. It's no secret she's slept with most of the married men in the apartment complex, gaining more than a few enemies. Her housemate, a registered sex offender, is fulfilling his weekly obligations with his parole officer and attending court-mandated classes.

I make it to her apartment door without encountering anyone along the way, and I fish out a pair of latex gloves. Trying the handle, I roll my eyes when I find it unlocked. This is almost too easy.

Stepping inside, I close the door gently behind me. The mess in the living room is immediately apparent—beer bottles and drug paraphernalia scattered across the coffee table, two lines of coke neatly cut and waiting on the glass end table, needles discarded on the floor. Aside from a worn teddy bear slouched on the couch, there's nothing in the room that indicates a child lives here, my stomach churns in disgust. I have to save Ansley from this situation.

"Jim, is that you?" a female voice slurs from the bedroom. "I've been waiting for you."

Jim is one of her regulars, but he won't be making it today. He's been otherwise held up. An anonymous call to his probation officer prompted a drug screen, which he failed, and he'll be spending a few weeks in county lock-up.

A tiny waif of a woman stumbles out of the bedroom looking at least two decades older than her thirty-one years. Her stringy red hair falls around her shoulders, and she wears a cheap negligee that leaves little to the imagination. The glaze in her eyes is heavy, and her arms bear the marks of repeated injections.

She stops short when she sees me. "Who the hell are you?"

"Your worst nightmare," I sneer, pulling my Glock from its holster and aiming it straight at her. "Now, here's what's going to happen. You're going to be very quiet and do what I say."

"Or what?" she challenges, though her fearful, uncertain eyes betray her bravado. "I'm not afraid of you."

"Sit down. We have some things to discuss."

"Who are you?" She stumbles back, her legs bumping into the couch, and she sinks down onto it. "You a cop? Another do-gooder DCFS worker? What's Ansley saying now? She's a little lying bitch."

I tilt my head as I stare down at her. "You know that's not true."

"Just look at the condition you've let her live in. She goes to school with dirty clothes and unwashed hair. Her behavior has been off lately, don't you think?" I glare at her, my eyes burning with hatred. "I wonder if it has something to do with the pedophile you moved in here. Have you been leaving her alone with him? Did she tell you he was hurting her? Did you let him touch her?"

Her eyes shift away, and I feel a hot rush of rage. This woman's depravity is beyond anything I could've imagined.

"You knew, didn't you?"

She refuses to answer, and I press the gun to her forehead. Her eyes widen in alarm, and she stammers out a weak, unconvincing excuse: "He pays the rent on time."

"He pays the rent on time?" My lip curls up in disgust. "You know what? Don't say anything more. The time for talking is over. Say another fucking word, and I'll blow your fucking head off. Grab the tourniquet," I instruct.

Her gaze falls to it, and she hesitates before reaching for the tourniquet with trembling hands.

"Tie it around your arm."

She does as I say and then looks at me. Reaching into my back pocket, I retrieve a syringe and hand it to her.

"What is that?" she whispers, fear creeping into her voice as the realization dawns on her.

"Exactly what you deserve," I say coldly, plunging the needle into the most prominent vein I can find. Within seconds, her face turns white, her skin becomes cold and damp. She lets out a series of gurgling noises, and her pupils—tiny dots—plead with mine for a fleeting moment before fading into a haze. Her lips turn blue, and vomit spills from the corner of her mouth. Her body convulses violently, and I find a chilling satisfaction as the light slowly seeps from her eyes. Her body slackens and slumps to the side.

A normal person might feel remorse, maybe even worry about the consequences of getting caught, but not me. I don't feel any of that. Instead, I feel an eerie sense of peace. The fear or guilt that should be there? It's nowhere to be found. And now there is one less monster in the world. Candice may not have set out to harm her child, but she didn't protect her, and she certainly didn't save her. Ansley will be better off without her.

Grabbing up her phone, I set it to speaker, dial 9-1-1, and place it next to her hand.

"9-1-1, what's your emergency?" the operator responds, clearly bored.

"I think I took too much," I whisper, trying to disguise my voice.

The operator hastily assures me that paramedics are on their way. I remove the tourniquet, leaving the syringe hanging limply from her arm. There's no need for any further countermeasures.

The police will discover a drug addict who overdosed on fentanyl-laced drugs. I holster my gun and head for the door, listening for any sounds in the hallway. It's silent, and I slip out of the complex unnoticed.

Outside, I discard the gloves in a dumpster behind the dollar store. I walk into the ladies' restroom, remove my hoodie, pull my hair out of the ponytail, and touch up my lipstick. After flushing the toilet for effect, I walk out, and head back to my cart.

Spotting an employee walking toward me, I clutch my stomach and twist my face into a grimace of pain.

"I'm so sorry. It's that time of the month, and something didn't settle right in my stomach. I wouldn't use the restroom just yet," I say apologetically.

With a sympathetic glance, she directs me to the Midol counter. After grabbing a box, I browse the tampon section, add a few more items to my cart, and head to checkout.

Two minutes later, I'm walking out with my two bags. An ambulance rushes by with its flashing lights and blaring sirens. Casually, I load my things into the backseat and climb into the car. Those lights won't be needed for much longer. By the time Ansley gets off the school bus, her mother's body will be long gone. I had Bryce take a look into her maternal grandmother and aunt, who live in Alabama. They'll no doubt take her in and treat her very well.

If anyone bothers to look at the security footage, they'll only see me entering and leaving. How could anyone possibly suspect me?

CHAPTER 16

Elijah

What a fucking week it's been. Nothing has gone according to plan. One problem after another has affected every job site. We're juggling three projects right now, and things are getting busier by the day. A warehouse delay has put one of the homes on hold because we're still waiting on the materials needed to finish it.

To top it off, I can't get Tessa out of my head. Just a taste, a hint of her sweetness, and I'm consumed by the need to claim her as my own. It's only a matter of time before I get her exactly where I want her—underneath me, naked, screaming my name as she comes.

The way she ran out on me at the bar only piqued my curiosity. I contacted an old friend of mine, someone with access to the information I needed.

Tessa Sparks, twenty-eight, daughter of Dillon and Nancy Sparks from the Buckhead district in Atlanta. No siblings. She kept her head down in school, got good grades, and had no boyfriends in high school. She graduated in the top ten of her class, which had over three thousand students, earning a full scholarship to UGA. Not that she needed it, judging by her parents' wealth and the hefty trust fund her grandfather left her.

From all I can gather, the day she left Atlanta, she severed contact with her parents. She has no other close family or friends aside from Allie and a guy named Bryce Hayes, whom she met in college. There's no record of any legal issues, not even a speeding ticket. The most interesting thing I found was the death of her first college boyfriend, nineteen-year-old Brady Collins. He was killed in a boating accident in Panama City Beach during spring break in her first year at UGA, with Tessa named as the sole witness. After that, she had a couple of short relationships, but mostly, she focused on her nursing degree. She graduated with honors before moving to Lake Falls a year ago.

She has little to no social media presence, though she appears in a few pictures on her friends' accounts. Her current residence is just a few miles from my place. She's an avid runner and volunteers a few hours a month at a local women's shelter. As far as I can tell, she hasn't been seeing anyone since she moved into town.

I wonder how much further things could've gone if those drunk assholes hadn't interrupted us. And why the hell did she run off? I know she wanted me as much as I wanted her. I still want her. It's her face and her body I've been jerking off to in the shower every day since.

I quickly change into jeans, a blue T-shirt, and work boots. I need to pick up some supplies from a couple of different stores. On top of work, I've got some ongoing projects at my own fixer-upper. When I first moved back, I stayed with Jace for a few months, then snagged a nice piece of property on the lake. I haven't decided yet whether I want to keep it or sell it. I'm aiming for renovations that will appeal both to me and to a potential buyer.

I see countless *Pinterest* photos from homeowners every week with extravagant requests that are often unrealistic given their budget. Or they can afford it and decide mid-project to change the design. I don't mind—I'll be compensated either way, and so will my employees.

Currently, I'm in the middle of a full remodel of my primary bathroom shower. The old toilet, tub, cabinetry, and tile have all been ripped out. I'm just waiting for the new supplies to complete it.

About thirty minutes later, I pull into the home improvement store in Billings. It's early, but the parking lot is already full. Parking my truck, I grab my wallet and phone, and head for the flooring section, hoping to find the perfect subway tile. I grab the durac, grout, and other supplies I need.

As I check my list and shift the items behind me, I realize there's one more thing I still need. As I round the corner, a warm body unexpectedly collides with mine. I catch her by the shoulders to keep her from falling.

Startled gray eyes meet mine. "I'm so sorry," Tessa stumbles, her cheeks turning a bright pink. She's stunning, damn near a fucking dream come true. I can't help but grin as I look down, taking in the view of her beauty from head to toe.

She's wearing a green tank top, tiny denim shorts, and brown Gucci flip-flops, showing off her pretty pink toenails. Yeah, I know Gucci when I see it. My mom's obsessed with shoes and probably has at least a thousand pairs.

"Well, hey there, Little Killer. Where's the fire?" I drawl.

"Sorry about that," she smiles sheepishly, her eyes shining with a natural brightness I haven't noticed before. "I wasn't watching where I was going."

Holding a handful of paint color samples, she looks a little embarrassed. "I'm trying to pick a color but can't decide. It's just a small home improvement project I'm working on. What brings you here? I figured you'd have people who shop for you."

She knows what I do for a living. Interesting. She must've asked around about me.

"I like getting my hands dirty," I say, winking at her. "I'm picking up supplies for a project at my place, a remodel of my primary bathroom."

"Those tile colors are beautiful," she remarks, glancing behind me at the palette of items.

"You should see it when I've finished working my magic. These hands are good at many things," I tease, watching her blush even deeper. Winning this girl over is going to be so much fun.

"So, about the other night—" she starts, then breaks off nervously. "I was a little tipsy and on edge. I can't believe I pulled a knife on you. Sorry about that by the way. You startled me. And for what happened after... that's not normal for me. I got caught up in the moment." She says, her tongue sweeping out to moisten her lower lip. My gaze fixes on them like a moth drawn to a flame.

"Hey, no harm, no foul." An easy smile spreads across my face. "Though I hated the way you ran off on me," I add, my voice dropping to a low murmur.

She bites her lip nervously. "It's just... I'm still new to town, and my career's just taking off. My public image matters to the community and I don't want to give anyone the wrong impression of me."

"I understand and have a solution to fix the problem," I say smoothly. "How about a proper date, just the two of us?"

"A date?" she sputters before adding, "No, I don't think so. I've already told you, I'm focusing on my career. I'm not interested in a relationship right now."

"Who said anything about a relationship? I'm just offering to treat you to a nice meal. It doesn't even have to be a 'date,'" I reply smoothly, making air quotes with my fingers.

Her smile is slow, almost reluctant, and I can feel her resistance weakening with each passing moment. I'm curious to learn more about her—her personality, her likes and dislikes, what makes her tick. She's not just a pretty face. I'm intensely drawn to her.

Glancing around, I notice no one paying attention to us so I lean in close, my breath warm on her skin, and whisper, "Come on? It's just lunch. Two people having a meal together."

As I speak, I tuck a loose strand of hair behind her ear, and she shivers, her whole body trembling slightly. The heat in her eyes is unmistakable, and I know she feels it too, and I can't let her get away.

Indecision is written all over her face as she seems to wrestle with the thoughts running through her head.

"I don't bite... unless you want me to," I add playfully with a wink.

She rolls her eyes and continues to scrutinize my face. Is she scared of something? Afraid to let down her guard? I need to know what she's thinking but I don't want to scare her off.

"Okay, one meal." She steps back and, after a deep breath, replies, "But we'll go Dutch."

No way in hell that's happening, but I nod in agreement.

"There's no time like the present. Want to grab some lunch? Rosie's makes the best Italian food in town."

Her stomach grumbles, and her eyes widen in embarrassment.

"I guess I could eat," she admits, begrudgingly. "I've got a couple more errands to run first, though."

"Meet me there at noon?" I flash what I hope is my sexiest grin.

"I should be able to make it by then," she says, "But only because I'm starving."

So am I. As she walks away, I can't help but notice how her shorts cling to her like a second skin.

One step closer to making her mine. I can almost taste the sweet victory on my tongue.

CHAPTER 17

Tessa

Over the last few days, I've been riding the biggest high. The rush from a kill and a good sleep are enough for me. A huge smile spreads across my face as I wake up this morning. Earlier this week, I turned on the news and heard a brief mention of Candice Smith's accidental overdose. *God, that was almost too easy.*

Allie called me yesterday to say Ansley was already on her way to her grandma's house in Alabama. According to her, Ansley is handling things surprisingly well, given the circumstances. She'll need therapy for a while, but Allie's referred her to someone local. Ansley will have a new beginning. The opportunity for a brighter future.

I went out early this morning to browse the home improvement store and run a few other errands. I've made up my mind—it's time to tackle some renovations, and an outdoor living space is something I've wanted for a while now. I haven't added any flowers or shrubs to my yard since I moved in last fall, except for the white rose bushes, of course.

Spring is almost over, and summer is quickly approaching. I love everything about lake life—the fresh scents, the melody of chirping birds, the breeze that rolls off the dock. Maybe I'll put in an in-ground pool. An infinity pool would be perfect, and I'm planning on repainting my sunroom. The previous owner picked a dull off-white color for the interior, but I'm considering something more vibrant—maybe sea blue or sunny yellow.

My day starts at the nail salon, getting a manicure and pedicure. I chose a lovely shade of pink with cute daisies. It's a bit girly, but I like to offset my darker side.

After paying, I head to the home improvement store, excited to see what they have to offer. I browse the patio and outdoor furniture briefly, then make my way to the paint section. I grab at least thirty color palette samples, and I'm flipping through them when I run into Eli.

"Well, hey there, Little Killer. Where's the fire?"

The scene at the bar has been replaying in my mind like a movie reel. I can't believe I gave in to him so quickly. I've always been careful about relationships—past experiences taught me to be. My side hobby is something I prefer to keep under wraps. You know, jail and all. I'd rock the shit out of orange, but I'd rather not spend the rest of my life behind bars.

Eli has an aura, a certain charm, that makes me feel inexplicably drawn to him. It's not just his rugged good looks, with his chiseled jawline and piercing blue eyes. *Though that definitely helps.* I hardly know him, but he makes me feel safe in an indescribable way—something I've never experienced. And apparently, my body is telling me it's been too long since I last got off with something besides my fingers and my vibrator.

And his mouth—lord help me. If we hadn't been interrupted at the bar, I'm certain I would've been riding his face by the end of the night. Just the thought of it has my panties soaked. I meant every word when I told Eli I wanted to make a good impression in Lake Falls. My profession requires me to be a good role model.

"I guess I could eat," I confess, amused over how he's charmed me into this so-called date. "I've got a couple more errands to run first, though."

Eli aims a sexy smile my way. "Meet me there at noon?"

"I should be able to make it by then, but only because I'm starving."

We part ways, and I next stop in the garden section and pick out a houseplant, lantana, and two rose bushes. White roses, with their delicate petals and sweet scent, symbolize purity and innocence. They have significant meaning for me. I have a garden full of them. One for each life I've taken. A rebirth of sorts.

I'm about to check out when a text message notification interrupts me. I grab my phone and enter my password, assuming it's from Allie, but it's from an unfamiliar number:

Little Killer, I'm not rushing you, but I've snagged us a small booth in the back at Rosie's. See you soon, beautiful.

How the hell did he get my number?

I type a quick reply: **Okay, Stalker. Be there soon.**

I arrive at Rosie's Italian Restaurant at exactly noon. This charming spot is known for serving some of the best Italian food in the state. I glance at the rearview mirror to check my appearance, and quickly finger-comb my beach waves and apply a small amount of lip gloss before heading inside.

A well-dressed gentleman, who I presume is the host, greets me with a friendly, "You must be Tessa. I'm Sam. Eli's waiting for you." He gives me a broad grin, followed by a wink. Eli probably knows everyone in the towns around Lake Lucia.

Feeling a little underdressed, I survey the other customers, relieved to see most are wearing casual attire.

"Our dress code applies only in the evenings," Sam says, as if reading my mind.

He leads me to a secluded table in the back, away from the crowd. The lighting is exquisite, soft and romantic, with the gentle glow of candlelight flickering across the room. As we approach the table, Eli stares at me intently, his eyes fixed on me as if I'm the only person in the room. The waiter pours water while I take the seat Sam pulls out for me.

"Thank you, Sam," Eli says, never taking his eyes off me as I join him. "You look even more beautiful in candlelight, just as I knew you would."

I've never been good at taking compliments, so I just roll my eyes. "I'm here. You can stop laying it on so thick."

He sits back casually. "I'm just calling it as I see it, Tessa."

"And how in the hell did you get my phone number?"

He smirks. "A friend of a friend."

"It's concerning that people are giving out my phone number to just anyone," I reply after the waiter takes our lunch order.

"Relax, I sweet-talked Allie."

He sounds so sure of himself.

"Oh really?" I say, raising an eyebrow in surprise over the fact that Allie gave my number out without even telling me. "So tell me about yourself. The only thing I know is that you're from Lake

Falls and run a construction company. That's about it." I keep my knowledge of his sister's kidnapping and murder to myself.

"Yes, that much is true. I've always been into building things—using my hands, that kind of stuff. It wasn't my first job, though. I served in the Navy, starting at age nineteen. After a few tours, I decided it was time to leave, and I came home and started a business with my friend Jace. You met him the other day."

I nearly choke on my water. He's *ex-military*? *SHIT.* I quickly compose myself.

"The Navy, huh? Wow, I'm impressed. Was it something you always wanted to do, or was it one of those commercials with the *'Honor, Courage, Commitment'* thing?" I say, half-jokingly.

His eyes flicker with brief pain and guilt, but he stares back unflinchingly. "I was going through some things, and the Navy gave me many opportunities."

I pause, unsure of what to say, but luckily, the waiter arrives with our meal.

I'm starving, so when I take a bite, I can't help but groan in appreciation.

"It's good, right?" Eli says, a slow, knowing smile spreading across his face. The darkness in his gaze has faded, revealing a lighter, more joyful expression.

"So very good," I close my eyes as the delicious taste of garlic and pasta sauce fills my mouth.

We eat in comfortable silence, the only sound being the gentle clinking of silverware, while my brain races to process everything I've learned about him. Getting involved with Eli could lead to trouble. He could easily stumble onto my less-than-honorable activities. The thought of him discovering my secret and recoiling in disgust makes my heart sink.

"Hey, is everything alright? You look a little pale." Concern flickers in his eyes as he reaches for my hand and gently rubs it.

I force a smile. "Everything's fine. I was just thinking about something that happened at work."

"Am I boring you?" he teases.

"No, of course not," I say evasively. "Did you have to kill a lot of people when you were in the military?"

"Yes, but only those who deserved it," he says seriously, before a smirk lights his face. "I'd tell you about it, but then I'd have to kill you."

I become aware of his hand still resting on mine, the gentle stroking sending shivers down my spine.

"So, tell me about yourself. You're a nurse practitioner, right? Do you enjoy it?" He takes a sip of water before continuing. "Trevor said you were the one who sewed up his finger after he nearly chopped it off with a table saw."

I relax into this question. It's easy to answer. I've wanted to be a nurse for as long as I can remember. My work is deeply rewarding because I genuinely enjoy helping those who need it.

Eli's intense focus makes me think he's truly interested in what I say and conversation flows so easily with him. I find myself sharing more about my house and my vision for the outdoor living area. He tells me about his work and how much he enjoys fishing. Before I know it, I've nearly cleaned my plate. I don't pretend to be embarrassed; I'm not ashamed of my appetite or my body.

Despite my objections, he insists on picking up the tab after our meal.

As we leave the restaurant, he places his hand on my lower back, startling me. "I'm just making sure you don't get away too easily," he murmurs. My body buzzes with electricity, and I feel a flutter in my core. Once we're outside, the sun warms my skin, and a gentle breeze caresses me. He walks me out, guiding me toward my car.

How does he know what I drive? My eyes narrow at him in suspicion. "I saw you pull in," he says with a shrug.

"Yeah, okay," I reply. Seriously though, has he been digging into my life? He seems to know a lot about me—more than he should.

I push aside the flicker of worry that rises within me. He's harmless. The man literally saved my life, and he's definitely not hard on the eyes. In fact, he's kind of easy to stare at. There's no reason to worry—at least, that's what I keep telling myself.

His eyes lock on mine, bold and unwavering. "Since we're friends now, when can I see you again?"

A smirk plays across my lips. "Friends? Why do I feel like you're looking for more than friendship?"

His gaze, filled with desire, drops to my lips as he pushes me back against my car, his body pressing against mine in all the right places.

"I'd have to be fucking dead not to want more. Not to want you. But I'll take what I can get." He pulls back, releasing me. "For now," he adds, his voice carrying an ominous edge as he turns toward his truck. "See you later, Tess," he says, climbing into his vehicle.

My knees wobble as I press the unlock button and sink into the driver's seat. Jesus Christ, what is this man doing to me?

As I start the car, I notice he's climbed into the cab of his truck and is waiting on me before he drives off. That is a gentlemanly thing to do, right? He doesn't move until I pull out of the parking lot, then follows behind me since we're headed in the same direction. I drive toward home, my thoughts firmly stuck on Eli. Perhaps I'm fighting this too much. A quick fling could be good for me.

Upon entering the city limits, he turns onto Main Street, heading toward the town center. Disappointment hits me like a wave, and a soft chuckle escapes me. Did I really think he was going to follow me home and fuck me senseless? The absurdity of my own thoughts makes me roll my eyes.

I continue for a few miles before turning left onto Deer Point Road. I adore this street and everything about the neighborhood. We have ample space, so our homes aren't crammed together like those in the newer, wealthier developments. It's elegant but not ostentatious. My neighbors are friendly but keep to themselves for the most part, just the way I like it.

I park in front of my house and start to get out of my car when something catches my eye.

The front door is wide open. I'm certain I locked it and set the alarm before leaving this morning. My fingers hover over my bag, reaching for my Glock, when I see Jane Hill, my neighbor, rushing toward me, waving her phone wildly.

I pause.

"Don't go in there, dear!" Jane shouts. "Cricket started barking while we were walking, and I saw a man sneaking out of your house!"

What the hell?

Had someone been in my house?

I tamper down the panic rising in my chest and turn to Jane. "Did you recognize the man?"

"I don't think so, but my Cricket scared him off," she declares with pride.

My gaze drops to the yappy Pomeranian snapping at her heels. I highly doubt Cricket could scare away a fly, but I don't argue.

"Thank you," I reply. "I called the sheriff, and they're on their way," Jane adds, bouncing a little too excitedly. "Don't worry, they'll track down whoever did this."

Jane has been watching too much *Law and Order* again, and at eighty-four, this is probably the highlight of her year. She is a sweet, harmless woman who recently celebrated her sixtieth wedding anniversary with her husband Fred.

The wail of sirens draws near, and I internally groan. Fuck. I would have preferred to handle this myself, without involving the police.

A black Dodge Charger with flashing blue lights pulls up, the gold *Sheriff's Office* insignia gleaming on its sides. Two officers emerge after the sirens are silenced. I recognize one as Marshall Randall, the sheriff's son. The *good* one, apparently. The other officer is roughly my height, with short blond hair and a cocky attitude I can see coming from a mile away.

Marshall tosses me a curt nod, and he and Mr. Cocky make a beeline for the house. "Wait out here."

"Okay," I reply, the word tasting like ash in my mouth as I paste on a fake smile. Inside, I'm fuming. I'm not some delicate flower or a helpless damsel in distress. *Stay here, where it's safe.* Sure. Okay.

Their guns are drawn as they cautiously enter the house. It doesn't take long. A few minutes later, Marshall and the other officer return, holstering their weapons.

"There's no sign of anyone, and nothing looks disturbed as far as I can tell. Could you check inside to see if anything's missing or out of place? Ethan will follow you while I speak with Mrs. Hill about what she saw."

I nod and head into the house. My security system is state-of-the-art. Bryce had installed it and assured me it was the best, which meant no one should have been able to get past it. The violation gnaws at me. How dare someone invade my personal space? I search through every room, searching for anything amiss.

"Does anything look out of place, ma'am?" Mr. Cocky asks, his tone laced with boredom.

"I don't think so."

"Anything missing? Jewelry, electronics, underwear—" he muses, jotting notes. "Anyone have a key or access to your security code? Any ex-boyfriends or family members that might have an ax to grind?"

"No. And no to everything else," I snap.

Marshall and Jane are standing near the island in my open-concept kitchen. The large picture windows frame a view of the backyard and lake.

"Jane gave me a description, but we don't have much to go on," Marshall says. "Tessa, are you sure you locked the door and set the alarm?"

Yes, dumbass.

"Pretty sure," I answer meekly, playing the fragile woman for now. I need them gone so I can check the indoor cameras.

They question me for another thirty minutes, and once I get everyone out of the house, I head into the library, access the safe room and enter the code and thumbprint ID. I keep everything in there from guns to knives to pharmaceuticals to my favorite hardback book collection. *What? My books need to be safe too.* Everything is secure.

I grab up my laptop to view the indoor cameras, and my jaw drops as I open the program and check the footage. My heart pounds. The video glitched for eleven minutes. The intruder used a key.

No one had a key.

Not even Bryce.

A chill runs down my spine.

I call Bryce to fill him in as my home alarm chimes—someone is pulling into my driveway.

CHAPTER 18

Elijah

A smug grin spreads across my face as I relive my date with Tessa. It was a date, whether she wants to admit it or not. The more time I spend with her, the more I want to learn everything about her.

Following behind Tessa as far as I can, the urge to keep going almost overpowers my need to make this next important stop. A long-overdue stop.

Turning onto Main Street, I drive toward the police station. It's been months since I've heard from Sheriff Randall about the investigation into my sister's death. My anger rises with each passing day, week, month, and year, and it's becoming harder to control.

Walking through the police station's front door, the familiar bell rings. I nod to Millie, who's been at the front desk for as long as I can remember, and she offers a pleasant smile, but I can't help but see the pity in her eyes. "Good afternoon, Eli. Did you come to see the Sheriff?"

"Yes, ma'am. Is he available?"

Millie nods and makes the call from her desk phone. "I'll let him know you're here."

Within seconds, Sheriff Randall emerges from his office, and motions for me to come in.

"Eli, how are you doing?" he asks, shaking my hand. "Sit down and make yourself comfortable, son."

The room is unchanged after all these years. Framed pictures cover the walls—many featuring him, other law enforcement officers, politicians, and even one showing him with Matthew McConaughey during a movie shoot in Georgia a few years back. Several photos litter his desk, all of them showing his wife and sons at various stages of their lives. Speaking of which, I need to talk to him about Wilson.

"Sheriff, I wanted to get an update on the investigation."

"Eli, you know as much as I do. After all these years we continue to hit nothing but brick walls, and more than anything we want to give you and your parents closure and get justice for Paisley."

My jaw tightens. "I have nothing but respect for this office, but the disappearances of underage girls in neighboring towns can't be a coincidence. There has to be a connection between those girls and my sister. They have to be related somehow."

My hand balls into a fist as the heat of frustration builds inside me. "Have you explored neighboring states? Consider contacting the FBI?" I grit out.

He bristles at my insinuation that he doesn't know how to do his job. "We've already requested assistance from the FBI, but they rejected our inquiry, and we've pursued every lead they would've offered."

It's no secret that the federal and local governments have a long-standing history of inability to work together. It's not that they don't trust each other, it's essentially a dick-measuring contest between the two.

This Saturday would've been Paisley's twenty-fourth birthday. "It's been a decade since my sister was abducted, sexually assaulted, mutilated, and killed. How would you feel if it were your own sister or daughter?"

The Sheriff's face betrays a hint of shame. "I can't comprehend the pain you've been through since your sister's death," he says with a heavy sigh. "We're still determined to find the person who took her life."

I can tell this conversation is going nowhere, and there's no use in arguing with him further. It's time I start looking into things myself. My father hired a private investigator a year or two after Paisley's death, but even he didn't uncover anything.

I can't shake the possibility of never knowing what happened. I refuse to.

Having nothing more to say, I shove off my chair, mumbling my thanks as I head for the door. Halfway there, I remember Wilson, but as I turn to give the sheriff an earful over his son, I hear Millie's voice over the intercom. "I'm so sorry to interrupt, Sheriff, but there's been an incident. Reports of a 10-62 in progress at 27 Deer Point Road. Marshall and Ethan have already arrived and secured the scene."

A wave of cold fear washes over me as I recognize that address. *Tessa.* Shit. I realize a 10-62 is a 'breaking and entering in progress.'

I burst out the door, ignoring Millie's startled yelp as I rush past her. Slamming my truck into gear I speed toward Tessa's house, the tires screeching on the pavement.

Keeping an eye on the clock, each minute drags by until I finally pull into her driveway. I breathe a sigh of relief, noticing the absence of flashing lights and sirens. The police have already left, and the lack of ambulances and body bags only deepens the sense of relief.

Exiting the truck, I hurry to her front door and ring the bell, my impatience growing. As I wait, I glance around, taking in my surroundings. The door swings open, and a gun is pressed to my head.

"Jesus. First a knife, now a gun?" My eyebrows shoot up in disbelief as she yanks me inside, the firearm steady in her grip. "What the hell?"

"You scared the shit out of me. What are you doing here, Eli?"

My eyes sweep over her, searching for any signs of injury. No cuts, no bruises—but something flickers in her gaze. Anger, maybe, but beneath it, I catch the glimmer of something else. Fear.

"I came to check on you, Tess. I was at the station when the sheriff got the call about your break-in. What happened? Are you okay?"

She takes a deep breath, then, with practiced ease, ejects the bullets from the chamber. The gun and ammo disappear into the drawer of the entryway table with a soft click.

"I'm fine," she says. "Someone broke in while I was gone. My neighbor saw them and called the police. They just left."

"Shit, Tess." I run a hand through my hair, exhaling sharply.

"I checked the whole place, but nothing seems missing. I don't know if my neighbor, Jane, interrupted him before he found whatever he was looking for... or what." She hesitates, briefly looking away.

"I saw the cameras outside. Did you recognize the guy?"

She shakes her head. "That's the strange part. The outside cameras caught someone in a hoodie using a key to get inside. He bypassed my security system somehow." Her voice wavers slightly. She looks up at me, her fierce eyes betraying the fear she fights to suppress.

"Nobody—nobody—has a key to my house. And nobody knows my security code." She hugs herself, arms crossing tightly over her chest as though to shield herself from an unseen threat. "I feel so violated."

Seeing Tessa vulnerable is unsettling. She is strong and capable. But now, something twists inside me—an instinct to protect her, to keep her safe. I swallow it down.

I cast a slow glance around the living room and kitchen. Her home is beautiful, a perfect blend of modern updates and warmth. I've been here before—long ago, when one of my grade school friends' parents owned it. They moved away a few years back, and the house eventually went on the market. Renovations breathe new life into the place.

Reaching for her, I invite her into my arms. She hesitates for only a second before stepping forward, surrendering to the embrace.

"I won't let anything happen to you," I murmur, my voice low, steady.

"Why?" she says, looking up at me, her eyes searching mine. "You don't even know me."

"I know enough," I reply with a smirk.

She smells incredible—jasmine and the sweet scent of strawberry shampoo. I shift slightly so she won't feel the growing hardness between us.

"Let me help you get the locks changed. I know a guy."

Releasing her, I pull out my phone and call Ed, a trusted locksmith I've used for years.

"He'll be here in about an hour," I tell her after ending the call, brushing a stray lock of blonde hair out of her face and tucking it behind her ear.

"Thank you," she says softly, pressing a gentle kiss to my cheek.

I smile, feeling the warmth of her lips lingering on my skin. "I can think of a few ways you can thank me," I joke.

She glances at my lips, then back into my eyes, her expression playful yet intense.

"I bet you can," she replies, her voice low and teasing.

This girl... she's fiery, and I can't get enough of it.

"Since I'm here, maybe you can show me what you want," I say, gesturing toward the back door.

"Huh?" she stammers, clearly flustered.

"Outside," I say with a wink. "The outdoor living area you want to redo. What did you think I meant?"

She laughs, shaking her head before motioning for me to follow. As we step onto the back porch, I take in the expansive yard and the lake stretching out beyond the fence. Her garden is a stunning display of white roses, and there must be at least a dozen blooming in a soft cluster, their petals glowing in the fading sunlight. This place is a prime spot—serene, quiet, a little slice of paradise.

She points out the areas she wants to renovate, and I can already picture the improvements in my head. The project would be easy enough.

"I see you have an outdoor shower," I say, nodding toward a small wooden structure in the corner of the yard. Dark-stained oak walls and pebble steps lead to the entrance, complementing the tranquility of the space.

"It was one thing I absolutely had to have," she replies, her excitement evident. "After a run or a swim in the lake, I love rinsing off before going inside."

We move closer to take a look, and as we do, she stumbles over the water nozzle.

Ice-cold water bursts from the showerhead, drenching us both instantly.

She squeals, her face flushing as she scrambles to turn the nozzle off. "Oh my God, I'm so sorry!"

Laughter rumbles up from my chest, the initial shock fading quickly. I glance down at her, and my breath catches—her white tank top clings to her curves, nearly translucent, the lace of her bra and the hard peaks of her nipples unmistakable beneath the soaked fabric.

Dragging my gaze back to her face, I find her staring at me, something darker in her expression now. Her lips part slightly, the air between us thickening.

Stepping closer, my chest brushes against hers, the heat of her body seeping into mine.

I'm not sure who moves first, but suddenly our lips collide, desperate and hungry. Her hand slides around my neck, pulling me deeper, her tongue meeting mine in a fevered rhythm. I trace my fingers down her cheek, along her jawline, then down her neck to her collarbone. She tastes like sugar and desire, and I can't get enough.

She pulls her mouth from mine and draws in a ragged breath, looking up at me with a hesitant expression.

"We should stop," I respond easily, taking a small step back. The last thing I would ever do is push her into something she isn't ready for.

"No. Don't stop. Please. Fuck me, Eli."

That's all the encouragement I need. I pull her wet tank over her shoulders and head. *God, she is fucking beautiful.* She's grabbing at my shirt and yanks it off, and then her hands are everywhere all at once. Peppering light kisses down her neck and collarbone, I keep moving lower until I reach her ample breasts, and I take her pebbled nipple into my mouth through the bra, sucking hard. She moans and grinds against me. I flick the other nipple with my other hand and slowly run my hand down into her shorts beneath her lacy thong. She's soaking wet for me. My cock's so hard I feel like I'm going to burst out of my shorts.

"God damn, baby," I growl. "So fucking wet."

"That feels so good," she moans when I shove two fingers into her tight pussy and rub circles around her clit with my thumb.

"I can feel how ready you are."

"Oh, dear god, Eli. I need you."

Tessa yanks my shorts down, and my cock springs out. She wraps her hands around my shaft and pumps it. She rubs at the precum on the head of my penis with a finger and smirks, taking the finger to her mouth and sucking it off. So fucking hot. So full of surprises.

"I need to go grab a condom."

"I'm on the pill."

I pause. "I've been tested, and I'm clean, but are you sure?"

"Yes. Please, I can't wait any longer. I need you to make me come," she pleads, her steel gray eyes darkened with desire.

Fuck it. I peel off her shorts and panties, lift her hips, and rub the base of my cock against her tight dripping entrance. Without further hesitation, I toss her against the shower wall and thrust deeply inside her, and we both groan with relief. She's so tight, it's like her sweet cunt was made for me. I capture her lips in mine and continue hard, fast strokes.

"That's right, Tess. Fucking come on this dick like the good girl you are."

Within seconds, her moans of pleasure spike, and she screams out my name, her pussy contracting around my cock. My balls tighten as I sense my building climax, and I push deeper inside her, filling her with my release.

"Oh, fuck," I groan as I let the euphoria wash over me. We're both gasping for air, our bodies still fused. I've never come so hard in my life.

I press my lips against hers, just as a truck horn honks loudly.

"Oh, my god." Her face is flushed crimson, and I've never seen anything more beautiful in my life.

I lean my forehead down against hers. "That must be Ed." I yank my wet clothes back on. "Wait here. I'll distract him while you get dressed."

CHAPTER 19

Tessa

What the hell did I just do?

This isn't like me. I don't act impulsively; I carefully plan everything. I'm cautious, meticulous to a fault. The last thing I need is to get involved with a local. I avoid attachments and steer clear of relationships. Whatever this is, I have to nip it in the bud before it goes any further.

But damn, he's going to be hard to walk away from. He makes me feel things I shouldn't feel, and don't even get me started on what he just did to my body. Today's events have left me buzzing with adrenaline, and my mind won't settle down.

I grab my dripping clothes from the floor, hastily covering myself as I slip through the back door and race up the stairs to my bathroom.

After the quickest shower of my life, I brush through my tangled hair, throw on a pair of jeans and an old Jason Aldean concert t-shirt.

The faint hum of a drill can be heard as I descend the stairs to meet the guy changing my locks. Eli's eyes—sharp and bright—connect with mine as I enter the foyer, and a slow blush creeps up my face. He's talking to a short, stocky man, presumably Ed, who looks to be in his late forties or early fifties. He pretends not to notice our exchange.

"Tess, this is Ed. He's the best locksmith around."

Ed flashes a light, friendly smile my way. "I'm the only locksmith you'll find in this area. But he's right—I'm the best."

"Thank you for coming so quickly."

Eli coughs, trying to contain his laughter, and I nearly die, realizing the double entendre I accidentally uttered. Instant mortification fills me as I long for the floor to open up and swallow me whole.

"I was about to lock up and head home when Eli called. It's impossible to refuse a Huntington," Ed tells me, completely oblivious to our inside joke.

Eli looks a little embarrassed but quickly dismisses it. "I'm sure it's got nothing to do with the amount of work I give you—or the six-pack of beer I promised."

Ed chuckles. "You know I like a cold beer at the end of a long workday."

Their easy comradery makes it clear they've known each other for ages. That's how it is in small towns.

He finishes changing all my locks quickly, and I reach for my purse. "How much do I owe you?"

"Not a thing. We already have it worked out." Ed smiles, glancing at Eli.

I shoot Eli a withering look. "I'm not letting you pay for me. This is my problem, not yours."

"Calm down, Tess. It's already taken care of."

With a huff, I fold my arms across my chest.

"Hey, if you want to make it up to me, we can figure something out," he says, his eyes gleaming.

I throw up my hands in exasperation. "We'll deal with this later."

Turning to Ed, I say, "Thank you so much," and wave goodbye as he leaves. Eli walks outside with him and returns moments later with my new set of house keys and a small duffle bag.

"What the hell is that?"

"A bag. I keep a clean change of clothes in my truck, just in case. I always like to be prepared," he responds.

"So, you like to be the knight in shining armor, coming to the rescue of the damsel in distress?" I raise an eyebrow at him. "Do you always fuck them too?"

The flash of anger and hurt in his eyes triggers a sudden wave of guilt within me.

"Actually, this is the first time," he replies sharply.

"I'm sorry. You're here to check on me, and I'm being an asshole." A frown mares my face. "I should have said thank you. I'm just really shaken up after the break-in."

"Tessa, listen to me." He gently places his hands on my shoulders. "Whoever did this could come back, and you shouldn't be alone tonight. We can finish what we started, or I'll crash on your couch, but I'm not going anywhere."

"Do you think I can't take care of myself?"

He takes hold of my chin, his gaze unwavering. "This isn't up for debate. I'm staying."

I let out a disgruntled sigh. "Okay, just for tonight, but at least get into some dry clothes. You can shower in the guest bathroom upstairs, first door to your right."

With a mock salute, he heads up the stairs, and I shake my head in disbelief. Making sure the doors are locked and the alarm is set, I reach for the TV remote and switch it on, craving the sound, some kind of distraction. Perhaps I should cook dinner for him, or maybe just order something in. After a quick peek into my empty pantry, it's clear—food delivery it is. Reaching into the fridge, I take out a bottle of wine to pour myself a glass, when a news broadcast on the television interrupts my thoughts. The reporter is talking about an investigation underway in Baker County after a teacher was accused of taping a fourteen-year-old student to their desk. Following allegations—Ronald Tweed, age thirty-four—has been suspended without pay pending the investigation. His parents say they discovered a recording of their son, who has special needs, posted on social media. The parents' faces, filled with anguish, are displayed on the screen.

"We were horrified and sickened to learn our son, who is autistic and non-verbal, was being tied to his desk. He uses his hands to communicate. We don't understand why this happened—" She breaks down in sobs, tears streaming down her face, and her husband finishes the interview.

Rage and heartache consume me. No child should be subjected to that kind of behavior.

"That's fucked up," Eli remarks as he comes down the stairs, freshly showered and carrying the scent of soap and my strawberry shampoo. It smells even better on him. "There's a special place in hell for sick people like that."

I nod somberly in agreement, a heavy sigh escaping my lips. Indeed, there is, and I look forward to speeding up the process by personally pushing them into the fiery pits of hell. I'm unsure what that means for me, I've never been particularly religious, and I doubt God would approve of my actions. I'll probably end up in the same place as those evil bastards. If that's the case, I look forward to terrorizing them even more.

"Want something to drink? I have water, wine, and beer."

"A beer sounds perfect," Eli replies. I grab a long-necked bottle from the fridge and hand it to him. The brush of his fingers sends a shiver down my spine, a thrilling heat spreading through me. Being around Eli awakens sensations within me I never knew existed.

"I'm ordering some food to be delivered. Do you have any requests?" I ask while navigating the app on my phone.

"It doesn't matter to me," his voice is husky, he licks his lips, scanning me like I'm a whole snack. "I'd rather devour you, Little Killer."

His words instantly spark a jolt of heat in my core, causing my thighs to clench involuntarily. Words fail me, and I find myself lost in the depths of his piercing eyes, my cell slips out of my hands clattering against the marble.

Eli inches closer, his body taut with tension, like a predator on the prowl. He corners me, pinning me against the cold, hard countertop. As he runs a hand up my arm, goosebumps rise in their path, like tiny beads of excitement.

Tracing my lower lip with his thumb, he whispers, "Would you like that? Me feasting on your pretty pink pussy?"

Letting out a soft moan, my tongue darts out to wet my parched lips, and he seizes the opportunity to slip his thumb into my mouth. "Suck," he commands, his voice firm. Without hesitation I comply, savoring the taste of him as I lick and suck on it, eliciting a groan from him, and I can feel the hard, unyielding pressure of his erection against my body.

He removes his thumb and scoops me into his arms, hoisting me onto the counter. His hands, warm and assertive, slide under my shirt, tracing a path across my stomach. I help him pull my shirt off, and he eases my jeans to the floor, leaving me in just a thin scrap of fabric. Feeling his fingers cup me, I become acutely aware of the moisture seeping into my panties. He yanks them down, slowly lowers himself to his knees, and lifts my legs over his shoulders. My arms are braced against the counter and Eli's gaze is molten with longing, his eyes burning with a fiery passion that catches my breath in my throat.

"You're so wet and ready for me," he groans, before teasingly licking and kissing my outer lips. My hips involuntarily buck, desperate for more. When his mouth finally reaches my clit, I'm overwhelmed by a cascade of sensations. His firm attention on my clit nearly brings me to climax right away.

"Uh-uh. Not yet," he murmurs before gently tracing his finger along my folds and sliding it inside me. He inserts another finger and moves them in and out slowly as he runs his tongue back across my clit.

"Please, don't stop," I whisper urgently.

As his fingers hit that special spot inside me, he increases the intensity of his thrusts. He devours me like a starving man, as if I'm his final meal.

"Oh, my God. Oh, Eli," I gasp before reaching my peak. My muscles tighten around his fingers, and a wave of sensation engulfs me as I tumble over the edge. Gradually slowing his thrusts, he withdraws his fingers from me, taking a moment to lick off my sweet essence.

"Absolutely delectable, Tessa," he says, his voice rich with satisfaction.

Eli helps me back down to the floor, my legs wobbly and unsteady. I cling to his shoulders for support, momentarily resting my forehead on his chest.

"Is that all you've got?" I smirk, letting a slow, sly smile play on my lips.

His eyes, filled with insatiable longing, meet mine. "We're just getting started."

I grab his shirt and begin to pull it off. My jaw drops as I really look at his chest for the first time, noticing his six-pack and the powerful muscles in his arms. I unbuckle his belt, unzip his jeans, and reach into his boxers to grasp his firm length. My body tingles with excitement, a thrill coursing through me like a jolt of electricity. His jeans fall as he steps out of them. His large, hard erection is impossible to ignore. Holy shit, he's even more massive than I remember. A bead of precum glistens at the tip, signaling his arousal. He kisses me hard, his lips consuming mine, the taste of minty toothpaste mingling with my own juices. *Huh, he must carry toothpaste around in his bag as well.* The sensation of him unhooking my bra snaps me back to the present. My bra falls to the ground, and my nipples harden in response.

"You are fucking beautiful. These perfect tits fill my hands as if they were made just for me. I could spend hours worshiping every inch of your body," he says softly as he cups my breast and toys with my nipple.

He moves his mouth to my other breast, sucking and nipping at my stiffened peak. A loud moan escapes my lips. As my hands roam over his body, they eventually find their way to his perfect cock, which is standing at full attention for me. I tightly grasp his firm shaft and begin to stroke it slowly, feeling the heat building between my legs. My pussy's drenched, my release seeping down my thighs.

I kneel eagerly, itching to take his throbbing dick into my mouth, but he stops me. "No, not like that," he growls. "I need to be back inside your perfect, tight cunt."

He lifts me and flips me over onto the counter, face down. His hands reach down to my slit, rubbing over my clit. I feel his hard cock pushing against my entrance. As he thrusts deeply inside me, I release a moan of pleasure.

"That's it, Tess. Take this dick like a good girl," he praises.

The room is filled with the intense sound of skin slapping against skin as he pulls out and thrusts even harder. With my face pressed against the counter, his movements grow more rapid, and his skillful hand massages small circles around my clit.

"You like it rough, don't you?"

Turns out, I have a praise kink. Who knew?

I curve my spine, allowing him to strike deeper.

"Yes, sir."

"Good. Fucking. Girl." Eli growls.

As the sensations grow stronger, I climax, screaming his name as I squirt onto his cock. I can feel his balls tightening as he grunts, spilling himself into me. Eli sinks against me, his weight a comforting pressure, and his lips brush softly against my shoulder.

I'm breathless, my heart pounding like a drum, but my body has never felt so sated.

"That was... unbelievable," I murmur, my body exhausted.

He gently pulls out, then grabs a rag from the hall bathroom. The damp cloth feels cool against my skin as he washes me up, then carries me to the couch. Pulling a throw blanket over us, he snuggles close, spooning me. His lips brush across my forehead. My eyelids grow heavy, and I can barely keep them open. As I drift off to sleep, his arms around me, all I can think of is how perfect this is. But it can't last. As much as I crave it, crave *him*, I know this moment is fleeting, that it will end. I have to make sure it does.

CHAPTER 20

Elijah

As Tessa sleeps, I watch her. Her breathing is barely audible. I could spend hours just watching her. Gently, I brush a stray blonde lock from her face and tuck it behind her ear. She's mine, though she doesn't know it yet. Now that I've tasted her, I'll never let her go. This feeling is unlike anything I've ever known.

I've had casual relationships, but none were significant enough for me even to consider bringing them home to meet my family. We respected each other, and I never let anyone think we were more serious than we were, no promises of forever. We'd go our separate ways but still be friends.

The only real entanglement was with my high school girlfriend, Molly. Losing my sister sent me spiraling. The pain was unbearable, and I started using drugs and drinking to numb myself. I blamed everyone, even myself. Molly tried to be there for me, but she couldn't understand why I couldn't just process it and move on. I isolated myself, refusing to answer her calls or texts. For months, she tried to reach out, including showing up at my house. I'd either ignore the doorbell or get my parents to tell her to leave.

Eventually, she gave up and went to college at Clemson, where she started dating a baseball player.

As for me, I let go of my football scholarship. I no longer believed I deserved the dreams I'd once held dear. My parents were wrapped in their own grief and couldn't support me. Dad buried himself in work, while Mom filled her time with charity events and book clubs. Sometimes, I'd wake to the sound of her cries, echoing through the empty house. Every time she cried, I wished I had died instead. If Jace hadn't pushed me to get my act together and the recruiter hadn't convinced me to join the Navy, I might not be here today.

Tessa shifts in her sleep, and for a brief moment, I worry she'll wake and catch me staring at her like a creep. Her eyes are still closed, and a contented sigh escapes her lips. One thing I know for sure, I'll never let Tessa down. She's mine now, she just doesn't know it yet. With my arm around her waist, her soft breaths lull me into a peaceful slumber.

I wake a few hours later, the first light of dawn casting long shadows across the still waters of the lake. Tessa is sprawled across me, her head resting on my chest, her blonde hair catching the early morning light. Our legs are tangled together, and the blanket has slipped down, revealing the soft swell of her full breasts. Within moments, my morning wood turns into a raging hard-on. She's sleeping so peacefully that I don't want to disturb her. While it might be tempting, I'm not into somnophilia. As I ease myself out from beneath her, she sighs softly and rolls over. I pull the blanket up over her, slip on my boxers, and head to the bathroom to take a piss.

The downstairs hasn't changed much, except for the kitchen and living room merging into one open space. It shines with a modern touch and is impeccably organized. The bathroom is painted in a calm blue hue, adding a sense of tranquility to the space. After I finish, I lower the toilet seat, like the gentleman I am. Turning around, I glance at the painting on the wall. It's a picture of a blonde toddler playing in the sand, building a sandcastle. Her smile beams up at the artist, her eyes sparkling a deep, nearly metallic gray.

As I leave the bathroom, something catches my attention. A tiny glimmer in the painting. It's a small camera, no bigger than a pinhole, hidden in the child's eye. *Why would Tessa have a camera in her bathroom?* I exit quietly and survey the kitchen, spotting three more cameras in various places: the smoke detector, an electrical outlet, and within a decorative plant. I'm completely confused by this—like trying to solve a puzzle with no pieces. Why would Tessa need all of these cameras? Is she trying to escape something or someone? She's hiding something from me, but I know without a shadow of a doubt that I'd kill anyone who even thought about hurting her. I need to uncover her secrets, and I'm determined to find the truth, no matter what.

Returning to the living room, I lay down on the couch beside her. Her delicate features and peaceful slumber make her seem like an angel. As she stirs, she unconsciously rubs her ass against my groin. Alright, maybe a wicked angel. My dick hardens, and she jolts awake, her eyes snapping open. She stares at me, a mix of shock and uncertainty in her gaze, though there's an unmistakable hint of longing underneath.

"Well, shit," she mutters.

With a raised eyebrow, I remark, "That's not the usual reaction I get after bringing a woman to orgasm multiple times."

She rolls her eyes and makes a dramatic face palm but then softens and leans her head against my chest. Her hard nipples brush against my skin, and my dick perks up, nudging against her clit. A soft, pleasurable moan escapes her as she rolls her hips in response. Her stare feels heavy as she lifts her head to look into my eyes.

"This is the last time," she whispers to herself.

That's what she thinks.

She grabs my throat, pushing me onto my back with surprising strength. Climbing on top of me, she presses her lips to mine, her tongue exploring my mouth as she straddles me. Her arousal is evident, dripping onto my stomach. Our tongues twist and tangle, deepening the connection between us. Reaching for my cock, she begins stroking. She lifts herself above me, arching her hips before slowly sinking down onto me, enveloping me completely.

"Oh, fuck, baby," I groan, mesmerized by the way her breasts bounce as she moves. "That's right, Tess, ride me like the dirty little slut you are."

She moans, and I spank her perfectly rounded ass. "Fuck, Eli. You feel so good."

"Touch yourself," I order, and she obeys, rubbing her clit in slow circles. I grab her nipple and pinch hard, and she screams as she comes, her walls clenching around me. I follow her as we ride the wave together before she collapses on top of me. I don't know how long we lie there, my dick slowly softening as I lazily caress her back.

I can tell she's deep in thought. She's probably trying to talk herself out of this—out of us. But I'm not going anywhere.

Her phone shrieks, making her jump off me and scramble to her feet. "Shit. What time is it? I'm going to be late for work."

With my arms folded behind my head, I watch her move around in her naked glory.

She grabs her phone, sighs in relief. "I still have an hour."

In that moment, she realizes she's standing naked in front of the window. She squeaks and retreats from the glass panes.

I grin, appreciatively. "No need to hide that gorgeous body."

"How am I supposed to walk into work knowing I might have flashed everyone?" She gasps, feigning shock and clutching her imaginary pearls. "The horror!"

"Did you just make a joke, Tessa?"

Her face lights up with a grin as she looks at me, her eyes sparkling with amusement. "I can be funny when I want to be."

My gaze falls to her pouty lips. Lips that would look quite nice wrapped around my cock.

"I need to get a shower," she says, shooing me away.

"I could join you." My voice is low and husky, as I move toward her.

"Um, no. Otherwise, this'll turn into round five." She spins around, fleeing towards the stairs. With a smirk, she tosses over her shoulder, "You can see yourself out."

Wait, what?

I know she didn't just say what I think she said.

"Don't forget, your clothes are in the dryer," she adds, motioning toward the laundry room as she heads up the stairs. "It was fun!"

My jaw drops, then stretches into a grin. She really thinks she can get rid of me that easily. I must have fucked her stupid. Grabbing my clothes from the dryer, I head to the kitchen. The rumbling in my stomach reminds me it's been a while since I had real food. Rummaging through her cupboards and refrigerator, I find the ingredients needed to make a couple of omelets and start cooking. I turn on the coffee maker. I'm not sure how she takes her coffee yet, but I'll figure it out soon enough.

About half an hour later, she appears at the bottom of the stairs, jaw dropped in surprise when she sees the food laid out.

"I believe I instructed you to leave."

"Actually, you said, 'You can see yourself out,'" I correct. "And I will. After I've fed you."

Tessa eyes me suspiciously as she reaches for one of the coffee cups. I watch her grab caramel *macchiato* creamer, *noted*.

"How do you take your coffee?" she asks.

"Black, two sugars. Thanks."

Her movements are simple but graceful. The dark blue scrubs she's wearing catch my eye. I never thought scrubs could be sexy, but those pants hug her curves just right.

"Come sit," I gesture toward the barstool. "I hope you like omelets."

"I love them," she replies. After begrudgingly taking a seat, she takes a bite, and moans in appreciation. "This is amazing." She takes another bite, glancing sideways at me. "Maybe I should have you cook for me more often."

I chuckle quietly to myself as I lower myself into the barstool beside her. Forking a piece of my omelet, I savor the flavors that hit my tongue. It's pretty damn good, if I do say so myself.

We proceed with our meal in a comfortable silence.

When we're finished, she takes the plates to the dishwasher, a faint blush coloring her cheeks. She turns back to face me. "So..."

"Yeah, I should get going. Jace is probably wondering where I am," I say, pulling out my phone as it dings with a text. I grab my duffle bag and toss it over my shoulder. "Let me walk you to your car."

With a sigh, she grabs her purse and car keys, heading for the door. I stay behind her as she sets the alarm, memorizing the security code.

As I hold the door open, she glances at me, dubious.

"This is your new key," I say, handing it to her. She doesn't need to know I had Jim make another copy.

She locks the door, and we walk to our respective cars.

"Tessa!" a voice calls out as a yippy Pomeranian runs toward us.

Tessa stops, eyes wide.

"Jane, hi," she stammers.

"Oh, hello, Eli," Jane says, eyeing us both with a knowing smile. "Tess, dear, I just wanted to check on you this morning. But it looks like you're in good hands." Her gaze settles on mine. "It's been a while since I've seen you, boy. How are your parents?"

"They're good, Mrs. Jane. How's Mr. Fred?"

Jane beams at Tessa, "Eli's always so polite."

Tessa looks like she'd rather be anywhere but here.

"We're doing alright. Fred had his hip replaced last fall, but he's recovering nicely."

"I'm glad to hear that."

"Oh, Eli, I've been meaning to call you. Our grandson owns the lot down the street, planning to build a house. Do you think you could stop by one day and give him a quote?" Jane asks.

I reach into my wallet and hand her my business card. "How about next week sometime? I'd love to chat further, but we need to get Tessa to work." I wink at them. "She has lives to save."

Tessa shoots me a glare. If looks could kill, I'd be dead.

"I do need to get to work, Jane. Thanks for checking in," Tessa says, rushing to her car. I'm on her heels.

She opens the door and eyes me warily. "Look, I appreciate all your help, but I don't need a babysitter or to be 'handled.' I can take care of myself."

"I know you can," I reply softly. "But you should think about letting people in. Letting me in."

I kiss her forehead and gently lift her chin, forcing her gaze to meet mine. "I'll see you later, Tessa."

She mutters something unintelligible as I walk away, grinning from ear to ear.

"Oh, and you should think about getting a dog," I call back over my shoulder as I climb into my truck.

"It looks like I already have one, Stalker," she yells, slamming her car door shut.

CHAPTER 21

Tessa

I slam the car door shut, huffing and puffing—the nerve of that man. To make it worse, I got busted by the next-door neighbor. Putting the car in reverse, I back out of the driveway, and Eli pulls out behind me.

"You should get a dog," I mock. Yeah, a golden retriever to match the one I already have trailing me. Frustrated, I glance in the rearview mirror, half expecting him to follow me to the hospital, but he turns off, heading east. I wonder where he lives.

Wait, no, I don't. I don't need any romantic entanglements. I don't. I really don't.

Maybe it will ring true if I chant that in my head long enough. I have to admit, I do feel lonely sometimes. I've been living alone for years now, and the few casual flings I've had never fully satisfied me.

Last night was incredible. Eli is the only man who's ever made me feel this way. The way he looks at me, the way he works his fingers and his dick. I can't remember the last time my body felt so satiated, so rested.

Did sleeping in his arms last night really keep the nightmares away? The only thing that has ever kept them at bay is after I've eliminated a target, and even then I'm lucky to go a couple of weeks without the nightmares. The intrusive thoughts, on the other hand, never completely go away, not for long, at least. I often wonder how different things would have been had *he* never happened. Had my parents not abandoned me when I needed them the most? Things weren't supposed to turn out this way.

I never thought I would become a killer, but then again, does anyone who finds themselves wandering down this dark path? The first time I took a life it had been an accident. An accident I have never once regretted.

It happened back when I was nineteen. Life had been going my way, and I felt happy for the first time in a long time. I had entered my second semester at college, and while my mother had attempted to reach out consistently for over a year, she had finally taken the hint to leave me alone.

And in those months is when I began a relationship with the tall, dark, and handsome Brady Collins. Starting pitcher on the baseball team, and the most gorgeous male specimen I had ever encountered. Brady had bumped into me in the cafeteria one day. Never one to trust strangers, especially men, it took him a little while to win me over. It was also hard for me, the self-proclaimed introvert, to believe that someone like Brady could actually be interested in pursuing a relationship.

But win me over he did, and never once did he make me feel uncomfortable. Always the gentleman, Brady would take me on dates where we would have a lovely dinner and then end the night with long romantic walks where he held my hand as we discussed our hopes and dreams.

Then the beach trip happened.

We had been dating for four months when the idea to visit the beach for Spring Break came to him. There were to be several of us, including his teammates and their girlfriends. It sounded perfect, and, in my naive head, the right time to take our relationship to the next level. I wanted my first 'real' time to be with Brady. He had been nothing but patient, never pressuring me to do more than I could handle.

One of the things Brady and I bonded over in the beginning was how we were both what you would like to call trust fund babies. Neither of us liked to flaunt our comfortable status in life, but when Brady told me he had rented a small yacht for us to have a quiet, luxurious overnight excursion together, I wasn't surprised. We enjoyed hanging out with our friends, but there were moments when we wanted to spend time together alone.

It makes me sick to think of how excited I had been, even going out and purchasing some sexy lingerie to wear under my incredibly tight red strappy dress. Brady had told me to meet him at the bar close to the dock, and when I arrived to see him and his friends waiting, I couldn't help but be a little smug when the group gawked as I approached.

But I shouldn't have been paying attention to that. I should have noticed how Brady's eyes appeared dilated, or how his friend Garrett handed him a small baggie before we left. None of it mattered to me then. I was too excited. Arriving at the yacht we were greeted by the captain, and a perky red-headed staff member holding a tray with champagne. Money changes everything in this world. When you have it, you can make the rules and break the rules, and that night the staff proved they understood.

Anything we wanted they gave us, including privacy, and after tossing our luggage off in the primary we found a sumptuous meal waiting on the top deck. When we finished, I found myself tipsy from the few glasses of champagne that I had consumed, but again, I ignored any good sense I might have possessed, and went excitedly with Brady to watch the sunset.

Up on the top deck, yet another perfect setting waited. Instead of champagne we had wine waiting, and with nary a staff member in sight, we made ourselves comfortable on the plush cushions of the larger lounger.

The memory of what happened next burns, and while it's a moment I don't regret, the residual emotions left behind continue to hold a sharp sting to it. The first kill is always the hardest, with the rest falling into the carved out pieces of your soul as they attempt to fill the void they created by those who make us into the monsters everyone fears.

However, make no mistake.

Brady had it coming.

Uncorking the bottle, Brady pours us each a glass of the heady red wine. His bloodshot eyes feast on me as he does, and the warmth from the blanket he's laid on the cushions keeps me warm when a chill coasts over me at the hunger I see there.

But I ignore it, and reaching for my hand I allow him to hold on, as I slide off my heels. Shaking off the snap of unease I settle in, and know that this is it. This is our moment.

My heart pounds, and my palms embarrassingly sweat when the nerves kick in. I'd heard of liquid courage, and go for my wine glass, gulping down the contents as he does the same.

Not knowing what else to do, I blurt out the truth. "I want you, Brady."

Reaching for me, he takes my lips, and I eagerly let him slip his tongue into my mouth. We kiss for a moment, and it feels.... nice. A slow burn begins to build, and I pull back to take a deep breath.

The heat that had been in his gaze cools instantly, and he pushes me down on the cushions. I'm totally taken aback, and when his hand begins its steady creep up my thigh, my insides recoil in disgust.

"It's okay, sleeping beauty."

That voice. Those words. It's like he's reached into my deepest, darkest depths and is attempting to conquer me by using the worst moment of my life against me.

"I'm a little nervous, Brady," I stammer, making an excuse so I can get ahold of my emotions. "Can we take it slow?"

"Haven't we been taking it slow for quite a while now?" he snarls. "I'm fucking sick of taking it slow. It's time you give it up, Tess."

Brady has never so much as raised his voice at me in anger before, and to hear him snap like this causes tears to roll down my cheek. "I'm sorry—"

He slams his hand across my mouth, shoving me back down again. In one swipe, he tears the front of my pretty new dress open, and roughly grabs a breast, squeezing it until I'm crying harder, only no one can hear my screams since they're muffled by his hand.

"Quit fighting me." He removes his hand from my mouth, dragging it down to wrap it around my throat. "You said you wanted this."

This isn't the Brady I know. This isn't the boy I had come to know. Or is it?

Had I missed all the signs? Had he been cruel this entire time, and I had been too awestruck that someone like Brady could be interested in someone like me that I hadn't noticed?

"Please... stop," I whimper. He glares at me, and that's when I see his pupils are heavily dilated. Brady is completely out of it, and once his powerful grip tightens around my throat I know I'm in trouble. "Don't do this."

Keeping me locked down on the cushions with his hold on my throat, he ignores the crying and goes straight for what he wants. "You'll thank me later. The quicker we get the first time over with, the quicker we can get to the fun stuff."

"I said, no!" I try to get up. "Get the hell off me."

My panties, he's shoving them aside, and I buck in a wasted effort to move him, but it just pisses him off more. He squeezes harder, cutting off my air supply, and I panic, reaching out for anything that can help me.

Spots are appearing before my eyes, and right as I am about to succumb to the darkness, my fingers connect with the wine bottle. I grasp the neck of the bottle and bring it down hard on the top of Brady's head.

"Fucking bitch!"

The death grip on my throat loosens, and I take the opportunity to kick out, hitting him dead in the crotch. I make the hit, and he stumbles backward and into the railing, losing his balance.

Horror erases the anger on Brady's face when he falls over the side. Surprisingly, a person doesn't make that much noise when they hit the water.

I clamp a hand over my mouth, stifling the scream threatening. I stare at the spot where Brady once stood, trembling uncontrollably as I rise to stand. Rushing to the side, I see nothing but the endless, inky blackness of the ocean. The yacht is still moving at a slow but steady pace, and when a minute passes, and then two, a calmness washes over me. It's followed by a feeling of euphoria, as if I've found my own personal drug, the thoughts in my head become clearer.

There is no guilt. There is no regret, no static that overtakes my thoughts.

There is only peace.

And wannabe-rapist Brady's body floating off to sea to hopefully become shark food.

I smirk when remembering how I had immediately gone into survivor mode. Chucking the wine bottle into the water, I waited the appropriate amount of time to scream for help. It had been so easy to convince the captain, and later the police, that Brady was drunk when he fell overboard. When questioned about my ripped dress, I confessed demurely that we'd had sex and then continued to drink until he was utterly wasted. Brady was a known prankster, living for cheers of the crowd, so when I explained that he had been climbing on the side of the railing, and lost his grip, no one thought it was strange.

Why would anyone suspect me of any wrongdoing? I was just a girl out on a yacht with my boyfriend. It was a horrible accident. Playing the heartbroken girlfriend wasn't difficult, considering he actually broke a part of me. And to this day, that's the story I have always stuck with. I'd waited for guilt to consume me, but it never came. All I felt was relief. He would never have a chance to hurt anyone else like he had hurt me.

Nobody knows the truth, not even Allie. I can never tell her. She wouldn't understand. Speaking of Allie, she's been awfully quiet since the bar incident. We've shared a few text messages but haven't seen each other since that night. She's scheduled to work today, so I'll track her down.

After pulling into the hospital parking lot, I climb out of the car and check the time on my watch. I've just barely made it on time. Jesus, Eli is throwing me off my game. I rush through the back entrance to the emergency department and toss my things into my locker in the doctor's lounge. Grabbing my stethoscope, I head out to begin seeing my patients. Before noon, I've treated a patient with acute appendicitis, two with the flu, a broken ankle, and an elderly woman with pneumonia.

When I finally stop to grab myself a water, I send a text to Allie. **Hey, Alls, want to meet up in the cafeteria for lunch?**

The message shows as read, and I watch the dots pop up, disappear, and then pop back up again.

Something's definitely going on. What exactly? I don't know, but I'll damn sure find out.

After another hour of no response, I let the nurses know I'm breaking to grab lunch. They know to page me if they need me. I take the stairs up to the third floor, where Allie's office is, bound and determined to get answers.

Despite the urge to bust into her office, I politely knock on the door, in case she's with a patient. I hear a shuffling sound for a few seconds, and then finally, Allie responds. "Come in."

I enter the office and find her sitting at her desk, her cell phone in hand, and her eyes wide. "Hey, Tess, I was about to message you back."

"Allie, where the hell have you been, and why haven't you responded to me?"

She averts her gaze and pulls at the hair framing her face. Her hair is parted differently than usual, shading the left side of her face.

"Things have been busy." She evades, looking down at her hands before chancing a glance up at me nervously.

"Busy? Alls, this isn't like you. You're my best friend. I know you as well as I know myself, and I sense something is wrong. Now spit it out. Or should I be talking to Dalton?" I say, grabbing my phone.

"No, wait, stop." Her eyes fill with fear and shame. She runs a shaky hand across her face and takes a deep breath before continuing. "That night at the bar, Dalton was so drunk. He was so angry with me, and I embarrassed him. I shouldn't have been dancing like that."

"What happened?" my voice softening with concern. But on the inside, I can already feel my rage building.

"He didn't mean to do it." A small sob escapes her lips. "I know he didn't mean to hurt me."

Through clenched teeth, I enunciate each word in my next question. "What. Did. He. Do?"

Her pale face goes green as she covers her mouth and rushes into her bathroom. I follow behind as she vomits into the toilet. I hand her some wet paper towels to wash her face with as she flushes the toilet and turns around to face me.

She meets my gaze and brushes the hair back from the left side of her face, revealing a fading yellowish bruise just below her temple.

"I'll fucking kill him," I gasp out. "Why did you keep this from me?" Literally, I'll kill him. His days are numbered and ticking down quickly.

"Because I knew you would react like this. You don't like him, and I know that. But he's never done this before. I- I really think he was going to punch the wall, so I grabbed him. He didn't mean to hit me. It was an accident."

"Allie. This isn't okay. This is assault. You deserve better than this," I seethe.

"Do I?" she lashes out angrily but then pauses to take a calming breath. "Look, he apologized for hours. He got on his knees, crying and begging for forgiveness. It was clear he was heartbroken about it. I know he meant it. Afterward, he grabbed a pack of frozen peas, pressed it against my cheek and later held me so gently in bed."

"And every day since, he's been doing more to help me around the house. He finally put up the bird feeder I've been wanting for ages. Our porch now has a new pair of rocking chairs that he bought. He's even been making me dinner."

"I'm sure he is sorry. And the next time, he'll apologize again. It's a vicious cycle we both see daily at work. You know this as well as I do," I say, tucking a loose strand of hair behind her ear.

"Tess, I need this to work out. I have to give it a chance."

A feeling of dread washes over me. "Why do you say that?"

"I-I think I'm pregnant."

CHAPTER 22

Tessa

I glare at the computer screen as if I could change what's staring back at me. It's confirmed, no doubt about it. After dragging Allie down to the ED and getting a urine pregnancy test—which came back positive—I also ordered a blood test.

Sighing, I head into the room where Allie's waiting. The nurse administered an anti-nausea medication per my order and hung a liter of IV fluids. Her eyes meet mine as I pull up a chair next to her bed.

"Do you have any idea when your last period was?" I ask softly.

"No." She shakes her head. "Everything's been so hectic, and I didn't even realize I missed it. I take my birth control pill religiously, but I guess I didn't notice I skipped the placebo pills."

"When did you start feeling sick?"

"A few days ago," she says with a slight tremor in her voice. "I thought maybe it was a stomach virus or something I ate. I can't believe this."

"Based on the hormone levels in your blood, it looks like you're about four to six weeks along." My voice takes on a clinical tone, the professional distance feels so wrong when I'm speaking to my best friend in the world. "It's too soon to see anything on an ultrasound, but we should get you in with an obstetrician in the next couple of weeks. If you notice any bleeding or stomach pain, come in immediately."

"Tess." Her hand clutches mine, eyes pleading. "I don't know what I'm going to do, but I need you to be here for me. Promise me—no matter how you feel about Dalton—you won't leave me."

I should be calling the police. Or stringing him up by his toes and gutting him like a fish. Instead, I watch her tears fall like rain, and I can't move, my heart breaking for her. A child won't make the situation with Dalton any better, but I know Allie, and she's always dreamed of being a mom.

"Please don't tell anyone. Don't do anything. Let me figure this out myself."

"Alright." I let out a heavy sigh. "I'll back off for now. But if he touches you again, all bets are off."

Her face brightens, and she gives me a real smile, the first I've seen today from her. "I promise, you'll be the first person I call."

The day drags on relentlessly as I struggle to mask the storm of emotions brewing inside me, desperately determined to keep my professional facade in place. I treat patient after patient, nothing urgent, just one minor thing after another. But I give each one the same care, as if they were the only thing that mattered.

I feel my phone buzz in my pocket and I'm hoping for a message from Allie, praying she kicked that asshole to the curb. But no such luck. It's not her. Yet, for some reason, my heart skips a beat.

Eli: Hey, what are you up to later?

I wait a few minutes before responding. There's no reason to let him think I've been waiting on him all day.

Me: Thinking of going home to get some sleep. I didn't get much last night.

Eli: I don't remember you complaining.

He's right. Still, I don't want him to read too much into what's happening between us. It was just sex. *"Sure it was,"* the devil on my shoulder mocks.

Me: Last night was really great. But things are crazy, so I'll have to get back to you. Oh, an emergency's coming in. Talk later.

I watch the bubbles pop up and disappear, waiting for him to respond. They don't reappear. Images of my time with Eli, in bed and out, play out like a movie reel in my mind. Forcing myself back into the present, I recall the breaking news report from yesterday.

I head to the doctor's lounge, dig through my purse for a burner phone, and send a quick text to Bryce. I need to know everything about my next target—Ronald Tweed—the low-life who abuses helpless kids.

After a long shift, I'm finally leaving the parking lot, mentally and physically drained. I get a ding on my phone. Siri reads me the message from Bryce, letting me know he has sent the information I need to the burner cell.

A wave of energy floods me, and I crank up the radio, singing along to my *Eminem* playlist. A few moments later, I pull into a driveway that doesn't belong to me. I'd gone to great lengths to find Eli's address, but I'd intended to go home.

Shaking my head, I park behind a silver truck and walk up the front steps. I ring the doorbell, suddenly unsure. What if I'm interrupting something? He could have another woman over. I did evade his attempts to meet up, and lost in my own what-ifs, I'm startled when the door swings open.

I can't help but notice he's wearing only a towel, droplets of water still clinging to his hair. There's a light stubble on his chin, which only accentuates his jawline. Those piercing eyes seem to stare into my soul. My mouth goes dry. I force myself to swallow.

"Who's the stalker now?" Eli teases, his grin knowing, as he leans against the doorframe.

"I figured you were too busy for me."

I hear Jace's voice behind Eli.

"Oh God, I should've texted or called first." My face flushes and mortified, I turn to flee, hoping to disappear before the embarrassment settles in fully. "I'll go."

Before I can take a step, his hand clamps around my arm, stopping me, and I spin back around. Jace is standing behind Eli, holding a beer. His emerald eyes flick between us with a wicked glint.

"I knew you guys were close, but..." I say with a raised eyebrow. Eli smirks. "Only in his dreams."

Jace bursts out laughing. "You couldn't handle this dick, Eli." He turns his gaze back at me, amusement glinting in his eyes.

"You two are something else," I say with a grin tugging at my lips.

"We were just having a beer and talking about casting a line to see if we could catch some perch. But I just remembered I had something to do. See you tomorrow, bro," he says, slapping Eli on the shoulder as he heads out the door. "Good to see you, Tess," he adds, climbing into the ATV I'd overlooked when I arrived.

So much for being the observant killer. I give a small smile and a half wave.

Eli pulls me inside and locks the door behind him. The towel remains snugly wrapped around his waist. I wish it would just fall off already.

"Like what you see, Tessa?" His gaze burns through me, following the path my eyes took.

Without thinking, I launch myself at him, standing on my tiptoes to pull his lips down to mine. I kiss him fiercely— desperately— like it's the only thing that matters. He responds immediately, deepening the kiss as his hands slide under my scrub top to unhook my bra. In less than five seconds, I'm topless, my pants and panties dropping to the floor. I step out of my shoes and climb his body like a tree. My legs wrap around his waist, and I moan at the feeling of his erection pressing into my clit. Shivers crawl down my spine. I've never wanted anyone like this. I'm not sure how I feel about it, but for now, I'm going to enjoy the ride.

I pull back slightly, locking eyes with him. "This is nothing more than sex. It can't be anything more."

"Keep telling yourself that," he replies as he pulls me back into a kiss, not breaking it as he carries me upstairs to what I assume is his primary bedroom. Tossing me onto the bed, the towel drops from his hips. His erection stands at full attention, a bead of pre-cum leaking from the tip.

He climbs on top of me, staring down, cupping my breasts. "Gorgeous, just fucking perfect." He takes one nipple into his mouth, kneading the other with his hand. I grind my hips against him, impatient. Reaching down, I grab his shaft, guiding him into my soaking entrance. He slams into me, my hips shifting to accommodate his wide girth. He buries himself to the hilt, then pulls out, sliding back in—at first with fast, rough strokes, then slowing to a steady rhythm. "Stop fucking teasing me, Eli." He growls, thrusting roughly, but I don't feel any pain—only the pleasure building rapidly. I explode, my pussy clenching around his cock as I ride out the orgasm. Following closely behind, a guttural sound escapes him as he finds his own release, his cum filling me up. After our breathing slows, he eases out of me, grabs a rag, and washes me gently. No one has ever done that for me before. He treats me like I'm special. Worthy. Something stirs inside me—something I've never felt before. He crawls back into bed, cradling me against his chest. As sleep lulls me under, I swear I hear him whisper, "Mine."

I stir awake, blinking slowly, trying to focus on my surroundings. Where am I? It takes a moment to realize I'm still cradled in Eli's arms, and I must admit, I feel safe here. Everything in me feels grounded. My racing thoughts are at bay, and there are no nightmares. I swallow a sigh—I'm in quite a predicament. What started as sex has quickly become something more. I need to leave, even though I don't want to. I disentangle myself from his embrace. He rolls over onto his left side, the sheets falling to his waist. Damn, if he doesn't have the tightest ass I've ever seen. Fuck, I'm ruined forever. I tiptoe to the bathroom to pee, wash my face, and search for my clothes. The shower is in the middle of a remodel, which looks remarkable so far. He has good handiwork. *Shit. Stop thinking about his hands. Get out of here now.* Silently, I ease out of the bathroom and bedroom, giving him one last glance before sneaking away. I grab my clothes, throwing them on. My phone reveals it's just after one in the morning. I rush to my car and drive home, scanning for any signs of danger. I've been more cautious since the break-in, and a glance over my security footage shows no unusual activity, inside or out. I grip the handle of my trusty pocketknife, just in case. Seeing nothing out of the ordinary, I head up the steps and enter the house. After securing the doors, and resetting the alarm, I rush through a quick shower and change clothes before retrieving my laptop from my secret room. Logging in, I pull up Bryce's file on Ronald Tweed. Here we go, motherfucker.

CHAPTER 23

Elijah

I wake up to my alarm blaring. Reaching for Tess, I find only an empty bed. I can still smell her scent lingering on the sheets, but it's clear she's been gone for a while. That she could slip out without me knowing leaves me unsettled. Even before I joined the military, I was a light sleeper. She's elusive, my Tessa.

After grabbing a shower, I get dressed and head downstairs. My phone dings with a new message, expecting it to be Jace or my mom—or perhaps a certain blonde goddess—I'm surprised to see Jonah Miles' name pop up on the screen.

Call me.

The message is short and to the point, just like Jonah. It's been nearly two years since I've heard from him. We first met during basic training and quickly became friends, both running from our troubled pasts. It was pure luck we ended up on the same SEAL team. When we left the Navy, I returned home to my friends and family, and he went to work for the FBI.

I try calling him, but there's no answer. After leaving a voicemail, I hang up the phone, thinking his lack of answering is strange.

Grabbing a bottle of water from the refrigerator, I notice a black
hair tie on the counter. I pick it up and run my finger across it,
savoring the image of Tessa's long blonde locks strewn across my
pillow last night. Every encounter with her makes my obsession
grow stronger, she's seeped into my thoughts and dreams, she's all
I can think about. It takes everything in me to resist going back
upstairs to rub one out, but I simply readjust my hardening length.
Now is not the time, big guy. Looking at my watch, I head out
the door and drive over to check on the renovation progress at
the Cunningham residence. Jace is already outside, talking to the
plumber. I glance over at what used to be the Johnson's home;
only black rubble remains. Days after the fire, it was confirmed that
Conrad did indeed succumb to his injuries. Good riddance.

What if I *hadn't* been here working on this house that day? How
much longer would it have taken for me to encounter my Little
Killer?

Little Killer. She's a sight to see with a weapon in her hand. If
I didn't know better—I'd say she's had military training. Maybe
she's a trained assassin. I snort at the ludicrous thought.

"Hey, man," Jace calls out. "Everything's going according to
plan. We should be able to wrap up in the next week."

"That's good. So, what else do we need to check on today?" I
ask.

"You mentioned that Jane Hill wanted us to do something for
her. We could swing by there. Maybe Tessa's at home. Or is she still
in your bed, keeping it warm for you?" Jace wiggles his eyebrows
at me.

"Man, grow up."

"Oh, so she's not in your bed, huh?"

"All jokes this morning, aren't you?"

"I'm just saying. You'd have to be crazy to turn that down. So, if you aren't interested—"

"Don't even think about finishing that fucking sentence. She's off-limits," I growl, glaring at my best friend, fighting the urge to punch him in the face.

"Bro, I was just messing with you," he says, backing away with his hands up mockingly. "I saw last night—there's something going on between you two. And it doesn't look like just sex to me," he adds with a sly grin.

He's far too observant for his own good. Changing the subject, I redirect the conversation toward safer territory, and we briefly discuss a few other projects we're working on. He can handle most of this shit on his own.

I pat him on the shoulder before heading out. "You seem to have everything under control."

"Hey, where are you going?"

I smirk back at him as I climb into my truck. "I'm going in search of a certain blonde."

As I leave, I check my phone and find another missed call from Jonah. Immediately, I call back. After three rings, he picks up.

"This is Jonah," he answers in a brisk tone.

"Hey, man, it's Eli. Sorry I missed your call. How've you been?"

"Eli, I'm glad to hear from you. I'm good, just pretty fucking busy with work, but that's nothing new. You?"

"Doing good. Living the small-town life, you know?" I chuckle. "Where are you these days? Still working with the FBI?"

"Yeah, hard to believe it's been almost eighteen months now. And that's partly the reason I'm calling you. There's something you need to know."

A sinking feeling hits my stomach.

"There are developments regarding the girls who have disappeared around Lake Lucia during the last ten years. My team and I are heading over there in a few days." Jonah pauses briefly before replying, "Eli, your sister's case is being reopened."

After recovering from the shock of what Jonah told me, I spend a couple of minutes staring at my phone before getting up to pace the room.

Jonah said he'd call when he arrives in town so we can meet up, grab a beer, and talk face to face. I tried to get more information out of him over the phone, but he wouldn't elaborate further.

I've known about the girls disappearing from counties bordering the lake every year, yet those girls never turn up again. Paisley's body was the only one found.

Grief and anger rise in me, but I try not to let it pull me under. Years of guilt and anguish regarding my sister's death have plagued me. Maybe we'll finally get some answers. I think of my parents, but hesitate to reach out. I should probably wait until I know more. There's no reason to make them relive their trauma before I have more insight into the investigation.

Desperately needing a distraction, I send a text to Tessa.

Me: How's my girl doing today?

Tessa: I'm not your girl. What do you want, Stalker? I'm working.

Harsh. I thought she'd be a little more relaxed today. Guess not.

Me: Not yet. But you will be. Stop running, and I'll stop chasing you.

Tessa: You sound awfully confident.

Me: Oh, I am. I'll win you over yet. How about dinner tonight?

I see the bubbles pop up, but it takes a couple of minutes for her response.

Tessa: I can't tonight. I have plans.

Me: What kind of plans?

Tessa: The kind that are none of your business.

Me: Damn, you wound me. And here I thought we were friends. Friends with benefits? We can be friends without benefits, I guess, but aren't the benefits more fun?

Tessa: For Christ's sake, I'll text you tomorrow. I have to get back to work now.

Me: See, you want me. You just don't want to admit it to yourself.

Tessa: Goodbye, Stalker.

I grin, shoving my phone into my pocket. I'll win her over. Soon. I have no doubts about it. Something has been nagging at me. Curiosity wins out, and I hop into my truck to head to her place. The best time for snooping is when she's at work.

As I turn down Tessa's road, I see her car backing out of the driveway, and a sense of dread rolls through my stomach.

What the actual fuck? She's supposed to be at the hospital, saving lives, but here she is turning right, heading in the opposite direction. I follow, keeping my distance.

Thirty minutes later, she pulls into a run-down rest stop. It's one of those shady places that people usually avoid. There are three other cars in the lot. She steps out of her car with a small duffle bag and heads toward the ladies' room while I slowly pull into a nearby convenience store parking lot.

I wait, tapping my fingers impatiently on the steering wheel, scanning the rest stop, as a woman walks out of the restroom. She has dark brown hair pulled into a ball cap, wearing black jeans and a tight black tee. I freeze, and a cold chill crawls down my spine. By all appearances, she could be a stranger. But I know that body—every curve, every contour.

What the hell is going on?

Cautiously glancing around, Tessa walks past her silver Lexus and slides into the driver's seat of a run-down black Mustang with tinted windows. I follow as she pulls out of the rest stop, my mind racing through a hundred different scenarios.

Twenty miles later, she turns onto a dead-end road two counties over. I can't risk her seeing me, so I take the first trail I spot and park. She slowly drives past a few rundown homes before reaching the end of the road and parking behind a tree. Climbing out of the car, she grabs the duffle bag and dons a black raincoat. I gaze up at the sky—heavy clouds are hanging low, and it looks like rain could pour at any moment.

She walks into the woods, and I give her a few minutes before following. Grabbing my gun, I slip out of the truck. I may not know this area well, but tracking someone is something I was trained for and have done many times before. She's good at covering her tracks, though; she's not making it easy. I spot a broken stick and the faint trace of a footprint and continue to move quietly behind her. Reaching the edge of a clearing, I stand behind a tree, watching. Waiting.

CHAPTER 24

Tessa

After exiting my car, I glance around cautiously, an eerie feeling gnawing at me. Something feels off today. It could be because this isn't my normal routine. I usually scope out a target more thoroughly before going after them, but today, I feel like I have constant eyes on me. I hated lying to Eli earlier. It didn't sit well with me, and the guilt has been gnawing at my stomach. And it's not like I could explain this. My hobby? He wouldn't understand. He may have killed people before on orders from his commanding officers, but I'm sure he doesn't go around killing random people, even if they really fucking deserve it.

Like Ronald Tweed here. The man sealed his own fate and should have never laid a hand on that innocent child. He never should have restrained him. And the fact that he filmed and posted it on social media? That says it all. He feels no remorse. The file Bryce sent showed even more evidence that this monster must die. Three years ago, his grandmother was found in the home they shared, suffering from severe malnutrition, bedsores, and near death. He was her guardian. He was supposed to care for her—ensure all her needs were met—but he let her rot. If not for a family friend stopping by randomly, she would have died. Now, she lives in a nursing home, and he hasn't visited her once. I might be a killer, but I'll never understand these monsters.

Ronald's whereabouts were easy to confirm. He's been holed up at home since his suspension, only venturing out to see his lawyer. He's ordered all meals and groceries to be delivered. It's unlikely he's even ventured out to check the mail.

I follow the trail through the woods, and his house comes into view. The quaint two-story home is painted a faded blue, and the yard is overgrown. Clearly, he neglects everything in his life. I pull out my Glock, bypass the front porch, and head to the back entrance. No security cameras. Not that I'm worried. I've altered my appearance. I'm not counting on a man I've never met to know who I am.

The clouds are thickening, darkening. Rain's coming. Perfect. It'll fit into my plans. Staying in the shadows, I move quietly until I reach his back door. I pull on a pair of latex gloves and try the handle. Unlocked. He might as well be inviting me in. Rolling my eyes, I open the door and survey my surroundings. The house is a mess—clutter everywhere. A few dishes sit unwashed in the sink, clothes are piled up on the sofa, and a fine layer of dust covers the surface of the furniture. The first floor is clear. In the distance, I hear moans. I pause, reassess, and realize the sounds are coming from his computer or television.

Slowly, I make my way up the stairs to a cracked door on the right. I see Ronald—a short, wiry man with mousy hair and glasses, jacking off in front of a laptop. Gross. I have the worst timing. But he doesn't deserve a good time. So, this ends now.

"Put your dick down, pervert."

His eyes widen in shock as he jumps nearly two feet into the air. "What the hell? Who are you? How did you get in here?"

I raise my Glock toward his head. "Did you not hear me? Put that thing away," I say, disgust radiating off me. "We'll get to the details soon enough."

He tucks himself back into his pants, pulls the zipper up, and lifts his trembling hands. "I don't want any trouble. What do you want?"

I raise an eyebrow. "What do you think I want, Ronald?"

"I–I don't know."

"You don't know?" I say, mocking him. "Well, you're about to find out."

He looks wary as I usher him down the stairs and out the back door. "To the dock. Now."

He glances back at me, fear in his eyes. "Where are we going?"

"You'll see."

I walk him up onto the aging deck overlooking the lake. I don't understand why he has a boat dock—he doesn't look like someone who knows how to use it. The deck and stairs have aged, but the metal railings are sturdy.

I pull out my bag of tools. "Grab the plastic tarp and lay it on the deck."

The alarm on his face is almost comical, but he obeys. Dread and fear radiate off him.

"Now, grab the rope and put it around your neck."

"No, please don't do this," he sobs, tears and snot running down his face. "Please, I'm begging you."

"Do it. Or I'll shoot you dead in the face." My patience is beginning to wear thin.

Slowly, he places the noose around his neck, and I direct him to tie the other end to the railing just under the deck. He follows my instructions, scooting back as far from the edge as he can, sobbing into his arms like a child.

I grab the syringe I've prepared and inject it into his neck. A cry escapes his lips.

"So, you like to hurt children and little old ladies?" I sneer. "You're about to experience what it's like to be helpless. To have no control over your own body." My hand clenches around the empty syringe as I stare down at him. "Did you think about that when you tied up that child? When you neglected your grandmother? Your own flesh and blood?"

"I'm sorry. I'm sorry. I shouldn't have done it. Please. Please don't hurt me."

"Any minute now, you'll feel what it's like to be paralyzed, unable to move."

His eyes nearly pop out of his head as the neuromuscular-blocking agent takes effect. The paralysis sets in quickly, and though he can feel pain, he can no longer move voluntarily. His attempts to speak are futile. The drug's effects are temporary—only lasting a few minutes—and it won't leave any trace in his blood once it wears off.

At that very moment, the rain starts pouring.

I tower over him, peering into his panicked eyes as his face turns a sickly blue, his breath shallow. "This is better than what you deserve. What you deserve is to rot in hell."

Grabbing the edge of the tarp, I shove his limp body over the side of the railing. "One, two, three...wee."

It's funny how random song lyrics pop into my head. Eminem's a classic.

His body jerks violently as the noose cuts into his flesh, his breath caught in his throat. I shove the Glock into my back pocket and descend to the next level. I don't want to miss a moment of this.

The blood vessels in his eyes burst, and I watch life drain from his gaze. The adrenaline rush hits, and I smile. Another monster removed from this world. He can't hurt anyone else. Too bad I couldn't draw it out longer, but this needed to be quick. And who's going to question that a sick bastard like Ronald Tweed took his own life?

I hum softly as I walk back up to the deck. I'm rolling up the tarp when a snap of a broken branch makes me freeze. I whirl around, my hand instinctively reaching for my gun. Shock and dread fill me as I look directly into a pair of shocked dark blue eyes.

Oh shit.

CHAPTER 25

Elijah

I'm not sure what I expected to find when I started trailing Tessa, but it was certainly not this. Taking in the situation and the gun pointed in my direction, I raise my hands.

"Tessa," I say slowly, locking eyes with her. Her gaze burns with a mixture of emotions I can't fully decipher before she shuts it down, her expression turning unreadable.

"Well, this is awkward," she says flippantly before pausing for a moment. "Wait, it was you—you were following me? You're fucking stalking me?"

As she speaks, her tone slowly turns to outrage, and she grips the Glock more tightly. *Tread carefully, Eli*, I think to myself.

"No, not exactly following you," I edge, wary.

"What do you mean 'not exactly'?" she deadpans.

"Is it not enough that I wanted to see you?" I ask innocently.

"Cut the bullshit. There's no way you should be here right now."

Her worry is palpable as she paces, her eyes wide with anxiety, her body tense. Her beautiful, perfect face. How did I miss this?

I should feel more horrified by what I've found, but I don't. Looking down, I see the purple hue of the man's dead face, his body hanging from a noose. I can't help but notice the sick irony of this situation, especially considering the nickname I gave her. Who would've thought my Little Killer was actually a killer?

"Baby, did this man hurt you?"

"What? No," she scoffs. "He preferred to terrorize innocent children and grandmothers."

Recognition dawns as I realize who the man is. The way Tessa is acting, it's clear she's losing control. I need to de-escalate this before it gets out of hand as I have no desire to face death today.

"Tess, can we put the gun down? I'm not going to hurt you, baby."

She startles at that. "*Baby*? That is twice now you've called me that. How can you even look at me right now? I can only imagine what you must think of me. This is why I don't do relationships. This is why we would never work. What am I going to do with you now?" Her eyes well with tears, on the verge of spilling over.

"We can talk about it. Let's take care of things here and go to my place or yours and talk."

Her eyes narrow with suspicion, seeming to calculate something. Finally, she makes up her mind.

"Did anyone see you?"

I shake my head slowly. "No, I was careful not to leave any tracks. We seem to have that in common."

She glares at me, muttering something under her breath, but puts her gun back in her waistband, I inwardly sigh in relief.

"Help me with this tarp." We roll it up, and she scans the area, checking for anything out of place. "Give me your cell phone." I hand it over to her, and she scans through it before sliding it into her back pocket. "So, did you drive here, or did you use your Spidey senses and leap over trees?" she asks, her voice thick with sarcasm.

"My truck is just down the road." Keeping my hands where she can see them, I lead the way back. She remains silent during the trek. I can feel her eyes boring into the back of my head and when we reach the path's edge, she swings me around, her eyes searching mine.

"How do I know I can trust you? You could leave here and drive straight to the police station."

"Have I ever given you a reason not to trust me, Tessa?"

"I don't know you."

Well, shit. She's not wrong, I suppose.

I try to reach for her, but she holds me at arm's length.

"No. Please don't touch me."

Stepping back, I stare into her steel gray eyes. "I'll never hurt you."

She holds my gaze for several moments before looking away, her eyes searching for my truck. "We're going to your house. I'll follow you." She draws in a deep, audible breath. "And don't try anything stupid."

Nodding, I head towards my truck, climb in, and crank the ignition. I pull out and wait until I see her headlights behind me before heading towards my house.

My heart races, adrenaline pumping as I try to process everything that happened. Fuck. Nothing in the background search I did of her indicated anything nefarious. I've encountered stone-cold killers during my time in the Navy. I've killed people.

It's not something I've ever felt guilty about—they were bad people. It was my job, my duty, and I was following orders.

My mind flashes back to images of Tessa, starting from when I first saw her walking by the Cunningham house. Wait. The Johnson's house. It was ruled an accident but could she have had something to do with the fire that took Conrad's life? Images of her in the coffee shop, wading in the lake, putting a knife to my throat at the bar, her eyes as I made her come with my tongue and my cock. I never would have thought her capable of murder, but it's all beginning to make sense. A feeling of foreboding and dread churns in my gut. She is not a psychopath, and that much is clear. She saves lives. But apparently, she takes them as well. One thing is for sure: she's been hurt before. Someone hurt my girl.

Parked in the driveway, I wait for Tessa to grab her things from the trunk. I open the truck door as she nears with the duffle bag slung over her shoulder and the rolled tarp in hand. The downpour that was so intense just thirty minutes ago has subsided to a light drizzle.

"Do you have a fire pit?"

"Yeah, I'll show you."

Leading her around back, I grab a couple of logs and tinder for kindling to start the fire. As soon as the flames rage, Tessa tosses the tarp in and watches it until it's completely consumed. She removes the ball cap and brown wig, throwing them into the fire as well. Transfixed, I can only stare as she peels off the black tee and throws it into the pit. She's wearing a thin, lacy black bra that accentuates her full breasts, and the light breeze hardens her perfect nipples. I stifle a groan as I readjust myself. Her eyes follow my movements, and her tongue snakes out to moisten her lips. She pulls out my phone and the Glock, placing them on the bench beside the fire. Unbuttoning her jeans, she kicks off her shoes and slides them down, keeping her eyes fixed on mine as she stands before me in just her matching bra and panties. She throws the discarded garments into the fire.

Leaning over and grabbing something from her duffle, she slowly heads toward me. I know we need to talk. We have a lot to discuss, but I can't find the words. She's never looked more beautiful than she does at this moment, her long blonde hair cascading over her shoulders, and her dilated pupils gleam with a mixture of desire and pure adrenaline.

Reaching for me, she grabs the back of my head, entwining her fingers in my hair and pulling my face down to hers. Her lips meet mine in heated passion, our tongues clashing, dueling together in a frenzy. I slide my left hand down to cup her ass, but I hear the metal click as it tightens around my wrist.

She pushes me back against the pine tree, pulling her lips from mine. "Hands behind the tree."

I swear my cock has never been harder as she handcuffs my hands behind the tree, leaving me entirely at her mercy. A knife appears out of nowhere. *Where the hell was she hiding that thing?*

Sliding the edge of the blade to my throat, she presses just hard enough for me to feel the sting without nicking the skin. She pulls back, drinking me in while dragging the tip of the blade down my chest to my abdomen, shredding my shirt in the process. She sinks to her knees. *Sweet Jesus.*

I feel the sharp prick of the knife as she makes a small puncture just above my belly button. Her eyes gleam as she looks up at me before running her tongue over the small wound, lapping up the drop of blood. It's all I can do not to come on the spot when she presses a light kiss over the cut before sliding my shorts and boxers down to my ankles. My swollen cock jerks to attention, nearly slapping her in the face as she tossed the knife aside to smile up at me. Her tongue flicks over the head of my penis, licking up the pre-cum. Her movements become more frantic as she takes me deep into her throat.

I can't stop the guttural moan that escapes me. "Fuck, baby."

She's a sight to behold, with her plump pink lips wrapped around me, tears running down her cheeks. Holding my dick in one hand as she sucks me deeper, the wet warmth of her mouth drawing me closer to the edge. Her other hand slides down beneath her panties, stroking circles around her clit. Her eyes flutter up at me, and her movements hasten. Just as she reaches orgasm, coming on her own fingers, my balls tighten, and I shoot ropes of cum down her throat. She greedily swallows before sliding her lips off my cock with a loud pop.

I drag in deep breaths as she wipes the tears from her face. She stands, pulls up my shorts, and tucks in my semi-hard length. Picking up her knife, she steps away from me and searches through her bag until she finds a change of clothes. I see the conflict playing out in her eyes as they lock on mine.

Slipping on a white tank, jeans, and flip-flops, she settles back on the bench to stare at me with an expression of indecision. "I don't know what I'm going to do with you."

CHAPTER 26

Tessa

Fuck. What am I supposed to do now? This is why I avoid relationships. I knew better than to get involved with Eli. His military background makes him more attentive to detail than most people. I knew the risks going in, and I should've been more careful. But somewhere between it being just sex and letting my guard down, I allowed him to creep his way into my heart. Does he hate me? Is he completely horrified by what he's discovered about me? What if he turns me in to the police? I can't go to jail, but I don't think I have it in me to hurt him.

I feel his stare before I see it. When I finally meet his eyes, they're stormy blue, filled with a depth I can't quite decipher. I study them, trying to figure out what he's thinking.

"Well, first of all, as incredible as that was, and as much as I enjoy these handcuffs—" He smirks, desire flickering in his eyes. "Not to mention that the memory of this tree will be imprinted in my head forever—do you think you could release me? We can go inside to talk."

His voice is low, teasing, but there's an edge to it that puts me on alert.

I keep the pocketknife in hand as I grab the key, unlocking the cuffs with a reluctant flick. He rubs his wrists, still watching me with an intensity that unnerves me. Honestly, I'm shocked he's still standing here. He could've tackled me and turned the tables at any moment. Why didn't he? I would have, if the situation had been reversed.

He reaches for my hand, his grip firm yet somehow reassuring, and leads me inside. We enter the living room, but I'm still on edge, unsure of what's coming next. Something inside me trusts him, though. I don't know why, but I do.

I sit on the couch as Eli pours two glasses of what looks like scotch from a decanter. He sets them on the coffee table before sitting beside me. I eye the glass warily. He wouldn't poison me, would he?

Noticing my hesitation, Eli raises an eyebrow and takes a long swallow of his drink. Seeing this, I follow suit, needing something to steady my nerves. The burn of the liquor slides down my throat, and I slam the empty glass onto the table.

"Tell me what you're thinking right now."

"I need to know who the fuck hurt you," he demands.

The words hit me like a punch. I freeze, shock flooding my system. Of all the questions, that's the first thing he asks?

"Tessa, answer me. Who. Hurt. You?" His eyes flare, intense with something between anger and concern. "You didn't just wake up one morning and decide to kill people."

A cold knot of nerves tighten in the pit of my stomach. "P—people?" I avert my gaze, unable to meet his eyes.

"The fire at Conrad's. That was you, wasn't it? You were there the morning after his house burned to the ground. The day I first laid eyes on you and knew I had to make you mine."

I laugh bitterly. "I bet you're rethinking that decision now."

"You *are* mine." His voice is low, possessive, his eyes burning with something that could be called love, if it weren't so intense. "I don't care what you've done—or why. Nothing would change my mind about the fact that you belong to me."

"You can't promise me that." My voice cracks, and tears fill my eyes. They spill over, streaking my face as the dam inside me threatens to collapse.

He cups my face in his hands, his touch gentle but firm. "Yes, I can." His lips brush against mine in a soft kiss. "Start from the beginning. Leave nothing out."

This is it. The truth—the raw, exposed truth—is about to spill out, and I know he'll finally understand how broken I am. He doesn't know it yet, but once he does, he won't want me. Who would? I'm damaged goods. Losing him... that might break me completely. I don't know if I could handle it. My heart is already a crumpled mess, and he's the last thing holding it together.

I shove the fear aside and close my pocketknife, placing it carefully on the coffee table.

"It all started when I was twelve."

Chapter 27

Tessa

I grab a throw pillow, cradling it against my abdomen, as if it could offer some comfort while I unburden myself of the darkest of secrets. I take a deep breath before continuing.

"For the first decade of my life, my childhood was picture-perfect. I never wanted for anything. My dad is a lawyer, just like his father before him, and his grandfather before that. My mom has always been the docile, socialite wife, deeply involved in the community. It wasn't until I was about nine years old that I realized my family wasn't as perfect as I thought. One night, I overheard my parents arguing—my dad berating my mother. It was the first time I had ever heard him speak to her that way. He'd been drinking, and when he was drunk, he was cruel. I've never seen him physically violent with her, but his words were brutal. He told her she was a pathetic excuse for a woman because she couldn't bear him a second child. A son. I remember the disdain in his voice. I'll never forget his words."

God, this is hard. I haven't felt this vulnerable in a long time. Eli's concerned gaze hasn't left mine as he waits for me to continue.

"She seemed to change after that night, becoming more distant, immersing herself in tennis lessons and multiple charitable organizations. When Dad wasn't working long hours at the firm, he was playing golf at the country club with his colleagues. More often than not, he came home drunk. He grew close to one of our neighbors, and soon, my mom became friends with his wife. Dinner parties and fundraisers became regular events at their house and ours, back and forth. They had two kids, and I adored them. They were like brothers. I loved Mrs. Tammy, William's wife, but I never felt fully comfortable around him."

My voice hitches on a sob, and Eli takes my hand, silently urging me on. "And then one night, I realized that my intuition was right."

Eli's face hardens, his jaw clenches as he spits out, "Tess, what the hell did he do?" Determined not to let my emotions overwhelm me, I fight to keep the tears at bay, telling myself it's not my story anymore, that I'm only retelling someone else's.

"We were at William and Tammy's house, and I was watching the boys. Babysitting was something I always wanted to do. I saw teenagers babysitting on TV, and I wanted to see what it was all about. That night, I was getting paid for it. I didn't need the money, but the desire to prove I could be responsible and earn something on my own was so strong. I thought it would make my dad proud."

"After putting the boys to bed, I fell asleep on the couch in front of the TV. The next thing I remember is waking up to that monster. I tried to get away, but he threatened to kill my parents. I was young and so scared, and all I could do was wish I was somewhere else. I desperately hoped it was a nightmare, one I could wake up from. But the next morning, when I got out of bed, I felt the unmistakable discomfort between my legs and the dried, sticky substance on my stomach." I shudder violently, the memory sharp and clear, as though it happened yesterday.

Eli's jaw clenches. "Did you tell your parents?"

"They didn't believe me," I say, unable to meet Eli's eyes. "They thought I'd had a nightmare and later accused me of making it up for attention. They lost my respect that day. I knew then that their reputation and their friends mattered more to them than I did. Their own flesh and blood." The silence in the room is deafening, louder than my racing thoughts. Still avoiding his gaze, I add, "I can understand if this is too much for you. I can go."

Before I can move, his hands firmly grip my shoulders, holding me in place.

"Tess," he growls, his voice rough and commanding, "look at me."

I meet his gaze, expecting disgust, pity, or something equally shattering. But all I see is sadness and concern.

"You're not too much. You could never be too much for me. Nothing will change that. Ever." He leans over and kisses my forehead before pulling me into his chest. "What happened to you wasn't your fault. You were targeted by a sick bastard who belongs in hell." I can feel his anger radiating, thick and palpable. He holds me tight in his arms, and the comfort he offers seeps into my bones. I finally let go, and the tears fall freely now.

After a few moments, I lift my head to look him in the eye, needing to get everything out. I don't want to keep any more secrets from Eli.

"A couple months after the incident, my parents sent me to summer camp here in Lake Falls, where I met Allie. After that, I spent the rest of my educational years at a boarding school. I was determined to do whatever I could to get out of that house— that loveless home. I worked hard to get the grades I needed to earn a full ride to a university far away from them. I haven't spoken to them since."

"What was college like?" Eli asks, resting his chin on top of my head.

"College helped me find a newfound sense of independence. No one cared about who my family was, and I made some friends, one of whom I'm still close to. My first romantic relationship started not long after that. His name was Brady, and he made me feel more than anyone ever had before. It only lasted a few short months, but I thought he could've been the one. But he wasn't…" My voice trails off.

"What happened?" he asks gently.

"I killed him."

CHAPTER 28

Elijah

It takes a moment for her words to sink in, but I immediately school my features to conceal my surprise. The puzzle pieces slowly start to fall into place in my mind. My stomach tightens, and I wait, bracing myself as she continues.

"It was an accident," she adds quickly. "But I don't regret it."

She explains how Brady had gotten drunk and high and tried to rape her. It's undeniably self-defense, and that motherfucker had better be glad he died by her hands and not mine. I relax my clenched fists and brush a stray hair out of her face.

All I want to do is protect her from the world—and burn it down in her name.

"Baby, the things that happened to you should never happen to anyone. At least he can never hurt another woman again," I grit out.

She scoffs, "I thought I'd feel some remorse, shame, horror. But not only did I feel relief, I felt exhilarated—almost euphoric. It felt good."

"But sadly, the feeling didn't last. I was soon plagued by regular nightmares, ones I must have repressed from my childhood. All I could hear was 'Sleeping Beauty' playing over and over in my head. It didn't matter how hard I tried to escape them; the only way I've ever been able to silence them, at least for a while, is by taking the life of a depraved soul."

I study her face for a moment, then ask, "So, what happened after that?"

She chews on her bottom lip before continuing. "A few months later, I came across my first target. A bartender, rumored to be slipping women roofies. It was my mission to save other women from what I experienced. One night, I dressed to the nines, went to the bar, pretended to get sloppy drunk, and watched as he drugged a young girl's beer. I couldn't stop myself from following him as he guided the girl out the back door after his shift. He helped her into his passenger seat and walked around to the driver's side. Sneaking up behind him, I snatched a shard of glass from the ground and shoved it into his jugular, watching as he bled out on the pavement. It was reckless on my part, but fortunately, there were no cameras or patrons nearby. The girl was passed out in the truck, and she was none the wiser. I slept like a baby that night—and for many months after."

"Jesus, Tess, what if you'd been caught?" I let out in exasperation, running a hand through my hair. "I'm sorry, babe. Continue."

She flinches, her eyes flickering away for a split second before meeting mine again. "From then on, I was more selective with my targets. I meticulously researched and planned each one. The more proficient I got, the farther apart the nightmares became.

Nothing else helped." Tessa pauses, her gaze filled with something inexplicable, yet intense. "Until you."

Stunned, my breath catches. "Me?"

"When I met you, I felt drawn to you immediately—and that scared the hell out of me," she admits. "I tried to keep you at a distance. I even tried for a casual fling, but I can't ignore that this is more than just a hookup. Your arms have been my sanctuary, keeping the demons at bay these past few nights."

Her words send a million emotions surging through me. My feelings for her are overwhelming. And if I'm being honest with myself, nothing she's told me makes me feel different about her. I'm not sure what that says about me, but it's how I feel. Every fiber of my being tells me she needs me right now. Needs reassurance that she's not a villain and, most importantly, that she's not alone. She needs to know how important she is to me.

"Well, that's good to know because I've already claimed you as mine," I say roughly, my hands sliding up to cup her cheeks. "Mine." My lips drop to hers, and my tongue plunges into her mouth, and she matches my intensity, kissing me as if her life depends on it. As if she thought it might be our last. Our kiss breaks, leaving us gasping for air. Trembling, I finally release the words I've been holding back.

"Tessa, I think I'm falling for you."

An hour and two orgasms later, she's wrapped in my arms, sated and breathless. What she didn't say in words, she shared during our lovemaking. The intimacy we experienced went beyond sex.

Tess's carefully constructed barriers are finally crumbling, like a dam breaking. It's for the best. I would have spent my whole life dismantling them, one piece at a time. I'll never let her go.

Her stomach growls, echoing in the silence, followed by her embarrassed gasp.

"Worked up quite the appetite today, huh?" I tease.

She playfully punches me in the arm, her laughter filling the room as she sits up in bed. It's the most beautiful sound I've ever heard. Her flushed skin and mussed hair are so captivating that I can't look away.

Her plump, swollen lips curve into a grin. "Well, feed me, Stalker."

"Anything for you, Little Killer."

The following morning, after returning the old Mustang and collecting her Lexus, Tessa revealed a business arrangement in which she borrows cars from a guy and pays him cash, which he uses to fund his drug habit.

We spend the rest of the weekend together, and on Sunday, we find ourselves at her house, nestled comfortably on the back porch, glasses of wine in hand. The water stretches out before us, and a light breeze cools the late summer air. We talk easily, occasionally lapsing into a comfortable silence, as we savor the simple beauty of the moment.

"There's something I haven't told you. About me. About my family. About my sister," my voice trails off as I think about Paisley. I see her innocent face as clearly as if it were yesterday.

She glances at me, placing her hand on my chest. "Allie told me you lost your sister." Sympathy is evident in her voice.

"It was a lot more than that. It was my fault."

Her steel-gray eyes implore mine, waiting for me to continue.

"I just had to throw that party. A last hurrah before leaving for college. Instead of doing what I was supposed to do—looking after my sister while my parents were out of town."

"It happened so fast. One minute, she was there; the next, she was gone. Her body was found a couple of days later. Someone raped and murdered her. The police have never found her killer. My mother never fully recovered. They say they don't blame me, but I blame myself. And I always will."

Her hands reach out, touching my face, wiping away the tears I didn't realize were falling.

"I'm so sorry, Eli," she whispers, her eyes filled with emotion, unshed tears shimmering in them. "But it wasn't your fault. You couldn't have known someone that vile was lurking, waiting to prey on a young girl."

"Maybe not. But I could've done more to find the monster afterward."

"You were what, eighteen? What could you have done?"

"I could've been stronger. But I ran away. Ran to escape the pain. To bury my grief. Joining the Navy was probably the smartest thing I did. I'm not sure if I'd still be alive if I had stayed on the disruptive path I was on. I kept myself apprised of the investigation, but the police found nothing. Her case is cold. I'm not sitting around waiting anymore, though."

"What do you mean?" she asks, her expression puzzled.

"The FBI recruited a former military buddy of mine after we left the Seals. He's been looking into her case. He hasn't found any MO matching her murder, but he's discovered that more girls have gone missing."

"Every year, two girls disappear in the counties surrounding Lake Lucia. All girls between thirteen and fifteen years old. They vanish, seemingly into thin air. On the night Paisley went missing, another girl disappeared. Of all the girls, only my sister's body was found."

Her gaze sharpens, taking in everything I've said. "So, the sheriff doesn't think the cases are connected?"

"Correct. However, Jonah and I have established a connection between all the girls. He's just received clearance a few days ago to officially take over the case."

"What's the connection, other than age?"

"Every single girl that was taken has been petite, with brown hair and blue eyes."

CHAPTER 29

Allie

This isn't how I pictured my life. Since I was a little girl, I've had a plan for how things should go. I would find the man I love, then walk down the aisle to marry him, wearing a picture-perfect white gown, all while surrounded by loved ones. Then, we would start a family.

That's it.

It was all I ever wanted.

In that order.

I glance down at the one-carat pear-shaped diamond solitaire on the ring finger of my left hand. It's still hard to believe I'm engaged. I was incredibly nervous telling Dalton about the pregnancy, but he seemed surprisingly calm, even happy. The next day, he proposed. While he may not be my knight in shining armor or my Prince Charming, I love Dalton, and we can make this work. There's nothing I want more than to build a happy and loving family to raise our baby in.

The morning sickness has been horrible, and I've noticed a slight bump developing as my body has changed over the last few weeks.

It fills me with utter happiness. After my visit to the obstetrician, my refrigerator now boasts an ultrasound of my precious peanut.

I can't wait for all the firsts. The first flutter in my belly. The first kick. Holding a healthy, happy baby boy or girl in my arms for the first time. I can't wait for the sleepless nights of nursing a newborn.

We'll have a small ceremony with family and close friends in a few weeks. I've been working on the guest list, but Dalton insists on keeping it short. He says we don't need a big wedding. As long as my parents, brothers, and Tessa are there, that's all that matters.

After cleaning the house and preparing supper, I head outside in search of Dalton. He's home from work today, and I haven't seen him in a while. He's converted an outdoor building into an office. I'm not supposed to go in there, because that's where he keeps secure work documents.

My hand hovers over the door, ready to knock, but a raised voice stops me in my tracks.

"Man, we have to get a move on this. We're already behind on the shipment. The boss is going to have our asses." The voice sounds vaguely familiar, but I can't quite place it.

"Keep your voice down. Allie will hear you." Dalton's voice is low, strained, and almost frantic. "Look, we'll get it done."

"Speaking of Allie, I hear congratulations are in order." The familiar voice sneers.

"I told you the plan is in motion. I know my assignment, and I've followed through."

"She doesn't suspect anything?"

"Of course not," Dalton scoffs. "Allie believes whatever I tell her. She won't be a problem."

"Okay, I'm trusting you with that. Let's get the girls tomorrow. We don't need to waste any more time."

Girls? What girls? Who are they talking about? Is Dalton cheating on me?

My mind races, but before I can process it, the door suddenly bursts open, startling me.

All of a sudden, I'm thrust back to a night that will haunt me forever.

"You didn't see anything here. Do you understand me?" The words I can never unhear—echoing in my mind, relentless, and still haunting me after all this time.

I stumble back, the blood draining from my face. *No.* It can't be.

They say evil hides in plain sight. And it's often true. You hear the stories of women married to rapists, serial killers, or pedophiles—people they never suspected. They lived with these men or women, never once guessing anything was amiss. I always scoffed at those stories. How could they be so naïve? How did I miss this?

Dalton steps out of the building behind Wilson, looking at me in shock. He hisses, "Allie, what the fuck are you doing out here?"

"It was you. It was both of you," I whisper, my voice hoarse. My hands tremble as they cup my mouth. Nausea hits my stomach like a lightning bolt, and I spill the little I've eaten onto the ground.

Dalton's eyes lock onto mine, and a sudden realization dawns on him. He knows I've connected the dots. He knows I know.

"Allie—" He reaches for me.

"No! Get away from me!" I back away, looking between the two of them. A hard, calculating glint flashes in Wilson's eyes. Dalton's are ablaze with unbridled rage.

"I knew you would fuck this up," Wilson says coldly. "Do I need to take care of this, or will you?"

"I've got it. Go," Dalton whispers harshly. Wilson turns to leave, quickly boarding his boat and revving up the engine.

I'm terrified. I sense what's about to come will be earth-shattering.

I turn and run toward the house, my heart pounding in my chest. If I can get my keys, or my phone, I can get help. I fumble with the back door handle, but before I can get inside, a hand grabs my hair from behind, and a scream rips through my throat. Hot tears stream down my face, my scalp on fire.

"Stop!" I beg, sobbing. "Please, stop!"

"You had to go and stick your nose where it didn't belong, didn't you? All I needed was for you to be a good little bitch and do as I say." He shoves me into the house, and I crash to the floor. He slams the door shut behind us, the heavy lock clicking with a resounding thud.

I scramble back, trying to get as far from him as possible, and I see my phone at the end of the kitchen island. If I could just reach it, maybe I can call for help, but I have to find a way to distract him.

"Why did you do it? Why did you kill Paisley? She was a child. An innocent girl."

"Shut the fuck up. You don't know what you're talking about. I never killed anybody." His voice drips with contempt.

"But I heard you. You talked about getting the girls."

His lips curl into a snarl. "I guess it doesn't matter what I tell you now."

"Wilson and I work for a man who has... certain needs. Certain preferences." He pauses, as if thinking.

"He likes them young, too. You would've been perfect. With your luscious brown hair and pretty blue eyes."

Oh, God. Bile rises in my throat. I inch away, horrified. "You're a sick bastard."

"It didn't have to be this way, Allie girl. You just had to be a nosy bitch. Again. You did this to yourself."

It's now or never. I spring to my feet, lunging for my phone, but just as I reach it, he grabs me and shoves me hard into the counter. Sharp, searing pain fills my abdomen, and I cry out. He knocks the phone from my hand, sending it crashing to the tile floor.

Before I can crumple to the ground, he jerks me up and slams my head into the marble countertop. Stars explode in my vision, the sharp pain flooding my skull. I'm not getting out of this alive.

Just as he tilts my head back to strike again, I hear someone shouting and pounding on the door.

Dalton lets go of me, and I crumple to the floor. The sound of a door opening and closing is interrupted by the deafening crash of the front door exploding inward. A frantic, urgent voice calls my name as everything around me dissolves into thick, suffocating blackness.

CHAPTER 30

Tessa

I t's been three weeks since I told Eli everything, and we've slipped into an easy rhythm. We haven't spent a single night apart. Some nights we stay at his house, where I help him paint and watch him tile his bathroom. Other nights, after a long shift in the emergency room, he has supper ready for me when I get home.

Admittedly, being held in his arms every night has kept my nightmares at bay. But I'm not sure I can change the person I've become.

I feel a little guilty that I haven't spent as much time with Allie lately. The douchebag Dalton actually proposed to her after she told him about the baby, and as much as I want to be happy for her, it's hard to hide my disapproval. She assures me he hasn't laid a hand on her again. Maybe I should do a drop-in to be sure she isn't lying to me, but I feel like she's being honest. Allie sounds genuinely happy about the pregnancy and engagement. She literally squealed into the phone when I admitted Eli and I are a couple. I suppose I'll do my best to suck it up—maybe invite her and the douche over for dinner.

And try not to call him a douchebag to his face. No promises there.

Since that night I killed Ronald, I haven't been actively hunting, but they still find me sometimes.

I'm in the middle of a hectic shift. About thirty minutes ago, we got the call: Lake Falls Penitentiary is bringing in an inmate who sustained injuries after an altercation with another inmate. This man made the news a decade ago after being convicted for the rape of six students at the University of Alabama. It appears serial rapists are shunned, even by the most ruthless criminals. *Who knew?*

The shrill sound of the ambulance siren slices through the silence, and I head instinctively toward the ambulance bay.

"Fifty-one-year-old male, burns from a gas fire to seventy percent of his body. IV line is in, fluids running. Blood pressure ninety over sixty, heart rate one hundred and fifteen, oxygen sats ninety percent and dropping," the paramedic fires off in rapid succession. We push him into trauma room two, and the nurses get to work stabilizing the inmate. I rattle off orders for labs as I intubate him while the respiratory therapist bags him. The protocol is to stabilize him and transfer him to a burn unit as soon as possible. Within minutes, he's connected to the ventilator, a machine taking over the work of his lungs, allowing them to rest.

"Grab some gauze, soak it in normal saline, cover the burned areas, and give one milligram of morphine stat," I call out.

Grabbing the chart, I document the orders I've just given and glance at the man. The major areas of the burn are his face, neck, trunk, and upper extremities. The skin is broken, peeling in several places. And yet, it's hard to feel any empathy for him. The burns could take months to heal, and he'll suffer excruciating pain, likely requiring multiple skin grafts and leaving horrific scarring. It's nothing less than what he deserves. But what if he survives all of that? Or what if the prison lets him out because they don't want to pay his extensive medical bills? I've seen it happen before. While unlikely, given the nature of his crimes, the possibility still exists.

I look up at the IV bag, fluids dripping rapidly into his right arm. Fluids keeping him alive. A man who doesn't deserve to take another breath.

The nurses move in and out of the room, completing the orders I've given.

Pulling myself out of my thoughts, I head to the nurses' station.

"Dr. Sparks, the patient in room seven has critical labs," Lucy says and hands me the chart.

"Mr. Winston's potassium levels are dangerously low. Start an IV drip of potassium to be administered slowly over four hours," I instruct, then add, "Be sure the patient stays on cardiac monitoring during the infusion."

Lucy nods, and a few minutes later, she draws up the potassium and adds it to the fluid bag. She places a label on it and sets it on her cart, beside a fluid bag of normal saline. Just as she's about to head down the hall, alarms blare.

"Code Blue, room ten." Lucy and John, a physician's assistant, run down the hall with a few other staff members. Since there are only two of us manning the emergency department today, I need to stay available for any other crises.

Seizing the opportunity, I glance around cautiously, ensuring I'm alone before walking to the cart holding the IV fluids. Quickly, I remove the potassium label and place it on the saline bag.

The beauty of the emergency department is that the staff help each other during crises. Moments later, a tall blonde nurse—whose name I've forgotten—grabs the potassium bag and heads into room two. I follow, ostensibly monitoring the patient's status, watching as she swaps the empty saline bag with the fresh one, the fluid running wide open. Because of the severity of his burns, he isn't on cardiac monitoring, and the alarms that would normally blare in the event of a heart arrhythmia will stay silent. Struggling to keep my expression blank, I exit the room and head down the sterile hallway to check on the next patient. It shouldn't be long now.

At the end of my shift, I head to the doctors' lounge to grab my things, my day of saving and taking lives over. The euphoric feeling still lingers, even though it's been nearly four hours since my patient's demise. He was found without a pulse, and resuscitation attempts were fruitless. Severe burn victims sometimes die unexpectedly. It was a stark scene: no tears, no family—just a sheet covering his burned face.

John walks over, touches my shoulder, and asks gently, "Tess, are you okay? It's hard when we can't save someone."

I roll my eyes, then face him with a forced, desolate expression.

In an effort to show emotion, I easily recall a memory of a former patient, a kind-hearted woman who frequently came to the ER due to cancer complications. A woman I tried desperately to save. Tears spring into my eyes as I look at him.

"I'm okay. It's part of the job, but it never gets easier." That isn't exactly a lie. Villains are the only ones who make it easy. The loss of an innocent life is almost unbearable, especially when it could've been prevented.

I pull my bag onto my shoulder, say goodnight, and make my way home. A broad smile spreads across my face as I pull into my driveway and park next to Eli's truck. This is something I could definitely get used to. How did someone like me get so lucky? I've spent so much of my life keeping everyone at a distance, not letting anyone near my heart or close enough to hurt me like my parents did.

Walking into the house, the aroma of cooking food fills the air. Eli turns, and his eyes light up. A light grin crosses his face. A wave of warmth and certainty washes over me, and I know, without a doubt, that I'm irrevocably in love with him. He pulls me close, his fingers tangling in my hair, and then his lips are on mine—soft and warm. My lips tingle as I deepen the kiss, and we're both left breathless.

"Damn, Little Killer, kiss me like that and we won't be eating supper until later."

I stiffen, caught off guard by his use of the nickname, the memory of that defining night fresh in my mind. Yet, his teasing, bright eyes—full of adoration and longing—electrify me. Complete devotion and hunger focused solely on me.

"As good as that sounds, I'm starved." I croak out a laugh and swat him on the ass.

Working together as if we've been doing it for years, we set the table. He places the chicken Alfredo on a hot plate, and just as he's pulling the garlic bread out of the oven, his phone rings.

He sets the pan on the stove, grabs his cell, and answers, "Hey, man. We're about to—what? Wait, slow down. Tell me what happened?"

My eyes shoot up to him as he turns to face me. The color drains from his face.

"Eli..." I look at him, a sharp pang of panic twisting in my stomach.

"It's Allie."

CHAPTER 31

Tessa

Jumping out of the car as it rolls to a stop in front of the emergency room, I dash inside without waiting for Eli to park the truck. The moment I step into the lobby, my eyes land on Jace, pacing with a worried look twisting his features.

"Jace?! What happened to Allie?" I rush toward him, the words tumbling out in a breathless rush.

"Tessa, she's in a bad way," he says, his voice thick with distress. "Her place is only a few houses down from mine. I was working on my boat when I heard shouting. A few seconds later, I heard her scream." His voice cracks, and he swallows hard, eyes glassy. "I ran over, but the door was locked, so I kicked it in. Found her lying there—unconscious, her head bleeding." He looks down, his breath shallow. "She looked so pale. So broken."

The weight of his words hits me like a punch to the stomach.

"Dalton," I mutter through clenched teeth, rage swelling inside me. I push it down. Now is not the time. Not yet.

"There was someone leaving out the back door when I got there. I wanted to chase after them, but I had to get help for Allie. It had to have been that bastard." His eyes flicker with anger, then darken with worry again.

"Have you heard anything? Any updates?" I press, desperate for any information.

"No," Jace shakes his head, frustration etched across his face. "They won't tell me anything because I'm not family."

Eli appears in the lobby then, his heavy boots echoing against the tile. I approach the nurses' desk, where the triage nurse looks disinterested, her eyes glued to her phone.

"Can you please provide an update on Allie Walker?" I ask, my voice sharp.

"Are you family?" she responds without even glancing up, her tone flat.

"Sarah," I deadpan, my eyes narrowing.

Her gaze snaps up, recognition dawning in her features. She stammers, "D-Dr. Sparks, I'm so sorry, I didn't realize it was you." She hastily reaches for a button and buzzes me through. "I'll let you back to see the doctor. I think she's in radiology right now."

I glance at Eli. He gives me a reassuring nod and gently guides Jace to a chair.

Rushing down the hallway, I push open the door to the doctor's lounge. John is at the table, casually sipping his coffee, but his grim expression falters when he sees me.

"Tessa. I suppose I know why you're here," he says, his voice heavy with concern.

"How is she? Please, tell me what her status is." My voice trembles, betraying the panic I'm barely keeping in check.

A frown deepens across his face as he scans the chart. "Allie is in CT right now. She sustained a contusion to the temporal lobe, and she needed a couple of staples. However, what I'm most concerned about is hemorrhage or cerebral edema. She was unconscious for a while, but she's awake now. The best-case scenario is that she has a concussion. We'll know more soon."

I nod, attempting to absorb the information, but my mind is racing with worst-case scenarios.

"John, Allie's pregnant."

His eyes soften with understanding, and he sighs. "Yes, she told us when she got here. I need to let you know she also suffered injuries to her abdomen. I've ordered blood work, and we'll do an ultrasound once we're confident she's stable."

Just then, Sarah pops her head into the lounge, a little sheepish. "Doc, the patient in room four is back from radiology."

"Thanks, Sarah." He looks at me, his expression tightening. "Go be with her. Let me know if she needs anything. I'll keep you updated once we get the results."

I nod quickly and rush down the hall to the trauma room where Allie is being kept. Worry and fear churn in my stomach, both equally heavy. The nature of my job has always demanded objectivity, emotional detachment when caring for my patients. I've prided myself on my ability to compartmentalize, to keep my personal feelings locked away—but with Allie, it's like a dam breaking. The emotions flood in, and I can't contain them.

Entering the room, my breath catches in my throat at the sight of her. Her body, so still and fragile. Tears sting my eyes, and I try to swallow the lump in my throat. A bandage covers her left temple, swelling already beginning to form beneath it. Her skin is pale, almost translucent. She looks so small.

An IV line winds into her left hand, while a nasal cannula delivers oxygen into her body. The steady beeping of the machines echoes, a haunting reminder of her fragile condition.

I pull up a chair and sit beside her, reaching for her right hand. She stirs, and her eyes flutter open, clouded with confusion.

"Tess?" she whispers, her voice barely audible, but I hear the fear in it.

"Alls, I'm here. I'm right here." I squeeze her hand, and we sit in silence. She closes her eyes again, squeezing my hand so tightly I feel the pressure all the way to my bones.

I'm awakened by a hand on my shoulder, and I find Eli standing beside me, holding a cup of coffee in each hand. He passes one to me, and I take a quick sip, and I check on Allie. Her eyes are closed, and she lets out a whimper before gasping as she wakes. The sudden beeping of the machine startles all of us, and she shifts her gaze, scanning the room, taking in Eli's presence before turning to face me.

Fear flickers across her face as she grips the edge of the bed, and her breath comes in shallow bursts. "Tess, something's wrong."

A nurse and a radiology tech enter the room then. The nurse quickly checks her vitals, adjusting the IV, while the tech prepares for the abdominal ultrasound.

"The obstetrician will be here soon, dear," the nurse says in a calm tone.

Eli's voice is steady, but his eyes betray his concern. "I'll be right outside." He places a hand on my shoulder, giving it a gentle squeeze.

I nod up at him. "Okay, thank you."

I help the nurse adjust Allie's gown, and my breath catches in my throat when I see the bruising blossoming on her abdomen, vivid and darkening by the second. The tech meets my eyes, a quiet understanding passing between us before she applies a thick layer of ultrasound gel.

Allie's body tenses at the sensation, and I grip her hand tighter. Her knuckles whiten as she winces in pain. We both watch the screen intently, anxiety squeezing the air out of the room.

A knock at the door interrupts the silence, and Dr. Ross walks in, carrying Allie's chart.

The moment Dr. Ross begins her work, I can't look away from the screen. My breath catches as we wait for the rhythmic sound of a heartbeat, but instead, we're met with silence.

"Dr. Ross," I say urgently, my voice shaky. "Please, take another look."

"What's wrong? Is everything okay with my baby?" Allie's voice breaks, and I can't stop the tear that falls from my eye.

Dr. Ross adjusts the transducer, her eyes scanning the screen with intensity. After a long moment, she lowers it with a heavy sigh.

"Allie, I'm so sorry to tell you, but there's no detectable heartbeat," Dr. Ross says, her voice soft but firm. "Your labs show you're suffering a miscarriage."

"No. No! You have to check again. Please, it must be a mistake!" Allie's cry is raw, a soul-deep wail that cracks my heart in two.

"Sweetheart, I'm so sorry. There's no mistake," Dr. Ross says, her voice gentle but resolute.

Tears pour down Allie's face as she releases another mournful cry. I lean over, my arms around her as I try to offer her comfort, though I can hardly breathe through my own sorrow.

"I'm so sorry, Alls," I whisper, the words a feeble attempt to ease her pain. Sobs wrack her body, and mine follows.

"I'll have the nurse bring her a sedative," Dr. Ross says quietly, before turning to leave.

Allie's cat scan comes back clear—no internal bleeding on her brain, just a concussion. They plan to keep her overnight for observation. After the Ativan takes effect, she calms down, and her body finally relaxes into sleep.

Eli and Jace come in to check on her, each trying to ensure she's okay, but I can't bring myself to leave her side. I'm terrified of what might happen if I do.

A sheriff's deputy arrives to take statements from Jace and Allie. Despite their efforts, authorities are still unable to track down Dalton, who has an active warrant out for his arrest.

The nurse enters with a tray of food—chicken soup and Jello—but Allie barely acknowledges it, staring blankly at the tray.

"Allie, you need to eat something," I coax, my voice gentle.

She shakes her head, her eyes distant as she turns to gaze out the window.

She whispers so softly, I can barely hear her. "It was Dalton."

"I know," I reply, my voice steady. "I heard what you told the deputy."

Allie's head whips back in my direction, her eyes boring into mine with an intensity that makes my breath catch. Her tone sharp and frantic as she speaks. Each word slicing through the air with a desperate urgency. "No, it was Dalton. H–he was the one at the lake that night. Dalton and Wilson. Wilson was the one who threatened me and my family." Slowly shaking my head, shock floods my system as my mind struggles to process her words, the gravity of the situation sinking in. "Oh my God, they're the ones who took Paisley."

CHAPTER 32

Tessa

S lamming my hands down on the steering wheel, I feel the rage I'd been trying to suppress fill my veins. This is my fault. I should have dealt with him sooner. If I had, this would never have happened.

I can't shake the guilt of what happened to my best friend. The attack, the miscarriage... it's all my fault.

But I can get revenge for her with my own twisted justice. Moments ago, the police still hadn't found Dalton. This is my chance.

Grabbing the burner phone from my console, I dial the one person who can help.

"Tess, it's good to hear from you—"

"Bryce, I-I need your help."

"Anything, babe. Are you okay?" Concern laces his voice.

"I am. But my friend isn't. Can you track a phone for me? I need to know where this piece of shit is and who he's contacted in the last six months. He's on the run, and I need to find him before the cops do." I grit the words out, my hands shaking with barely-contained anger.

"I'm on it. But promise me you won't do anything reckless before you hear from me."

"Not sure I can do that."

"Promise. Me." His tone is firm.

Inwardly, I groan. I'm not one to sit and wait. "Okay, Dad, I promise."

"I'm holding you to it. I'll get back to you as soon as I can."

"Thanks, Bryce." I hang up.

A sharp rapping on my window makes me jump. I press the unlock button, and Eli slides into the passenger seat.

"Tessa, what are you doing?" His eyes burn with a mix of concern and anger as he grabs my chin, pulling my face toward his. "I step away with Jace for one minute and you're gone. Dalton's still out there somewhere. We don't know what his mindset is right now. I need to know you're safe."

"I'm sorry, Stalker, but it's none of your business," I snap, my voice sharp.

"Anything to do with you is my business. Did you forget the part where I said you are mine now?"

"Look, I'm trying to keep you out of this. I don't want to drag you into the dark parts of my world."

His eyes soften. "You are my world. I want to be in every single part of it." His hands slide to the back of my neck as he pulls me closer, kissing me gently on the lips.

"I had to make a call," I sigh, my voice filled with exhaustion. "The police have had hours to find Dalton, and they still haven't. So I have someone on it."

"You mean your friend Bryce?"

"How do you know about Bryce?"

"I'm your stalker, love. Do you really think I didn't look into you after we met?" Eli looks at me skeptically. "Bryce Hayes, twenty-eight years old, lives in Cummings, Georgia, with his partner, Gabriel. You and Bryce met in college and have been friends ever since."

"Well, I guess I passed the background check," I reply sarcastically.

"You were always going to be mine. You just didn't know it. What's the plan?" He smirks. *He actually smirks at me.*

I take in his words. Words I've never heard before meeting him. This man understands me and accepts me for who I am. If I had any lingering doubts before, they're gone now.

"As much as it pains me, we wait. If anyone can track down Dalton, it's Bryce."

"Okay, then we wait. But we wait together." He takes my hand, pressing a kiss to my knuckles.

"I need to grab some things from my house. And a shower," I grimace, eyeing my disheveled appearance.

"Alright, let's get out of here."

After showering and throwing on leggings and a black tank top, I go downstairs to find an empty house since Eli left to grab some clothes. I suppose I should give him a drawer, maybe even a small section of my closet. He's wormed his way into my life, and I've accepted that—I want him in it.

I still haven't heard from Bryce, and it's driving me crazy. Pacing the kitchen doesn't help, but when the alarm sounds, and I glance at my phone to see Eli pulling into the driveway, I feel slightly better that he's returned. He has a key, and I've given him the code to get into the house. It's hard to believe that I can let my guard down so completely, but with him, it feels different. It feels right.

I flip on the TV as he comes through the door carrying a pizza. The smell of cheese and garlic fills the air, and my stomach grumbles in response. I can't remember the last time I ate.

"That smells amazing," I moan.

I can't help but notice how his shirt hugs his tanned, muscled arms as he sets the pizza box onto the counter. He catches me staring, and a slow smile spreads across his face as he pulls me close, pressing a kiss to my forehead.

"You need to eat, love."

The feeling I get every time he calls me "love" is indescribable. I grab some paper plates, and we settle on the couch in front of the TV to eat. He flips through the channels while I focus on my pizza, my mind still flitting between Allie and Dalton.

He stops on a local news station, and my stomach drops when I see the man on the screen.

"Governor Hunt, thank you for being with us today. Could you tell us about your current project for underprivileged youth?" A young female journalist beams at him, eyes shining with adoration.

"Thank you for having me, Sandra. We're building a—"

His voice fades as a ringing in my ears grows louder. My blood runs cold, my stomach tightens, and the pizza slips from my hand back onto the plate.

Eli's eyebrows shoot up in surprise, his gaze narrowing with concern.

"What's wrong?"

"I-It's nothing. I'm fine." My stomach churns with unease, and I force a weak smile, pushing the plate away with a trembling hand.

He looks like he's about to argue when the burner phone rings. Saved by the bell, I snatch it up, putting it on speaker.

"Bryce, what do you have?"

"Dalton dumped his phone behind the *Blue Lagoon Bar*. I pulled up the security feed and saw him leaving in a red Mustang."

Eli looks as if he's about to say something, and I wave him off.

"Where did he go from there?"

"Finding that wasn't easy," Bryce grumbles. "Lake Falls needs more security cameras."

My stomach sinks. "So, you lost him?"

"I didn't say that. I hacked into his phone records, found the number he called last, and traced it to a local resident named Wilson Randall."

My eyes dart upward, locking with Eli's.

"His number last pinged at an old, abandoned warehouse on Central Street. At first, I thought his phone died or he'd shut it off because there was no signal, but then I realized he was using a raptor."

"A raptor? You mean, like a cell phone jammer?"

"Exactly." Concern tints Bryce's voice. "I'll send you the coordinates. I'm not sure what you're about to do, Tess, but be careful."

"Always," I reply, ending the call.

"No need to look at the coordinates," Eli says solemnly. "I know exactly which warehouse it is."

"You do?"

"Yeah, it belongs to my uncle."

CHAPTER 33

Elijah

Tess's steel-gray eyes, wide with shock, meet mine.

"The property is one of many owned by my uncle Alvin."

"Wait. Alvin Walker? As in Allie's *father*?"

"Yeah," I reply. "But why would they go there, and how does it relate to my uncle? No one's used that warehouse in years. Alvin and Elizabeth moved to North Carolina after the twins graduated high school."

I can see the wheels turning in Tessa's mind. "Come with me. I have something to show you."

I follow her up the stairs and past her bedroom, and we enter a room filled from floor to ceiling with bookshelves. Shelves packed with hundreds of books. She reaches behind a copy of *Butcher and Blackbird*, and the unit swings open. My mouth falls open when I realize it's a door. A hidden room behind the door contains a large, impressive collection of firearms, knives, and other weapons.

"Damn, this is quite a collection you have here."

She smirks at me as she reaches for a revolver and spins the empty cylinder with a wicked glint in her eyes. Shit, I wouldn't want to be the person about to face her wrath. She's so damn hot right now.

Tessa's expression turns serious. "Grab a few things, and let's go find the fucker."

We decide to take my truck. I don't know what plan she has in that beautiful head of hers, but since the warehouse belongs to my family, it would be more logical in case anyone becomes suspicious.

She appears uneasy, but I don't think it has anything to do with Dalton.

"You want to tell me what's bothering you, Tessa?"

"Yeah, there is one thing."

"Okay…" I wait for her to continue, and she looks at me with somber eyes.

"You're not going to like it." She chews on her bottom lip nervously. "I believe Dalton and Wilson had something to do with your sister's kidnapping."

"What are you talking about?" I grit out as I slam on the brakes and pull over to the side of the road. My heart is in my throat. The image of Paisley's face flashes in my mind.

She takes a deep breath before continuing. "I don't know quite how to tell you this, but I need you to hear me out."

I grind my teeth as she fills me in on what Allie saw the night of Paisley's disappearance.

"Why didn't she tell someone?" I shout in outrage. "Why didn't she tell me?"

"One of them threatened to kill her and her family. She was terrified." I glare at her, and she flinches. "How long have you known about this?"

"About what Allie saw that night? Only a few weeks. The thing is, she didn't realize it was them. Allie only figured it out yesterday, just before Dalton assaulted her. I haven't been able to ask her more about it, and we can't right now. She's already devastated about the baby."

"Fuck!" I hurl myself from the truck, my fist connecting with the tailgate in an explosion of fury. "How could you not tell me?"

Tessa follows me out of the truck. "Eli, please stop and talk to me."

"Talk to you? Oh, now you want me to talk to you when you couldn't be bothered to tell me about this possibly monumental thing until now?"

"I'm sorry, I'm so sorry." She wraps her arms around me tightly, and I instantaneously feel the anger slowly fading into a low simmering rage. Guilt starts churning in my gut, I shouldn't have yelled at her. I hate secrets, but it wasn't Tessa that held this from me for years, it was Allie. Leaning into her embrace, I rest my head against hers. A few deep breaths later, I pull back and tuck a strand of blonde hair behind her ear.

"I'm okay."

She sees the damage to my right hand and gasps. "I hope you didn't break anything. Let me take a look."

Reaching for my hand, she examines it as I extend my fingers, allowing her to inspect my knuckles.

"It probably isn't broken, but let's ice it to reduce the swelling."

Despite everything going on right now, I let out a slow grin. "You're sexy with all that doctor talk."

Flushing a little, she clears her throat, and my smile broadens. "I know you probably don't want to hear this from me, but maybe you need to step back. Your emotions may interfere with your reasoning."

"And you have your emotions in check, baby?"

"Maybe not," she admits. "But I have a little experience with this."

"You forget, Little Killer, I've been in combat. And I have quite a bit of experience with torture and interrogation."

Heat fills her eyes, her gaze dropping to my lips and lingering there. I lick my lips, and her eyes follow the movement. Instantly hard, my cock strains against my zipper.

Down, boy.

"Stop looking at me like that, Tessa, or I'll fuck you right here in front of God and everybody else."

She smirks. "Maybe I would like that."

My mouth crashes down onto hers in a rough, brutal assault, and I reach between her legs to cup her pussy, soaking wet through her leggings, eliciting a low moan from her.

We pull apart, panting. "You *would* like that, wouldn't you, Tess?"

She kisses my neck, biting down into the flesh. "Yes," she breathes out. "But we have things to handle first."

Dropping a quick kiss on her lips, I back away, and my mind returns to the task at hand. I'm going to make Dalton wish he had never laid a fucking hand on my sister or Allie.

"Let's do this." She heads to the passenger door to get back into the truck. "Oh, and Eli? I love you too, Stalker."

Barely having time to process her words, I hop into the driver's seat, and we take off toward the warehouse. She reaches for my hand, careful not to touch my knuckles, and I glance over and see her eyes shining with emotion.

At that moment, I knew our love was meant to be, regardless of our depravity.

As the warehouse comes into view, I pay close attention to our surroundings. The building was previously used to store boats owned by locals. But a few years ago, when the marina was bought out and upgraded, most of the business went there, and my uncle moved on to other ventures.

"I don't see any sign of the car that your friend said they were in."

She reaches into her duffle and pulls out a pair of binoculars. And not just regular binoculars, but ones with thermal imaging. They're military grade, not a pair the average citizen could legally purchase.

"Christ, where do you get those?"

She side-eyes me. "I have my connections."

Laughing, I shake my head, and her face turns serious as she aims the binoculars toward the warehouse.

"There is someone here, but I'm only seeing one person."

"Maybe Wilson took off?" I reply, and she shrugs.

"We're about to find out. You're sure about this? You're stepping into my world now," she says hesitantly.

"I'd follow you to hell and back, Tessa. Never doubt that."

Weapons in hand, we walk silently together to the side entrance. My instincts tell me it's Dalton in there and not some vagrant looking for shelter or a rebellious teenager hiding out from their parents.

Twisting the knob, I find the door unlocked, and we quietly enter the building. I step out in front of her, and she glares at me.

Shrugging, I hang back and let her take the lead. I look around the warehouse—there's a dank smell in the air and old equipment sits covered in dust, appearing untouched for many years. This building has several hiding places. A few boats were left behind; either the owners passed away or moved away and didn't bother to pick them up. There's an office, an electrical closet, and a small bathroom at the opposite end of the warehouse.

"The heat signal is in that direction," she whispers, pointing to the room where the office is located.

We slowly edge toward the room, my senses on high alert. I approach from the left and Tessa from the right.

Grabbing a rock off the floor, I heave it through the window, and a startled shout rings back before a figure walks out of the office with a pistol in his hand. I make sure he sees me and not Tess, and sure enough, Dalton immediately aims the gun in my direction.

"Eli, what the fuck are you doing here? Stay back," he screams at me.

"Dalton, I'm just here to talk, my man."

"Put the fucking gun down." His hands tremble just slightly, and a bead of sweat rolls down his forehead.

I lower the gun to the ground and kick it away, raising my hands in the air.

"How did you find me?" he demands. "Did someone tell you I was here?"

"Who would tell me that, Dalton? Wilson, maybe?"

Dalton's wild, outraged eyes meet mine.

"Wilson? That fucking traitor," he sputters out. I know I need to handle the situation quickly, but I don't particularly like a gun pointed at my face.

From the corner of my eye, I see Tessa inching closer, and I try to think of a way to distract him.

"Look, man, I know you didn't mean to hurt Allie," I say cautiously, while taking a non-threatening stance, and forcing a cynical smirk. "I'm sure the weak bitch deserved it."

Dalton eyes me with confusion and a touch of suspicion. "I thought you two got along. Being cousins and all."

"I tolerate her for the sake of my parents You know, family sticks together," I scoff. "Look, I can help you."

"Help me how?"

"The police are looking everywhere for you. I can help you get out of here."

His eyes bore into mine. "You would help me leave?"

"Yes, now can you put the gun away?"

"Why should I trust you?" he asks.

"Because I'm fucking Allie's best friend, and I just want this situation resolved. If Tessa is happy, I'm happy. And with you out of the picture, she will be."

He relaxes his arm down, not dropping the gun, but it's no longer facing my direction.

At that moment, Tessa sneaks up behind him. Before he can react, she presses her Glock to his temple and clicks the safety off.

"Oh God, what the fuck!"

"Definitely not God, because he isn't here right now."

Dalton tenses up, his eyes wide with panic and fear. "Tess?"

"Now, drop the gun, or I will put a bullet straight through your skull," she says coldly.

The gun falls to the floor with a loud clatter.

"Kick it away."

He complies, kicking it out of reach. Before he can say another word, she pulls out a syringe and stabs it into his neck.

CHAPTER 34

Tessa

Dalton falls unceremoniously to the floor, his body hitting the hard concrete with a dull thud. I replace the needle cap and slip it into one of the pockets of my leggings. Adding pockets to leggings was a stroke of genius, and I should send a thank-you note to whoever thought of it.

"Took you long enough," Eli deadpans.

"But did you die?" I respond, my voice dripping with sarcasm. Inside, though, I'm trembling. My heart's racing as if running a marathon. That could have ended badly. What if Eli had gotten hurt—or worse, killed? It was a reckless decision to let him come and I've never been more frightened for anyone in my life. The thought of losing him is too horrible to contemplate.

"What were you thinking, using yourself as a distraction? That was an amateur move," I add, deliberately picking a fight, as I try to grapple with the realization that I've never felt this level of terror over another person.

"It worked, didn't it?"

Damn it, he has a point.

I kick Dalton, even though I know he's out cold, thanks to the sedative. The kick is just the beginning of what this piece of trash deserves.

I survey the room as I strategize my next move. From the high windows, the setting sun casts long shadows across the room as dusk creeps in.

"Alright, we wait until dark, then move him. I don't want to leave anything behind in case the police figure out he came here the same way we did."

I enter the office he'd left. The room is cluttered, but given the dust is just as thick, Dalton must not have disturbed much.

Bryce said Dalton's phone was tossed in a dumpster, but surely that wasn't the only way he was communicating.

Leaving the room, I find Eli propped up against the wall, anger radiating off of him as he glares down at the unconscious piece of shit. "I want him to talk," he mutters, running a finger through his hair. "And then I want to watch him suffer."

A man after my own heart. "That's my specialty, Stalker."

After securing Dalton's hands and feet with zip ties, I check his pockets, pulling out a burner cell, a wallet, and a small key. The key looks like it belongs to a lockbox or something similar. I pocket it and pull out a pair of latex gloves, grabbing Dalton's gun and placing it in a Ziplock bag, thinking it might come in handy later.

We wait until it's nearly dark outside. Eli does a quick perimeter search, then pulls the truck back to the docking area.

Working in sync, we load Dalton into the truck's back seat, sliding him across the floorboard. We cover him with a blanket, making sure he has enough room to breathe. I can't have him suffocating on me.

"Eli, I think we've reached the point in this relationship where I show you my basement."

CHAPTER 35

Tessa

B y all appearances, the room resembles a finished basement
with a theater system on one side. Decorative stones, varying
in size and shape, adorn the adjacent wall. It's quite beautiful, if I
do say so myself.

The keypad on the inside of the basement door gives the illusion
that this space could serve as a panic room. It can, but that's not
what I use it for.

I type in the code, and a door behind the stone wall slides open
to reveal a small, eight-by-eight-foot space.

The room is soundproof, and on the back wall, shackles and
chains are fastened to a wooden rack. On the opposite wall, a
collection of torture devices is neatly displayed. I turn around and
watch Eli's face as he takes in the area—and my toys. If I'm not
mistaken, his eyes reveal a hint of admiration, which is better than
the horror I expected to see.

After I secure Dalton with shackles and chains, I cut away the
zip ties and strip him down to his boxer briefs. Stripping someone

of their clothing messes with their psyche. He's still unconscious, his head lolling forward on his shoulders.

As much as I want to rip his head off right now, I need to bide my time. Eli has questions. He needs answers. In the past, with the exception of Brady, I've always felt a sense of detachment from my victims. But this is personal. My emotions are heightened in a way I haven't felt before. This monster attacked my best friend, and he will suffer in ways he can't possibly imagine.

Eli is pacing, deep in thought, and his body rigid with tension. "I need to know everything that happened to my sister."

I give a hard nod in Dalton's direction. "Let's find out what he's hiding."

He abruptly walks over and punches Dalton in the jaw. "Wake up, motherfucker."

"What the fuck?" Groggy eyes snap open, and Dalton spits onto the floor as he wakes. He struggles against the shackles, unable to break free. "Where am I?"

"Your own personal hell," I say coldly.

"Are y'all crazy? You can't keep me here like this."

"Can't we? What are you going to do? Call the police?" Eli taunts, holding up his phone. "There's a BOLO out, and I know they'd love to know where you are. Here, let me dial the number for you. I'll put you on speaker." He types in the number.

"Wait. Stop. What do you want?" Fear flickers across Dalton's face.

"Answers." Eli smirks, slipping the phone back into his pocket. "I want to know what happened to my sister."

Dalton pales. "W-what? Why would I know anything about her?"

Walking over to a shelf on the wall, I reach for a revolver. I load a single bullet, making a show of spinning the cylinder. His eyes widen as I press the barrel to his temple.

"Let's try this again. He asked you a question. Answer it."

Dalton swallows, looking at Eli with pleading eyes. "I don't know what happened to her."

Click.

"Okay, okay." He flinches, drawing in a ragged breath. "It was a job. We didn't know it was your sister."

Eli's brows are drawn together in a scowl. "Who's 'we'?"

I press the gun harder into the side of his head. "W-Wilson. Wilson Randall."

"So, what? You two grabbed her, raped, and murdered her?" Eli walks over and places two hands on the chair's arms, caging Dalton in while he shouts in his face. "Was it just for kicks? A dare?"

"Wait, what?" Dalton says, a puzzled expression on his face. "No! We didn't kill her."

Click.

Eli glares at me, and I innocently shrug, raising my eyebrows as if to say, 'Oops, sorry.'

"Stop! Listen. We were on an assignment. Each year, we take a couple of girls. All we do is take them. We never killed anybody," Dalton insists vehemently.

This catches my attention. "What do you mean 'take them'? Where do you take them?"

"I can't tell you that."

Click.

"Tsk, tsk, tsk. There are only three chambers left, one with a bullet." I tilt my head forward, meeting Dalton's gaze. "I suggest you spill everything now, or I'll blast your brains across the wall. That would be awfully messy."

Resigned, he sighs. "It all started in high school. Wilson and I were running dope when we got a call. We met up with a guy for what was supposed to be a drug run. He had evidence on us. He said he'd turn everything over to the feds if we didn't do exactly what he wanted."

"And what exactly did he ask you to do?" My patience is wearing thin. This fucker needs to spit it out already.

"Once a year, we take two girls. They have to match specific qualifications: between thirteen and fifteen years old, petite, brown hair, and blue eyes. Wilson and I each scout out a girl, then we round them up and deliver them."

Anger erupts within me. "Round them up? They aren't fucking cattle."

Click.

Dalton flinches violently, his eyes widen with fear. "We deliver them to the warehouse you found me at. That's all we do. I swear. We leave the van there and go. Neither of us knew it was your sister. Our target was supposed to be another girl and some friend of hers. We choose girls who won't be missed."

"My uncle's warehouse." Eli's face drains of color. "You're trafficking children at my uncle's warehouse."

Dalton looks ashamed for the first time. "After that first run, we went home to find money deposited into our bank accounts. The following year, he contacted us again. We said we'd work for him if he destroyed the evidence of what we'd done."

"Do you have any proof to back this up? Who the fuck do you work for?" I grind out.

"I can't tell you that. I won't. Just fucking kill me."

"Okay." Shrugging, I pull the trigger. Twice.

"Fucking hell, Tessa!" Eli exclaims, an exasperated look on his face.

"What?"

Dalton lies unconscious before us, his dark hair hiding his face, his body still. The only sound is the gentle rise and fall of his chest.

"I didn't kill him. I just wanted to scare him a little."

And it worked. I gesture toward him, noting the urine running down his legs. Disgusting. What a pathetic pussy. He can use his fists on women and kidnap children without a second thought, but he can't handle shit when it's dished back at him.

I meet Eli's gaze. "You didn't really think I left a bullet in the revolver, did you?"

"Yes." Annoyance flashes across Eli's face. "Yes, I did."

"He'd be too lucky to get off that easy."

When Eli continues to scowl at me, I wrap my arms around his waist. His body loosens, and he returns the embrace, relaxing into me.

"None of this makes sense." Eli rests his head on top of mine. "Why was my sister murdered when none of the other girls were found dead?"

"I don't know. But we're going to find out what happened to her. I promise you." And I mean every word. I won't stop until we have all the answers.

A few minutes later, Dalton stirs again with a groan.

"Please, let me go. I'll turn myself in. I'll disappear. Whatever you want," he pleads.

"What we want is to know who is behind all of this," Eli grits out. "And why my sister was murdered."

"I r-really don't know why she was killed, Eli. I swear. The girls are usually just gone. Never heard from again."

Feigning boredom, I shrug. "Well, if that's all you've got, I don't see what use you are anymore."

I pick a dagger from the wall and aim it at him like a dartboard. Dalton screams as the dagger impales his right leg. "My safe. Look in my safe! You'll find financial records from the account that deposits our payments. I'm sure you'll find something there."

"Where is it?" Eli growls.

"My shed behind the house. The safe is behind the Matthew Wong painting." He rattles off the code. "Please, let me go."

"I'm not finished with you just yet." My voice is hard as steel as I dig my fingers into his shoulder. "Do you think I'd simply let you walk away after you attacked Allie? After you killed your child? Nah. I think we'll keep you a little longer."

"Who are you? Who are you really?" Dalton eyes me, fear and confusion swirling in his gaze, as though he's seeing me for the first time

"I'm the one you should fear the most."

"Eli?" Dalton whines, looking at Eli, hoping for some sign that he has a chance to escape his destiny.

Eli lands another punch to his face. "The first one was for Allie. That one was for my sister."

CHAPTER 36

Elijah

I glance down at my reddened knuckles. It wouldn't take much to lose control and end this bastard now, but we leave him shackled, bloody, and bruised. Tess hits play on a Spotify playlist and *Enter Sandman* by Metallica blares on loop. As we leave the room, she cranks the volume.

I love a good Metallica song, but on repeat at full blast? That could drive a man crazy.

When we reach the outer room, she seals the door shut, and blessed silence greets us. I've seen my fair share of torture techniques from my deployment, but that's something I've never taken part in. I've got to give my girl props for her variety. And remind me never to play darts with her.

"We need to deal with Wilson. The longer he's out there, the higher the chances he runs to his father or disappears," Tess says as we walk upstairs.

"Let me message Bryce to confirm his whereabouts." A few minutes later, Tess gets a text back and shows me the location.

"That's his address," I confirm. "We can take my boat to his house."

She thinks for a moment. "Yeah, that works. Let me grab a few things." She returns with her black duffle bag. Her hair is piled up in a messy bun, and she is still the most beautiful thing I've ever seen. Her eyes shine focused and determined. Despite everything happening right now, I want to lay her down and fuck her senseless.

When we arrive at my house, it's still pitch black. A light breeze has picked up, and ripples run across the water. The only light guiding us is the moon. I know this lake like the back of my hand.

We use the trolling motor to glide quietly toward the middle of the lake. Then, I pull it out and start the boat motor as we head to Wilson's cabin.

I alert Tess that we're getting close, and she prepares herself. Cutting the motor, we drift quietly toward the edge of his property. While I secure the boat, she pulls out her thermal imaging binoculars and gestures in the direction where Wilson is sitting.

As we approach, I see his silhouette in a chair, facing a small bonfire, surrounded by several empty beer cans. His back is to us, making it easy to sneak up unnoticed.

"Wilson," I say coldly.

Wilson jerks around, looking over his shoulder in our direction. "Who's there?"

We silently move forward, into his line of sight.

"What is this? Eli? And you're that nurse. No, doctor. Nurse practitioner." He snaps his fingers toward Tess. "Ah, yeah, you are tapping that shit! Right on, man," he slurs, leering at her. I want to rip his eyes out of his head.

"What are y'all doing out my way?" he asks, oblivious to the rage burning in my chest.

"We're here to talk," Tess says, her voice steady. "Or rather, you're going to be the one talking."

I only now notice the latex gloves she's wearing.

Where the hell did those come from? Shit.

We should've gone over the plan on the way here, but part of me couldn't shake the feeling that maybe I didn't want to know the full truth. That part of me was afraid of what I might have heard. She's nothing like I expected. I thought I had everything figured out, but she's shattered every expectation. In the most overwhelming way, she's consumed me—every thought, every breath. She's become my obsession, my reason for everything. My soul feels tethered to hers, and I can't untangle the two of us, even if I wanted to. Tessa is my everything now. Mine. I'll be by her side until my last breath. No matter what comes, I'll face it with her.

Tessa draws a gun and clicks off the safety. "Now. Tell us everything about Dalton, the drug trafficking, the *human* trafficking, and what Eli's sister's murder has to do with it." Wilson stills, staring at her in disbelief. His mouth drops open in stunned silence. Tessa sneers at him. "Did I stutter? Use your words, asshole."

"You've been talking with Dalton. He was supposed to be long gone—" Wilson cuts off abruptly, realizing what he's just admitted.

Tess smiles, sinister and cold. "He will be soon."

The gravity of the situation hits Wilson all at once. His eyes harden, and there's no remorse or guilt in them. No emotion at all. We're standing here with a psychopath in the most literal sense.

"I'm not telling either of you shit," Wilson grits through clenched teeth. The anger in his voice is raw, and the defiance in his posture is unmistakable. He's not going to crack.

Tess must have come to the same conclusion as I have because before I can say a word, a single gunshot rings out.

The force of the round knocks Wilson backward, and he clutches his chest, blood spilling out. He goes down with a shocked expression, and as he opens his mouth to speak, Tessa silences him permanently with a bullet through his forehead.

CHAPTER 37

Tessa

G lancing at Eli, I try to gauge his reaction. Killing Wilson might have been a bit rash, and I'm still expecting Eli to walk away. Any sane person would. "He wasn't going to tell us anything. I doubt they used him for much more than muscle. Our best chance is Dalton." What I see makes my stomach flip. His eyes are filled with an unmistakable hunger as they scan me, moving deliberately from head to toe, and a familiar warmth spreads across my skin, igniting a flush that I'm unable to hide.

"Damn, Little Killer. You continue to amaze me." His heated gaze locks with mine. He's turned on right now. A shiver runs down my spine as heat floods my core. I can see his cock, rock hard.

"Down, boy," I tease, laughing as I give him a hard kiss. "We have things to take care of first." Dancing out of his reach, I carefully slide Dalton's gun back into a plastic bag.

Eyeing Wilson's car, I look back at Eli. "Okay, here's the plan."

As I pull out of the driveway, I take a sharp left toward the interstate. Frowning in disgust, I eye the old food containers and bottles littering the passenger-side floorboard. I roll down the window, trying to air out the stench and the wind hits my face, tangling my hair. With a deep inhale, I embrace the cool rush of fresh air.

After a couple of miles, I pull onto the side of the road. It's still pitch-dark, though dawn is edging closer. With latex gloves on, I retrieve the gun from the bag. Making sure no one's watching, I toss the weapon into the trees. Dalton's prints and gunshot residue are on it, and now some of that residue is on the steering wheel of Wilson's car.

I climb back into the car and head to my next stop. Turning up the radio, I blast an old country song. The words are ironically fitting—revenge against a man who harmed women. Wilson had this coming. A world without him is a better place, especially for the girls he trafficked. And God knows whatever else he got into given the company he keeps.

Coming up on a steep curve, I force my muscles to relax and press the gas, feeling the car's power beneath me. I close my eyes and silently pray to any God willing to listen as I ready to act on my plan.

I leap from the car, landing hard on the pavement as the red car crashes into the side rail and tumbles down the embankment. My shoulder throbs, but I rotate it slowly, testing the range of motion. It doesn't feel dislocated, but I can already tell it's going to leave one hell of a bruise. My shirt is torn, the fabric jagged where it's been ripped. I brush off the dirt, wincing as I do, and quickly scan myself for any other injuries. A few scrapes, but nothing too serious, and I exhale in relief. This part of my plan was impulsive, but some of my best ones have been. There's a thrill in taking risks, even if it means facing the consequences later. I take off on foot, heading a couple blocks away, knowing I've got only a few moments of darkness left. Just north is an old mechanic shop, I scan the area for cameras but find nothing. Moving toward the back of the shop, I toss the gloves into the dumpster.

I pull out my burner and text Eli to pick me up. While I was setting up counter-forensics, Eli drove the boat back to his house, careful to wipe away any traces of our presence.

Moments later, he pulls in with his lights off and I grin. Only an ex-military, born-and-bred country boy could pull that off.

"What the actual fuck, Tessa?" His eyes assess my torn clothing as he reaches out, touching my cheek. I feel a stinging sensation. A piece of gravel must have scratched me.

"I'm fine."

His expression tightens with concern. "You're bleeding. What happened? Where's Wilson's car?"

"About half a mile back," I say evasively.

"Do I even want to know?"

"Nope."

We slip away quietly before any early morning workers arrive, and once we're back at my house, I make my way downstairs to check on Dalton. Taking in his haggard appearance and bloodshot eyes, I can't help but smirk as I turn off the music. I guess that's enough torture for today. There's always tomorrow, and my man is waiting for me upstairs.

As I enter my bedroom, exhaustion hits me as the adrenaline that had been coursing through my veins ebbs away almost instantly. I collapse on the bed, and Eli's arms wrap protectively around me, and within moments, I succumb to the peaceful embrace of sleep, the world outside fading into nothingness.

The shrill ring of my phone wakes me. I roll over to answer it. "Hello?"

"Tess, I'm being discharged today. Can you pick me up?" Allie's voice sounds small, unfamiliar. Not at all like the strong woman who has been my best friend for ages.

"Of course. What time do I need to be there?"

Allie rattles off the details, her words short and to the point. "Okay, I'll see you soon, Alls. Thanks."

I hear the click of the phone as she hangs up, no other words. Sighing, I roll onto my back to face Eli. His eyes are alert, meaning he overheard.

"You know she can't go home, right?"

"Yeah, I know," I say softly, staring at the ceiling, as the first light of dawn begins to creep in through the windows, casting soft rays across the room. "Let's go get our girl."

CHAPTER 38

Tessa

I knock on Allie's hospital room door while Eli goes to fetch the nurse and grab a wheelchair. Stepping inside, I see Allie sitting in the bedside chair, wearing a pair of pale blue sweats—some fancy designer brand she loves. A few personal items are packed into a clear plastic bag on the bed.

She sits, staring out the window. Her dark hair falling in waves, framing her face, likely an attempt to cover the bruises. Allie possesses a natural beauty, her features perfectly symmetrical, with full, pouty lips and a pert nose. I step further into the room, yet she hasn't acknowledged my presence.

"Alls?"

Her striking blue eyes snap up to mine, confusion flickering before clearing, as if she's been lost in thought. Or dissociating. That wouldn't surprise me, given everything she's been through.

"Hey," she murmurs, unshed tears flooding her eyes before she bites her lip and looks away.

The nurse bustles in to go over discharge instructions while Eli hangs back with Allie. As he looks at his cousin—my best friend—the sadness and concern in his eyes only make me more certain of my feelings for him.

Love. The word still feels so foreign in my brain but that's what this is. Eli is a good man who accepts my darkness, while also nurturing my need to right some wrongs in this world, and if anyone can save me from falling too deeply into the abyss, it's him.

"So, Dr. Sparks, Allie will be in your care?" the nurse asks, snapping my attention back to the present.

"Yes." I nod as Allie says, "No."

I look at her, confused.

"I want to go home."

"Alls, I don't think that's a good idea. I don't want you to be alone right now."

"But I want to be alone," she snaps, her eyes flashing with defiance. It's the first sign of fight I've seen in her in days, but I wish it weren't directed at me. She's not going to win this battle. Not today.

"Allie, please. Don't argue with Tess about this." Eli speaks softly, but there's authority in his voice.

She looks at him, surprise written all over her face. "No...I don't want to be in the way. I don't want to intrude on you two."

"You will not be intruding. We want to be here for you," he replies firmly and then turns to address the nurse. "Yes, she'll be going home under Tessa's care. And mine," he adds.

And there he goes again, shocking the hell out of me. I love this side of him—the side he rarely shows. His authoritative tone might offend some women, but I'm practically melting. And so is the nurse, judging by the quick intake of breath and the swoon in her eyes.

"Oh—yes, okay. Let me grab that prescription for painkillers, and she can be released," the nurse stammers, cheeks flushed. I smirk at her. If only she knew how much I understand her reaction. But the difference is, he's mine.

Allie looks at Eli with an unreadable expression before relenting. "I'll stay for a day or two until I figure out what I want to do next."

The young nurse's attempts to flirt with Eli on the elevator ride down are cute but dissipate abruptly when he wraps his arm around my waist. It's a smart move on his part, as I'm two seconds away from stabbing her with my thoughts alone.

As if reading my mind, Eli flashes a knowing smile in my direction before taking my hand as we exit the lobby. After ensuring Allie is seated comfortably in the back seat, the nurse smartly returns to her shift, and we pull out of the parking lot.

"I need to go to my house and grab a few things," Allie says, her voice barely audible.

"Are you sure?" I ask. "I can always go pack a bag for you or order some things to be delivered."

"Yes. I need to do this."

"Okay, we'll go there first," I agree, nodding at Eli's silent approval. I know she needs this for herself. I'm just grateful she's agreeing to come to my house willingly. Kidnapping her isn't on my to-do list for today.

We arrive at her house, and I see the police tape across the door. The cops have come and gone, but the tape remains—an ominous reminder of the depravity that occurred here. I've already arranged for a new front door to be installed later today.

Allie hops out of the truck before I can get out and stands, staring at the doorway. Her eyes are haunted. I reach over and squeeze her hand, silently offering my reassurance. She takes a deep breath, swallowing back her emotions while Eli cuts the yellow tape off the door.

Pushing open the busted door and entering the house I gasp at what I see. My gaze lands on the dried blood on the floor, and my blood starts to boil. The living area and kitchen are destroyed.

Allie looks away, making a beeline for the primary bedroom, while I survey the damage. Cushions from the couch are strewn about, and drawers are upended.

"Did the police do this?" I ask Eli, my voice tight.

"No. Somebody else has been here."

I pull the key I've been carrying out of my pocket. "We need to get to his office out back." Peering down the hall, I see Allie going through her armoire. I signal to Eli, and we head quietly out the back, and through the backyard. I've never looked that closely at the building before now— it's a modest-sized structure with weathered white vinyl siding and a tiny porthole window. The entrance faces the lake. When we enter the man shed, or what Dalton calls his office, the area is in the same disarray as the house was. The desk drawers are open, and papers litter the floor.

I immediately go to the painting and pull at it, trying to figure out how to open the safe. It doesn't budge so I try pulling it from the left, then from the right. Frustration seeps in as I run my fingers around the edges, looking for a latch or something that would open it.

"He could've lied about the safe being here," Eli says, checking the room as well.

"No, that doesn't make sense. I held a gun to his head. Even a dumbass like Dalton values his life more than anyone else's."

I plop down in a chair and stare at the painting. Something about it draws me in. I study it closely, and then I spot it. Pulling the key from my pocket, I look between it and the painting, realization sparking in my mind.

I get up and run my fingers over the image of a lock. Feeling a hardened ridge, I press the key to the opening, and it slides into an actual lock. I hear a click, and the safe opens. The safe isn't behind the painting—it's part of the painting.

"Oh my God."

"Jackpot," Eli says.

"Somehow, I don't think we'll find the pot of gold we're looking for," I murmur. "But I think we've found something."

On the top shelf are bundles of cash, fake passports, and what appears to be some sort of heirloom. Bypassing all of that, I find a manila folder.

I walk over and spill the contents onto the table. The folder contains photographs and a zip drive. Trepidation fills me as Eli grabs one of the photographs. His face drains of color, and the intense pain in his stormy blue eyes is unmistakable as they lift to meet mine.

"It's Paisley."

CHAPTER 39

Tessa

W e leave Allie's house, bags packed and loaded into the
truck. Yes, bags. With Allie, it's never just one bag. The
noon sun blazes brightly overhead, and the skies are a clear blue—
a sharp contrast to the weight and gravity of the situation.

She hasn't said much, and didn't even flinch when she saw us
come back inside from the shed—Eli holding the manila envelope,
his hands gripping it tightly.

This is unlike anything I've ever seen from her, and I don't know
how to comfort my friend. It's as if she's just a shell of the person
I know, almost like her soul has been lifted from her body.

A breaking news alert snaps me to attention, and I turn up the
volume on the radio.

"Police have arrived at the scene where a body, believed to be
Wilson Randall, has been found. Wilson is the son of local Sheriff
Bob Randall, who is unavailable for comment at this time. Police
are investigating and are scheduled to hold a press conference later
today."

I glance at Eli before checking the rearview mirror, gauging Allie's reaction.

"What? W–what? Wilson is dead?" Allie stammers, panic lacing her voice. "What about Dalton? Where could he be? Is he coming for me?"

"Allie, you're safe. You're safe with me," Eli insists, reaching behind to rub her hand for comfort. "And with Tessa. We won't let anything happen to you."

Tears spill down her face. "But why?" she implores. "Why would you help me? It would be best if you hated me. For everything. For the things I didn't tell you."

Eli doesn't flinch. "I could never hate you. What happened to my sister, to your cousin, was not your fault. You were just a child. I love you, Allie. Nothing will ever change that."

"I love you too, cuz," she replies, weeping quietly.

We get Allie settled into my guest room. It's next to mine, so I can hear her if she needs me. She crawls under the covers without unpacking, curling in on herself. I try to coax her to eat something, but she refuses. So I leave a bottle of water and a granola bar on the nightstand.

I hold back the urge to act impulsively, to go downstairs and end Dalton's life right now, but I know Eli needs me to restrain my urges. This isn't about me, nor is it only about Allie. We have direct evidence linking Dalton and Wilson to his sister's disappearance, but there's still so much more to uncover.

I find Eli on the couch, staring at the photos. Going to the sidebar, I pour him a glass of whiskey, grab a bottle of water for myself, and settle beside him with my laptop.

"I've been waiting for answers for years but now all I have are more questions," his voice cracks, filled with despair.

"I know. We won't stop until every evil bastard is accounted for, and their justice served."

He grabs another photo. "This girl. She disappeared the same night as Pais."

"You said two girls, similar in appearance, have disappeared every year around the same time. These must be the other girls." I lift another photo and look at it closely before picking up the thumb drive and connecting it to my laptop. Eli leans in, watching over my shoulder as I pull up the documents, one by one. Some are photos, others are emails and phone records.

"Dalton must have been gathering data on everyone involved. Maybe he was collecting blackmail material in case his involvement was exposed?" I suggest.

"There are some big names here. Doctors, lawyers, CEOs... The fucking mayor?" Eli exclaims, his voice shrill. "God damn it."

When the next photo pops up, I freeze, and a shiver runs down my spine.

"Wait, is that Governor Hunt?" Eli asks, his tone tight.

Bile rises in my throat, and I fight the urge to vomit. My body shakes uncontrollably, but I can't look away.

This isn't happening.

This can't be happening.

"Tess? Tessa!!" Eli's voice is laced with panic.

All I can do is look at him, apprehension pooling in my stomach. I see the moment when it all clicks for him.

"It's him. He's the fucking monster who touched you? He's a dead man!" Eli snarls, slamming his fist onto the white oak coffee table.

"I could have stopped this. These girls... this is all my fault," I mutter, my arm sweeping toward the photos. Horror and understanding settle into me like a weight.

Jumping off the couch, I pace, cursing myself for not seeing it sooner. I should have known my attack wasn't an isolated incident. All these years, I thought I was just a victim of convenience.

What else have I missed?

Eli grabs me, holding me in place.

"I don't know how many times I have to tell you, or Allie, but this is not your fault. These men didn't act alone. This has been going on for a long time, and we're going to end it," he says, his voice growing louder with each word.

"We need to deal with Dalton," I respond, my voice hard. "We have everything we need from him. It's time he pays for his sins," I whisper harshly.

Eli freezes, his eyes locked behind me. I turn, finding Allie standing in the doorway, her eyes wide with shock, her face so pale it's almost gray.

"What do you mean 'deal with Dalton'? What's going on?"

"Alls—" I start.

"No. No more secrets. No more lies. I knew you two were hiding something." Her whole body trembles. "Oh my god, is he *here*?"

"Yes." I straighten, pulling myself together, and resist the urge to flinch as her eyes fill with horror, her hands covering her mouth. "He's locked in the basement."

Chapter 40

Allie

There are moments in life that you never see coming. Shocking moments of betrayal that lead to a pain so acute, it changes you at your very core. People aren't always who you think they are. They surprise you in both good and bad ways, but once the big reveal happens, you know, deep down inside, that nothing will ever be the same. And after everything that's happened in the last two days, I should be prepared by now. I didn't see this coming.

I try in vain to sleep, then finally give up and go to the bathroom. When I come out, I hear Eli and Tessa talking downstairs and something in her tone prickles my awareness. I'm not intentionally eavesdropping, but when Dalton's name is brought up, I need to know what's being said. Quietly, I make my way down the stairs, straining to catch the words drifting up from below.

"I don't know how many times I have to tell you. Or Allie. This is not your fault. He didn't act alone. This has been going on for a long time. But we're going to end it," he says, his voice growing louder with each word.

"We need to deal with Dalton. We have everything we need from him. He has to pay for everything he's done. It's time he pays for his sins," Tessa replies with a harsh whisper.

Breathe, Allie. Breathe. This is Tessa. You didn't wake up in the middle of a John Wick *movie.*

"What do you mean by 'deal with Dalton'?" I ask, a sick feeling curling in my stomach.

Tess turns to face me. "Alls—"

"No. No more secrets. No more lies. I knew you two were hiding something," I say, my body trembling with shock and disbelief. "Oh my God, is he *here*?"

"Yes. He's locked in the basement."

Horrified, a gasp escapes me, my hands instinctively covering my mouth.

Tessa simply watches me, and my skin prickles with alarm. "He was trying to run away. I couldn't let him escape after what he did to you."

"So... what, you kidnapped him?"

"When you put it like that, yes, that is exactly what I did." Tessa shrugs, no sign of remorse in her eyes.

Oh my God, this is a John Wick *movie!* I pinch myself desperately, trying to wake up. *Ouch, that hurt.* Panicking, I back up slowly, but she raises her hands and speaks in a reassuring tone. "Alls, it's me. I need you to give me a chance to explain myself here." I eye her warily before nodding at her to continue.

"He was running from the law, and they were doing nothing. Nothing, Allie. I had to stop him." She locks hands with Eli. "We had to stop him."

I look at Eli. "You were in on this, too?" My mind races, trying to put all of this together and make it make sense.

"Dalton hurt you. He almost killed you. He killed—" He breaks off suddenly.

Heavy emotions roll over me. My hand instinctively goes to my abdomen. The loss I feel is unbearable. It's as if there's a weight on my chest, making it hard to breathe. I have to focus on something else. I can't think about the baby. Not right now.

"How did you find him?" I ask, struggling to regain my composure. "Where was he?"

"He was hiding out in an abandoned warehouse." Tessa's gaze slides away from mine, as if she's leaving something out. "We grabbed him before he could leave town."

I look at my friend, slowly trying to process everything. I'm scared to ask more questions, but I need to know. "Tess, tell me why you brought him here. Why didn't you call the police?"

"Because there are others involved. It isn't just Dalton and Wilson. There are people in high places who will do anything to protect themselves," she says forcefully. "I had to get as much information out of him as I could. We have to get justice for those girls. I have to get justice for you."

"M-me?"

"Dalton is a bad man. I can't let him hurt anyone else."

"What are you going to do?" I ask, fear creeping in.

"Do you really want to know? I mean, *really* want to know?"

"No. Yes. I don't know," I sob. "Just tell me."

"He has to die."

Understanding dawns on me as I recall the news release of Wilson's body being found. "Dalton was here. He couldn't have been the one who killed Wilson."

"Wilson was a bad man, made bad decisions, and didn't feel an ounce of remorse. The world is better off without him."

My mind races. What did Tessa do? "Oh my god, so you're...what? Some sort of vigilante?" I gape at her, disbelief flooding through me. This isn't the Tessa I thought I knew. But if what she is telling me is true, Wilson and Dalton are monsters.

Biting my lip in indecision, I finally steady myself. "I want to see him. Dalton," I say firmly. "Take me to him."

We go down to the basement. I've always loved this theater room. We've spent several girls' nights drinking margaritas and watching rom-coms. I'm not sure I'll ever see this room the same again.

Tessa types into a keypad, and a door opens.

My mouth drops. *What the hell?*

Walking in, I gasp. I see Dalton shackled. He stirs as we enter, his eyes widening when he sees me.

"Allie! Please help me. You have to get them to let me go, doll."

Ugh, I hate that nickname. It was always *Allie-girl* or *doll.* I take in Dalton's appearance—his brown hair sticking to his forehead, his hazel eyes that I once thought were beautiful. Now I know they are just hiding the evil within him. He has bruises and swelling on his face, and the skin under his left eye is black. There's also a knife sticking out of his leg. My stomach churns at the sight. I walk up to stand in front of him.

"How does it feel?" I ask coolly. "Being beaten to hell and back."

Even I'm taken aback by the venom in my tone. His eyes plead with mine. "I'm sorry, Allie. I'm so fucking sorry."

"Are you sorry that you hurt me, or that I heard what you did?"

He glances away, evading my question.

"Why, Dalton? Why did you do it? I thought you loved me." My voice quivers.

Disdain crosses his face. "Did you think I was with you because I wanted to be?" he spits. I gasp, heat flooding my face as color rises to my cheeks. "W-what?" "You were an assignment, Allie girl," he sneers. "I was ordered to wine and dine you. To make you fall for me, and even to get you knocked up so I could keep an eye on you. Make sure you stayed quiet."

"What are you talking about? Assignment?" I exchange looks with Tessa and Eli, who seem just as flabbergasted as I am. "I don't understand."

"You just had to go snooping into your cousin's disappearance two years ago. You started this," he snaps.

My stomach drops as my mind immediately flashes to the tearful woman who had come into my office a couple years ago, experiencing a mental breakdown and desperate for answers about her daughter's disappearance. It had triggered a response in me, and I had asked questions, probed around, digging into her case—and then inevitably, into Paisley's disappearance as well. But at every turn, I was shut down. Now I know why.

"Oh, God," I whisper, a tremor running down my spine, the weight of this revelation sinking in.

"I mean, don't get me wrong, you're a nice piece of ass. A little too vanilla for me, but that pussy's tight."

"You motherfucker," Eli growls harshly.

Stunned and reeling, I slap him hard in the face.

"I loved you. And it was all a lie." I can feel myself breaking more than I realized was possible. "But you didn't have to take my baby from me."

Something akin to regret flashes in his eyes, but it's fleeting and replaced with a darkness I've only seen a few times before. He truly is evil.

A numbing calmness washes over me. All doubts I felt walking into the room wither away.

"Do what you want with him. I don't care." I turn to walk out of the basement door, glancing over at Eli and Tess. "But I want nothing to do with it."

"Allie, wait. Wait!!" Dalton screams out.

"Rot in hell, asshole."

And with that, I leave the room without another word.

CHAPTER 41

Tessa

Allie's reaction is something I never could have expected. I thought she would beg for his life. Instead, she gave me more ammunition to use against the sick bastard chained to my basement wall.

"I think she's just given us her seal of approval, right, babe?"

"Yeah, I'd say she did," Eli taunts.

Grabbing a bat off the wall, I stroll toward Dalton. His eyes bulge. It's not just any baseball bat—it's a design I created, something that looks like the spiked bat from *The Walking Dead* TV series, affectionately known as *Lucille*.

Negan would be proud of my baby Lucy. She's beautiful. The metal gleams devilishly in the light as I admire my creation, the spikes protruding with menace from the barrel. The unyielding weight of it is oddly reassuring, and it feels as if it belongs in my hands, like an extension of myself. I've been waiting a long time to unleash Lucy—she's dangerous, lethal, and all mine.

"Please, please don't," Dalton begs, tears and snot running down his face.

"Is that what Allie said? Did she beg you to stop?"

"I bet she did, but did you listen? No." I swing the bat, the satisfying crunch as it connects with Dalton's left knee ringing in the air. Blood oozes from the punctured, flayed skin.

He howls loudly, and Eli watches me with an intensity that floods my system with more euphoria than I ever thought possible.

"You know, I played softball when I was younger, but this is way more fun."

"You are fucking crazy, b— "

Eli grabs Dalton by the neck in a chokehold silencing him. "I suggest you don't finish that fucking sentence, D."

Dalton struggles to breathe, turning purple before Eli lets him go. My God, that was fucking hot. I clench my thighs together.

"I'm a righty, but I always thought I could be ambidextrous," I muse, winding up for a left-handed swing toward his right kneecap. "Yeah, I think so."

Dalton sobs, looking down at his shattered kneecaps. I've never been particularly violent, preferring less aggressive methods with my victims. But this? This is cathartic.

"Tell me how you hurt Allie. I saw the bruises. Did you punch her in the abdomen, or slam her into the countertop?" I whirl the bat around, landing the blow to his abdomen, and I grin at the blood pours from his shredded skin. "I guess it doesn't matter. You're about to feel much worse." Dalton screams, the sound grating and relentless.

"Christ, you are such a pathetic excuse for a man." I motion for Eli to grab a gag off the wall so he can shove it into Dalton's mouth.

"As much as I enjoy hearing you scream, you're giving me a headache." I cock my head, smiling coldly. "Speaking of headaches.

Did you notice the damage you did to Allie's face? You could have killed her. But that was the plan, wasn't it? She realized what kind of monster you are, and you had no qualms about ending her life."

I stare at Dalton, but he's no longer looking at me, his eyes are unfocused, his breath is ragged, and his shoulders are slumped. Blood drips from his legs, pooling on the floor in a crimson puddle.

"Well, I have no qualms about ending yours, douchebag," I say, lifting the bat. All the anger that has built up in me is now at its peak, spilling over uncontrollably, as I bring it down hard on the side of his head. Again. And again.

"I think you got him, Little Killer." Eli smirks, bringing me out of my daze, and that's when I realize tears are streaming down my cheeks. He takes the bat from my hands, and I look back at what remains of Dalton Jones.

I take a deep, steadying breath before turning to Eli. "Can I borrow your boat?"

While Eli is gone to grab the boat, I shower and order pizza. Allie sits curled up on the couch, a glass of wine in her hands. The television plays a sitcom, but she's not watching it. She's withdrawn into herself, and I'm starting to get really concerned about her. I couldn't get her to eat anything, but I leave a plate beside her anyway. She loves pizza as much as I do.

All I can do is be here for her when she's ready to talk.

I hear the roar of a boat engine and walk outside, watching Eli tie it up to the post on the dock. As he walks closer, the fresh scent of soap wafts toward me. I pause to inhale his fragrance.

"Hi, handsome." I smile shyly as he cups my cheek and drops his lips to mine. Eli deepens the kiss, before nipping my bottom lip, and I whimper. He wraps his other arm around me, pulling me closer, and I shamelessly press against his growing erection. I need to have him, and I need to have him now.

"Are you soaking wet for me, baby?" he groans, his lips moving to my neck. He kisses and sucks his way down until he takes my hard nipple into his mouth.

"Y-yes," I gasp, arching my back to give him better access. His teeth clamp down, and I feel a rush of pain mixed with pleasure.

"Oh, my God."

"I need to taste you, baby." His words send shivers through me, and my knees weaken. I've never experienced pleasure like this before, this instantaneous mixture of lust and deep emotional connection.

Pausing abruptly, "Wait! Allie..."

Understanding dawns in his eyes and he grabs my hand, pulling me toward the boat dock. We giggle like a pair of teenagers, stopping every few moments to kiss, we can't keep our hands off each other. Safely out of sight from the house, Eli presses my back against the railing, a slight breeze from the lake teases my skin.

He pulls my leggings and panties down, exposing me, and I spread my legs open for him, feeling completely unashamed. I've never considered myself an exhibitionist, but the idea of someone watching us excites me more than I can explain. Eli is awakening things in me I never knew I wanted.

He drops to his knees, gazing up at me in awe.

"That's my pretty pink pussy," he moans, a guttural sound escaping his throat.

His tongue flicks my clit, and my knees threaten to buckle under me. He feasts on me like a starving man.

"Yes, oh yes, just like that." I grab his hair, pulling his face closer.

"You taste like pure heaven."

He sucks my clit into his mouth as he thrusts two fingers deep inside me. His mouth works its magic, and his fingers curl into me, hitting just the right spot. I feel my orgasm building rapidly. The tension snaps, and I scream his name as I ride out the waves of pleasure that only he can give me.

His tongue licks up my essence, helping me come back down slowly.

The high I feel right now is like nothing else. I don't know if it's the combination of the kill and Eli consuming me—worshiping my body—but I've never felt so euphoric.

He slides my panties and leggings back up. "Wait, what about you?"

"This wasn't about me, Little Killer. This was all for you. I see you, Tessa, all of you. And you're all I've ever wanted, and more."

I swallow hard, tears threatening to fall. He presses a kiss to my lips.

"But you can thank me later," he winks, standing back up. I slap him playfully and giggle as he tosses me over his shoulder, carrying me inside. We wait until dusk before leaving. I sent Eli to grab some items we'll need from my shed. We've already loaded up some fishing poles, just in case we meet anyone else out on the lake.

I find Allie passed out on the couch, an empty wine bottle beside her, and the uneaten pizza still on the end table. Sighing, I cover her with a throw.

When Eli returns, I motion for him to be quiet. Dalton is wrapped in a tarp, secured with rope. I don't want Allie to witness us carrying out her dead boyfriend.

Once Dalton's secured in the boat, we head out onto the lake, traveling several miles away from the more populated areas.

"This is a good spot, I think," Eli says. He picks up the anvil from the back of the boat. "Jesus, this thing is heavy. Where did it even come from?"

"The previous owner, I guess," I shrug.

Together, we chain Dalton to the weight and toss him into the water. I watch as he sinks below the surface, ripples and bubbles rising as his body is pulled down into the deepest part of the lake.

"See you in hell, you fucking bastard." I mutter, unable to feel even an ounce of regret.

The ride back is uneventful. After ensuring all the evidence is gone, I rest my head on Eli's shoulder as we slowly head back to his house. The breeze runs through my hair, and I sigh, completely relaxed, knowing I've found my happy place. Eli is home to me, my safe space. I'll never let him go.

CHAPTER 42

Elijah

I breathe in her scent—strawberries and vanilla. The feeling of her relaxed against me is indescribable. My obsession with this girl continues to grow. I wrap an arm around her shoulders and steer the boat toward my house. The house no longer feels like a place I want to live. Maybe it never has. My home is wherever Tessa will be.

I dock the boat and help my lady out—not because she needs it, but because I need my hands on her. My life revolves around her now.

After grabbing a few changes of clothes, we head back to her house. We may not have always been close, but my concern for Allie is growing. And I know Tess is worried about her too.

We find Allie still asleep on the couch, and I lift her gently to carry her to the guest bedroom. She stirs, whimpering in her sleep, when I tuck her into bed. Brushing a strand of hair from her face I tuck her under the comforter just as Tess enters with a bottle of water and two aspirin, placing them on the nightstand.

"I'm so worried about her," she whispers, concern shining in her eyes as she watches Allie.

"I know, me too." I gently guide Tess out of the room, closing the door silently behind us. "Let's get you to bed."

She doesn't argue, as I expected. Exhaustion from the events of the past few days is evident on her beautiful face.

I strip down to my boxers and toss her one of my t-shirts. Shedding her clothes she throws it on, and as much as I'd love to sink into her, we both need sleep. I pull her into my arms, her head resting on my chest. Within moments, her breathing is slow and steady. I follow her lead, letting sleep claim me.

Screams jolt me awake.

Tessa's startled eyes meet mine, and we jump out of bed, heading for the guest room. In there, Allie is thrashing on the mattress, fighting off some demon in her nightmare, and I've got a good idea of who that demon might be. Fortunately for her, he's floating at the bottom of the lake. He'll never hurt her or anyone else again.

"Allie," I shake her lightly. "Allie! Wake up!"

Her eyes pop open, and she shrinks away from me, scooting to the far side of the bed. "Please don't hurt me. Don't hurt me."

"Allie, it's me. It's Eli."

Recognition slowly dawns in her eyes. She looks around the room, realizing where she is.

"You were having a nightmare, cuz. It's okay, I'm right here."

She places a hand on her abdomen, and a sob rises in her throat before she throws herself toward me. I hold her tightly as tears stream down her face. Tessa settles on the other side of the bed, wrapping her arms around Allie as we do our best to comfort her. She eventually falls asleep, and I ease myself away from her, careful not to wake her. Tess has also fallen asleep, so I cover them both and head downstairs.

I feel so helpless, and that's a feeling I fucking hate. It's like everything inside me is tied in knots, my pride, my control, all slipping away. If I could bring Dalton back to life and kill him all over again, I would. I was fine with letting Tess take control, but deep down I wish I'd gotten a few more licks in. A tremor runs through me, a low hum of barely contained fury, as my rage slowly builds.

Never again will I let anyone harm those I love.

Unable to sleep, I give up and put on a pot of coffee since it's just after five in the morning. While I wait, I walk outside and call Jace, knowing he's always awake this early.

"How is she?" Jace asks as he answers.

"She's physically okay, but emotionally, not so much." My tone is somber.

"Fuck," he mutters.

I've known for a while that Jace might have feelings for my cousin. He's never voiced it to me, but I've seen the way he looks at her, and the death glares he's given Dalton.

"She'll be okay. She just needs time."

"Is there anything I can do?"

"Yeah, sort of. I need you to keep handling things with the business. Keep Trevor and the guys busy."

We talk about some of the jobs and plans for the week before I end the call. Jace is nothing if not reliable. He's always had my back. I've just started breakfast when Tess walks into the kitchen. Her hair is messy, but she looks amazing in my t-shirt, which falls to mid-thigh. After making herself a cup of coffee, she takes a seat at the island, crossing her legs and leaning back in the chair, grinning at me. It's really nice seeing her like this— so relaxed and happy.

"A man cooking me breakfast is sexy as hell."

"We have to keep you fed." My lips curl up into a smug smile. "You burned a lot of calories yesterday." She rolls her eyes. "Just another day for me. I need to go for a run. I've been slacking the last few days."

We banter lightly as I finish cooking the eggs and plate our food. I set aside a third plate, hoping we can get Allie to eat something this morning.

"Oh my God... this is so good," Tess moans.

"You're going to have to stop making those sounds unless you want me to fuck you on this table right now." My dick twitches, and I groan. Her eyes widen in desire, and she tangles her legs with mine under the table.

Tessa picks up another bite, grinning wickedly at me. She takes a slow bite, moans again, then licks the fork clean.

"That's it!" I pull her out of the chair, tickling her stomach. She giggles and tries to escape, but I corner her against the island. My hands slide up her thighs as a loud thump pulls my attention away.

A suitcase lands at the bottom of the stairs, and Allie is glaring at us from the top.

"Can you two keep your hands off each other for more than five minutes?" Her irritation is evident in her tone.

Tess startles, her face flushes as I slowly pull away, kissing her forehead. "Allie, what's going on?"

"I'm leaving."

"What?" Tess straightens. "Why?"

"I can't be here anymore. I just can't."

"Is this about me and Eli?"

"No, Tess. Everything isn't about you." Allie glares defiantly. "I need to get out of Lake Falls. I'm going to stay with my parents for a while."

"Okay, if that's what you need, we'll do it. Eli and I can drive you."

"Yes, we will. But you need to eat something first." I nod my head toward the plate of food.

"I'm not hungry," Allie argues, sticking her chin in the air.

"Please, just a little something," Tess pleads. For such a badass, my girl has a soft heart when it comes to Allie. "Eli is a great cook."

"Fine. I'll try, but then I'm leaving."

"Okay, here," I say, as I grab the plate and place it in front of her while Tess makes Allie a coffee in a to-go cup.

Allie takes a few bites of eggs and bacon before setting the fork down and rising from the bar. "I'm going to grab the rest of my things," she says before leaving the room. I can see the worry in Tess's eyes, and I'm sure they mirror mine.

"Do you think this is the best thing?" Tess asks.

"I think we have to let her try to do this herself. She needs time away."

A few hours later, we pull into my aunt and uncle's driveway. I'm still reeling from the possibility that my uncle might be involved in human trafficking and possibly my sister's death. I don't want to believe it, and I'm hoping by seeing him, I can uncover the truth.

Aunt Liz comes outside to greet us, throwing her arms around Allie.

"My baby girl, I'm so sorry." Aunt Liz's voice wobbles, her eyes bright with unshed tears. "I should've been there."

Allie is stiff at first but relaxes into her mother's embrace. "Hey, Mom."

Liz's eyes meet mine and widen in surprise. "Eli? Honey, it's been too long since I've seen you. Thank you for bringing my baby home and being with her when I couldn't. Our flight back from Houston was delayed."

I nod briefly. "Good to see you, Aunt Liz."

"Come on, sweetheart," Liz ushers Allie inside. "Your father should be home any minute now."

She gives a sincere smile to Tess. "It's good to see you, Tess."

"You too, Mrs. Walker."

I grab Allie's things from the car and follow everyone inside. After sitting them down in the guest room Aunt Liz directed me to, I return and find a spot on the couch next to Tess, casually draping my arm around her.

"Baby, can I get you anything? I made your favorite—chicken and dumplings."

"I'm not hungry, Mom," Allie says, despondent.

"Let me at least get you a glass of sweet tea." Liz jumps up anxiously and heads toward the kitchen. She's never been one to sit too long, especially when she's worried or anxious. "I'll bring some for everyone."

As soon as my aunt is out of earshot, Allie turns to us. "You made him suffer, right?" Her voice is barely audible.

"Yes. He'll never be able to hurt anyone else again," Tessa replies.

"Good," she whispers. I hear the front door open, and Uncle Alvin rushes in to hug his daughter. "Daddy," Allie's voice breaks, her shoulders shaking as her father holds her. "It hurts so bad, daddy."

"I'm so sorry, my sweet baby girl," Alvin's arms tighten around her. "I've got you."

Tess looks at me with sadness in her eyes. I know it's hard for her to see her friend like this.

"Help yourselves, kids." Aunt Liz comes out with a tray of iced tea and sets it on the coffee table. She watches her husband and daughter fondly. "She's always been a daddy's girl."

Alvin glances over at us. "Thank you both. For everything."

"We were happy to help," I reply stiffly. It's hard sitting here acting as if nothing's wrong, all the while wondering if he's responsible for my sister's death. I have so many questions sitting on the tip of my tongue, just waiting to spill out, but now isn't the right time.

Aunt Liz settles into an armchair, her eyes bouncing between Tess and me, a sparkle of interest in her gaze before she focuses back on her daughter. Alvin asks about my mom, and how the construction business is coming along. Allie grows increasingly restless and stands. "I'm really tired. I think I'm gonna lay down for a while."

Tessa and I stand to hug Allie. "Call me if you need me, cuz. I love you."

"I love you too, Eli," she says, sniffling as she pulls out of my embrace and reaches out to Tess.

"Thank you," she whispers so her parents can't hear. "Thank you for being there for me. You've been the best friend I've ever had. I love you to the moon and back."

"I love you to the moon and back, Alls," Tess whispers. "Never forget it."

CHAPTER 43

Tessa

T he drive home is uneventful as both of us settle into a
comfortable silence. I know it must have been hard for Eli to
hold back from questioning his uncle. Every part of him probably
wanted to demand answers, to push for the truth, but the timing
just wasn't right. I could sense his internal struggle, even though
he hid it well. We stop for dinner, and when Eli goes inside to pick
up our food, my phone buzzes with a text from Bryce.

Bryce: I have some information you need to see.

Immediately, I grab my burner phone, power it up, and check
my email. Bryce has sent me a link to a news article announcing
a major fundraising event and my jaw drops as I read further. It's
hosted by none other than William Hunt, and it will take place two
weeks from now at his private residence.

The event is expected to draw politicians and wealthy business
owners from all over the country and the fundraiser will support
a non-profit that's already in the works. My stomach sinks when I
realize it's for underprivileged youths. Innocent children. Potential
victims.

Me: Message received.

My mind starts racing, already formulating a plan. This is the perfect opportunity to get to him, make him pay, and stop him once and for all.

Over the next week, despite everything, life resumes. Eli and I slip back into our new normal. We haven't spent a night apart from each other, and for the last few days, we've been staying at his place.

There hasn't been a discussion on the specifics, but I love my house, and Eli has no attachments to his. He's still working on his remodel after work and on weekends. Hopefully, if I get the nerve to ask him to move in with me, he can put his house on the market soon. Not that money is a concern, but my house is no longer a home unless Eli is in it.

Operation William Hunt Elimination is officially in motion. Everything is lining up just as it should. It won't be long now. The plan is to ambush him at his private home during the fundraising event being held this Saturday. An unexpected renovation was necessary after a pipe burst at the Governor's mansion, which led to a change of venue. The security will be less stringent. It's the perfect opportunity to get him alone, and with a few alterations to my appearance and a fake identity, I'll be able to blend in with the crowd. It's imperative that every aspect of the plan goes off without a hitch, and so far everything seems to be lining up just as it should. Once I've shown Hunt the evidence we have against him, it won't be difficult to draw him out to a new location to finish him off. I have something special in mind. The stakes are high, but the end result is that William will suffer immensely before meeting his maker.

It's Wednesday evening, and I'm finishing up my shift at the hospital. Nothing too exciting happened today, and I'm looking forward to getting out of there. Once home, I shower and towel-dry my hair, letting it fall in loose waves down my back before I throw on a camisole and shorts. Tonight, we're having fast food takeout and watching a movie. It's his turn to pick, so it'll probably be an action flick.

I smile to myself. With all the craziness in my life, Eli has become my rock. I don't deserve him, and I definitely never saw him coming. He bulldozed his way into my world and stole my heart.

We're on the couch, watching—surprise, surprise—*The Equalizer*, when my phone alarm goes off. I glance at the time. It's well after ten.

"Are you expecting someone?" Eli asks.

"No, not at all." I pull up the camera app to see a black sedan pulling into my driveway. Two men step out. One wears a gray hoodie, his face obscured, and the other man looks vaguely familiar.

Pressing a hidden button on the armrest, a secret compartment opens to reveal a pair of Glocks, and I pass one to Eli.

Why have one when you can have two?

"Christ, Little Killer, do you have weapons hidden everywhere in this house?" Eli's expression is incredulous.

"Can't be too careful these days," I reply flippantly, smirking at him.

We move silently toward the front door, each flanking one side, and when the doorbell rings. I raise an eyebrow, wondering what kind of cold-blooded killer would ring the doorbell.

Taking a deep breath, I open the front door with Eli right behind me. I know he wants to take the lead, but I'm perfectly capable of protecting myself. Still, it's sweet. The two men are standing on my porch. A familiar pair of brown eyes meet mine; I squeal and launch myself into his open arms.

CHAPTER 44

Elijah

I watch, stunned, as my girl jumps into the arms of a man I don't recognize.

What in the actual fuck?

The man in the gray hoodie has short blonde hair and deep, dark eyes that exude warmth. His smile is genuine, effortlessly charming, and directed at my girl, who's currently in his arms. Standing beside him is another man with olive skin, his gaze piercing and observant. He's dressed in a green sweater and slacks, his posture is relaxed but cautious.

"Tess," I growl, my voice like thunder.

A murderous rage fills me as I do everything I can to restrain myself from putting a bullet in this asshole's head for touching what is mine.

"Eli," she says, mocking me, before she lets go of Blondie. "Settle down, cowboy. This is Bryce." She turns to the other man with a warm smile. "And this is his partner, Gabriel."

I relax just enough to shove the Glock into the back pocket of my jeans. I'm still not happy with this situation, but there's no immediate threat. Not from them, anyway. I'm still contemplating chopping off pretty boy's hands and shoving them up his ass.

Tess is practically bubbling over with excitement. "What are you two doing here?"

"You didn't really think I was going to let you do this alone, did you, love?" The inflection in Bryce's tone tells me he's got a mix of British and American in him. "I'm not about to let you storm the castle without backup."

"But—" she starts, but he interrupts her.

"Shh, Gabe knows. I trust him more than anyone else in the world. You can too."

Bryce steps around Tess and extends his hand to shake mine.

"It's a pleasure to meet the man who tamed my dear Swallow."

Swallow? What the fuck kind of nickname is that? I grind my teeth, returning the handshake with more force than necessary.

Tess smirks at him. "Can you not poke the bear, Bryce?" She playfully punches him in the arm before grabbing my hand. "I don't think I can let this one get away." She looks up at me, adoration in her eyes. I feel my body relax a little as I wrap my arm around her possessively.

"Sorry, sorry." Bryce raises his hands in surrender. "That's a story for another day."

"We just wanted to let you know we were here," he continues. "We booked a room at that cute little lakeside B&B."

The name of the bed and breakfast is, ironically, Lakeside B&B.

"Absolutely not!" Tess exclaims. "You're staying here. With us," she says matter-of-factly. "Right, Eli?" She looks up at me, as if I have a say in the matter, and while I appreciate the sentiment, we both know I'll ultimately do what she wants.

"Of course. Can I help you with your bags?" I offer begrudgingly. She squeals and claps her hands together in excitement. Just because she gets what she wants doesn't mean she doesn't owe me for this. She heads upstairs to prepare the bedding in the guest room while I step outside with the guys to grab their belongings. And once Tess is out of earshot, Bryce turns around to face me.

"She cares deeply for you. Do not hurt her."

He's serious, and my initial misgivings about him fade. The guy's got some balls to say that to me, especially when I tower over him by at least four inches and thirty pounds. He knows everything about me, and he knows I'm not someone to fuck with.

"Never. I'd rather die than hurt a hair on her head."

Bryce nods, offering me a genuine smile. "We're going to get along just fine."

After their things are settled upstairs, we all head to the kitchen. Tess pulls a bottle of wine from the fridge and four glasses from the cabinet. I've never seen two men with so much luggage. And that shit was heavy, too.

Gabriel is the polar opposite of Bryce. Where Bryce is outgoing and cracking jokes, his partner has a quiet seriousness about him. Yin to yang. But I don't miss the tender looks they exchange.

Tess and Gabe are deep in discussion about a book they've both read. My Tessa is a sight to see when she gets excited about something. And she loves books as much as she loves killing shitty human beings. Her blonde locks shine as she gestures animatedly, and with Gabe's olive skin and shockingly blue eyes, they make quite the pair.

Bryce nods toward Gabe. "He's mine," he jokes, ripping a surprised chuckle from me.

"And she's mine," I reply, my gaze locking with Tess's. A smile lights up her face. "Forever and always. Why the hell does my girl have the nickname *Swallow*?" I growl, turning back to face Bryce. "Tread carefully, bro."

Bryce laughs. "It isn't anything like what you're probably thinking. I met Tessa in my freshman year of college. I'm not sure I'd still be alive if not for her." He pauses. "My childhood wasn't exactly easy in a small town, not everyone understood or accepted my lifestyle choices. My parents were supportive, thank God, but kids can be assholes. Bullies tormented me throughout most of high school. When I left for college, it felt like a fresh start."

He looks thoughtful as he pauses momentarily. "Seems some of those assholes leave small towns, too." His eyes darken with a hint of sadness.

My brows furrow. "What happened?"

"Things were going well. I had a roommate who wasn't afraid I'd 'turn him gay'." He snorts. "One day, I'm walking out of the library, and I see some guy berating a lesbian couple. He's spewing hate, calling them all kinds of names. The girls were crying. And then—bam—this fiery blonde bombshell appears out of nowhere. Within seconds, she's got him writhing on the ground, holding his groin."

"That sounds like my girl," I say with a wry grin.

He sighs dramatically. "Honestly, it's the only time a female has ever turned me on."

I shoot him a scathing look, and his eyes widen. "Hey, hey, I'm just being real with you. She's the most beautiful woman I've ever met, inside and out, but I've never seen her as more than a close friend."

"Smart answer," I mutter, giving him a quick nod before motioning him to continue.

"A few days later, I see her again at the gym. She's beating the hell out of a punching bag," he says proudly. "I could tell she was going through something, although it would take me months to get it out of her. After my treadmill session, I saw her entering a martial arts class, and I joined too. She was standoffish at first, but I charmed my way into her life with my devastatingly handsome looks and irresistible personality." He grins. "After that, we were inseparable."

"You still haven't told me why you call her *Swallow*." I can't help but ask again.

"Swallow... like the bird. Swallows represent spring, new beginnings, and loyalty. Tess embodies everything that the symbol of a swallow stands for." I absorb what he's telling me. And I have to agree, Tess has been my new beginning, my fresh start, helping me navigate through the pain of my past and giving me hope for the future—our future, together. She can keep the nickname.

"That sounds like my Tess," I murmur as she heads our way with a sly smile. "More wine?" she asks, her voice light and teasing.

We all gather, glasses in hand, and start preparing for the task ahead. All the light-hearted banter fades as we get serious. Bryce pulls out his computer and starts laying out details. It turns out Gabriel works for a private security company that's handling security for Governor Hunt's fundraising event.

My anticipation grows as I listen closely to the unfolding plan. She doesn't know it yet, but I will be deeply involved in this hunt. *Pun intended.* This motherfucker is going down.

CHAPTER 45

Tessa

We've been in Atlanta for the past three days, staying at the Waldorf Astoria, where I booked the penthouse suite. The bustling city has been almost suffocating, but it's given us the perfect cover. The four of us have been doing recon from every angle, analyzing every detail. Now, we're ready. Tonight is the night we make our move.

I smooth the seams of my evening gown. The gray color would match my eyes perfectly if not for the green-colored contacts. I finish curling a strand of my auburn hair into loose waves that cascade down my shoulders. It's a wig. I couldn't bring myself to dye my own, and the woman staring back at me in the mirror looks nothing like me. I went to the spa this morning for a facial and a "makeover." I pretended to be interested in a new makeup brand, so now I have a lovely, painted face I didn't have to apply myself.

Admiring the dress in the mirror, I spin slowly. The strapless gown hugs my curves, and my boobs look amazing. The shimmering fabric is gorgeous with a slit that runs up my left leg, scandalously landing at my upper thigh. I may have to keep this dress. But the three-inch heels? Hell no. My feet will be killing me by the end of the night.

Hearing the bedroom door open, I turn to see Eli enter. His eyes rake over me. "I prefer your blonde hair, but you make a sexy redhead," he says, his voice thick with desire.

"Don't worry, it isn't permanent," I reply breathlessly, unable to keep my eyes off him. He looks dashing in that tux.

"What I want to do to you right now... You can't even imagine. I want to taste those luscious lips more than you know."

"Don't you dare mess up my lipstick!" I protest, pushing my hand against his chest, which is suddenly in my face.

He drops to his knees and smiles wickedly. "Not those lips."

Sliding my dress up to my hips, he plants light kisses along my thighs as he pushes my thong aside. Warmth floods me, and I'm immediately soaking wet for him. He flicks his tongue out, licking at my entrance.

"So responsive for me, aren't you, love?" He groans as his tongue brushes over my clit, and I brace myself against the wall

"Such a pretty pink pussy," he groans, and my knees buckle as my eyes flutter closed, letting the sensations roll over me.

"Eyes on me, Tessa," he growls. I jolt back and look down at him. "Good fucking girl."

He teases me with his mouth and tongue, slipping one finger, then two, inside me. The pressure rises, building. "Oh, God," I call out when Eli bites down on my clit, and I can't stop the orgasm that surges through me like a tidal wave. He eases his fingers in and out as I ride the crest, slowly coming back down.

He laps up my arousal and withdraws his fingers, bringing them to his lips as he sucks them clean. "So sweet, baby," he groans.

He pulls my thong back in place. I reach down for his rock-hard length, but he bats my hand away. "Not now."

"B-but—"

"We have a villain to take down."

I take a deep breath and nod in agreement. How can this man flood my mind and body so completely that I'm distracted from something that's been coming for a long time?

"Swallow! It's time to go, love," Bryce calls loudly from the other room.

Tugging the dress into place, I smooth the fabric with my hands to straighten it.

We're heading out the door when I swear I hear him mutter, "Swallow... I have something you can *swallow* later."

Pulling into the driveway of the obnoxiously large mansion in my rented Range Rover, I'm pleased to see that the fundraising event has attracted a large crowd, which is good for me because I can blend in easily. As far as anyone is concerned, the rental is in the name of Anna Davenport. I climb out of my car and hand my keys to the valet. He's too busy staring at my breasts to take much note of my face—typical man behavior. I inwardly groan and hold back my usual feminist retort. Another man scans the evite invitation on my phone, courtesy of Bryce. It helps to have a hacker for a friend. Tonight, I'm playing the role of the wife of an entrepreneur with new money who is eager to rub elbows with the elites. He nods at me to go through.

There must be nearly five hundred people here. The expansive grounds are littered with men and women dressed to the nines. The butler opens the door, and I enter the foyer. A server carrying a tray of champagne walks by, and I grab a glass. I'm not particularly nervous, but this is a dangerous game I'm playing, and this isn't my typical method of hunting.

"Take a deep breath," a voice sounds in my ear. It's Bryce. A small earpiece keeps me updated with any information I need. I almost feel like I'm in a *James Bond* movie. I catch a glimpse of Gabriel out of the corner of my eye. He looks quite dashing in his security attire. No wonder Bryce fell hard for him.

Most guests are in the large ballroom, but several canopies are set up outside around the expansive inground pool. Perfect white tablecloths and fine dinnerware cover large rectangular tables, probably costing more than my annual salary.

Scanning the crowd, I seek out my stalker, who is conversing with an older couple. Our eyes meet briefly before I look away and continue my search. We decided to arrive separately. I'd hoped he would stay at the hotel with Bryce, but he insisted on attending.

It's inside the ballroom where I find him, William Hunt, the bane of my existence. The monster who stole my innocence and haunted my nightmares.

It's been sixteen years, but he seems to have barely aged. Botox probably. He's about fifteen pounds heavier, but still in good shape for a man in his late fifties. At his side is his loving wife, Tammy. My heart hurts for her. She has no idea what kind of man she lives with. At least, I hope she's unaware. A touch of guilt hits me, knowing the fallout from this will affect her. But he must be stopped. He will not live to see another sunrise. Trying to blend in, I move through the crowd, pausing only briefly to chat with a few guests. But when I head toward the ladies' room, I freeze, and my breath catches in my chest. Before me stands a familiar couple—a man with steel-gray eyes and dark hair streaked with silver, accompanied by a petite blonde wearing a stunning plum-colored evening gown.

It hadn't occurred to me they would be here. Of course, my parents would be at an event like this. Panic surges through me, and I hurry to the restroom. To my relief, it's empty, and I quickly slip into a stall, my stomach tied in knots. If anyone could recognize me, it would be them.

"Bryce," I hiss quietly. "You didn't tell me my parents were on the guest list."

"Shit, I didn't think they were coming. They didn't RSVP. Sorry, Swallow."

Eli's voice cuts in. "Breathe, baby. You've got this. And I'm nearby if you need me."

"I'll check the cameras to make sure no other unexpected guests are here," Bryce responds apologetically.

"Okay, okay. We move forward." I'm not sure who I'm trying to reassure more, them or myself. "It's just that seeing them took me by surprise."

The sound of a door opening startles me, but relief washes over me when I hear a couple of women chatting about the fundraising event. After taking a calming breath, I flush the toilet— which I hadn't used— and move to the sink to wash my hands. Satisfied with my appearance, I head for the door, only to come face to face with a pair of familiar pale blue eyes. I step back, unable to hold her gaze and look away.

"I'm so sorry, dear. I didn't mean to startle you," she says, offering a serene smile as I meet her eyes again.

"No worries," I reply, offering a quick smile as I inch around her and toward the door.

"Wait. Do I know you?"

A knot forms in my throat. "I don't think so." She looks puzzled. It's been ten years since I last saw my mother. She's still slim—only a hundred and twenty pounds soaking wet—but she's aged. Fine lines, wrinkles, and a hint of sadness in her eyes.

"I'm sorry, dear. My mistake. You look so familiar."

Offering a polite yet indifferent smile, I say, "You have a wonderful evening," as I dash out. That was far too close.

I discreetly move to the sidelines to watch the scene. The coordinator speaks into the microphone, praising Hunt and all the generous donations they have received. The speech drones on, but finally, he's introduced and addresses the audience.

My eyes track his every movement as I inch closer to the front of the crowd. Drawing from the two acting classes I took in college, I brace myself for what's coming. It's difficult because just hearing his voice makes my skin crawl.

I saunter forward, letting my hips sway. I want to be sure I'm in his line of sight. The man is a fiend, and will fuck anything that walks, with or without their consent. The thought of William being around children is sickening, he'll have unobstructed access to them and the perfect opportunity to target those that fit his needs and the needs of his clientele. His eyes land on me mid-speech, and I smile slyly as I take a slow sip of my champagne. He pauses briefly, and I don't miss the flare of his nostrils before he continues speaking. I make my way to the bar as he walks offstage. It's hard not to cringe as I feel him staring. *You can do this, Tess.* Pretend this is just some average Creepy Joe looking to get his rocks off.

I'm sipping a martini from the bartender when the scent of cologne hits my nostrils. I stifle a shudder as memories from my childhood flood me.

"Hello, darling. I don't believe we've met," William drawls, his voice thick as molasses. Swallowing, I turn toward him. His blue eyes wander down from my lips to my ample curves.

"Governor Hunt," I gush. "It's such an honor to meet you."

"The pleasure is all mine."

He takes my hand, pressing a light kiss to my knuckles. From all appearances, this is typical gentlemanly behavior that seems innocent in a room full of people. Only I, and maybe the bartender, paid to look the other way, can see the leer in his gaze.

"I'm Anna."

"And who are you here with this evening?" he asks coyly, glancing discreetly around us.

"It's just me tonight. My husband is out of town on business." I finish my martini and pull the olive off the stick, sucking it into my mouth in a move that I hope seems seductive—because now, it's all I can do to keep the contents in my stomach where they belong.

His eyes darken with lust as he watches my every move.

"Hey, William," a gray-haired man calls, beckoning him to join a group of men.

William glances back at me, regret flashing in his eyes, though the lingering lust remains. "It was lovely to meet you, beautiful. Maybe I'll see you again later tonight?"

"I sure hope so," I reply, my tone sultry, as I lightly trail a finger down his arm.

He turns and walks over to join the group of men.

"How are you holding up, Little Killer?" Eli's voice is soft and just hearing that comforting tone eases some of the tension in my body.

"I'm making it," I reply, turning to whisper back as discreetly as I can.

"I'll cut off his fucking hands for touching you."

A thrill shoots up my spine, and I clench my thighs. His possessiveness is just one of the many things I adore about him.

I order another drink, asking the bartender to lighten the alcohol. I sip it slowly, watching the room, waiting for the right moment to reappear. Tammy heads toward the backyard with my mother. Dinner's at nine. Glancing at the enormous grandfather clock, I note it's just after eight.

"It's time," Bryce's voice whispers in my ear.

Spotting William, I casually stroll by, heading toward the patio. I stumble, falling hard into him. My drink sloshes onto the side of his shirt and spills onto the floor. His dark glare is immediate, but he quickly masks it.

I gasp, looking up at him with feigned horror. "Oh my god." Frantically, I pat his shirt with my napkin, trying to clean the mess. "I'm so sorry, Governor."

Hunt gestures for the wait staff to clean the floor and remove my now-empty glass. "Darling, it's fine."

"But I've ruined your shirt. I insist on paying for the dry cleaning," I say, my voice trembling, my eyes filling with fake tears.

"Absolutely not. It's just a shirt. I have thousands more."

"There must be something I can do to make it up to you," I whisper, lowering my voice so only he can hear.

William stares at me for a moment before calling over one of his security team. He whispers to him, and the man gently takes my elbow.

"The Governor wishes to meet with you upstairs in his study." He escorts me down the hall and ushers me into a room I've seen countless times before.

"He will be with you shortly," the guard says curtly, giving a professional nod. I suspect he knows exactly why the boss is pulling me aside. He shuts the door, leaving me in the large room.

I walk over to the shelves lined with law books. There's a door leading to what I know is a private bathroom, and an oversized desk made from a deep cherry wood sits as the focal point of the room. Two chairs face it, and a loveseat sits near the window, draped with heavy champagne-colored curtains.

I perch myself on the edge of his desk, the slit in my dress sliding dangerously high.

The door creaks open, and William steps inside, locking the door behind him. He's changed into a pale blue button-up shirt, similar to the one he wore earlier, and as his eyes scan me, desire flashes through them.

"You said something about repaying me?" he jeers, as he comes to stand in front of me.

I smile mischievously and reach for the straining bulge through his pants. Groaning as I stroke him, his head falls back in pleasure. He moves to grab me, but before his hands can reach me, a cold knife presses against his throat, freezing him in place.

"Shit, it took you long enough," I grumble, my voice void of mirth.

"Sorry, love," Eli says with a grin. He stands behind William, his blade pressed to the man's jugular. "Scream, and I'll gut you like a fucking fish."

"Who are you? What do you want? If it's money, I have plenty in the safe over there." William points behind the desk.

"Money?" I scoff, incredulous. "You think this is about money?"

I tap my nails against the desk. "I have something you might be interested in. May I borrow your laptop?" I ask sweetly. "Well, I suppose I don't have to ask, do I?"

Eli tosses me a pair of latex gloves. I slip them on quickly, then grab the laptop.

"Password?" I demand.

Hunt grunts but stays silent until Eli digs the blade into his neck, breaking the skin. A drop of blood forms. "Alright, alright," he mutters, rattling off the password.

Access granted.

I reach into my bodice, pull out a small disc drive, and insert it into the laptop. A few clicks, and images flash across the screen.

William's eyes widen, and his jaw slackens as evidence of his numerous indiscretions unfolds before him.

"What is this? Blackmail?" he spits out, his face draining of color.

"Something like that," I reply, my voice dripping with satisfaction.

"Now, this is what's going to happen. You'll receive a text with further instructions after midnight. Speak to anyone—anyone—and I mean it, this information goes viral immediately," Eli states, his tone cold and final.

William swallows hard and nods in agreement. "Oh, there's one more thing you should know." I pause for effect, enjoying the fear etched on his face. "Your wife and sons have been dosed with a biochemical agent. It has some rather nasty side effects. If it isn't treated within twelve hours, it will lead to an excruciating death." I'm lying of course, I would never hurt his family.

His face pales further, his lips trembling.

"Don't worry." I pat his cheek twice, feigning sympathy. "I have the antidote. As long as you follow the rules, no harm will come to them. Not a word to anyone, and make sure you come alone. We have eyes and ears everywhere, so don't try anything stupid."

"Understood," he whispers, his voice barely audible.

Eli releases him, and William rubs his neck, his fingers tracing the nick.

"Okay, then. Carry on," I say, clapping my hands together. "You have guests waiting."

CHAPTER 46

Tessa

H unt leaves the room quickly, with not even a backward glance. It's almost comical. I'm not concerned about him staying silent; I've slipped a small listening device on him, just to be safe. Bryce is controlling all the cameras and erasing the evidence of our little excursion. Eli exits through a side door as I reappear at the party. As I pass the security guard who escorted me back, I wink. He smirks, clearly thinking I'm just another one of William's floozies, sucking him off while his wife is mere yards away.

I lock eyes with William, and he looks away quickly, heading outdoors with his guests to sit down for dinner.

Smiling graciously at the men at the door, I offer Gabriel a discreet nod as I move toward the valet for my car. I tip him generously before sliding into the driver's seat as exhilaration pulses through me in waves. My phone rings, and I tap the screen on the navigation.

Bryce's voice comes through the line. "Well, it looks like the plan is working. He has barely touched his food. He hasn't said anything, and based on the cameras, hasn't made any strange gestures or movements."

"And the footage of Eli sneaking in and out of the study?" I ask anxiously.

"Wiped clean and replaced with earlier footage."

"Perfect. I'll see you soon."

Back at our hotel, the elevator dings as I reach the penthouse. Stepping inside, I'm met with the aroma of food. I hadn't realized how hungry I was, and I can't even remember the last time I ate. Breakfast, maybe?

"I ordered food. I know you love steak and fries after a busy day of tormenting people." Bryce smirks.

"You're not wrong."

Grabbing a fry from the plate, I head into the bedroom to change out of the dress, and Eli's pulling on a black tee when I walk in. I march up to him and grab his face, pulling him down for a kiss.

"Now, can you help me out of this gown? Careful, though, I want to keep this one."

"Of course, love."

He unzips the back of my dress, his hands grazing my skin, sending tingles up my spine and leaving goosebumps in their wake. He peppers kisses down the side of my neck before stepping back.

His eyes are filled with desire. "I'll let you handle the rest, or I'll bend you over that bed and fuck that tight little cunt," he says, as he walks out of the room.

My mouth hangs open as I watch him walk away. And here I thought he couldn't resist me. I guess his restraint is better than mine. What a tease. I huff at myself as I dress in dark jeans and a red tank. Maybe it's not the best color to blend in, but it would hide blood pretty well.

I return to the living area and fix a plate, deliberately ignoring Eli, who's sitting on the sofa. Plopping into a chair at the dinette, I slice into my medium-cooked steak—just how I like it. I take a bite and can't stop the moan that slips from my mouth. Well, I probably could've stopped it, but I chose not to. As I take another bite, I glance at Eli. He's staring at me with raw hunger in his eyes. Smirking, I take another bite. Two can play this game.

Bryce is seemingly oblivious to the tension or simply chooses to ignore it. Gabriel has to stay at the Hunt's home until the event ends. It's already eleven, so the party should clear out in the next hour but I'm sure there'll be an after-party for the younger crowd somewhere nearby.

At midnight, the encrypted burner phone vibrates with the text. Seriously, between Bryce and Gabe, their tech beats anything else. Brains and brawn. Together, they could run one hell of a mercenary team. The thought makes me pause as I glance at my best friend. Nah.

"The address has been sent. He'll be there at one. We're ready, Swallow," Bryce says, excitement in his voice, making me glance sideways at him again.

"Here the fuck we go."

Before leaving the room, I don a dark hoodie. Having left the Range Rover two hotels away as a countermeasure, we borrow a black Jeep parked on the second-floor lot. The genius who owned it left the keys in the sun visor.

We arrive at the destination fifteen minutes later. The setting is perfect—secluded and still developing. The three-story building proudly displays *North Atlanta Youth Center*, and trees surround the area, providing cover. We park next to a large work truck, obscuring the jeep from view. Now, we wait.

Shortly before one, headlights appear. A sedan pulls up beside the building. A man steps out, and even in the dark, I can make out his figure. As instructed, he turns off the car but leaves the driver's door open, lighting up the interior to ensure no one else is in the vehicle.

"I'm here," Hunt shouts into the dark. "Now what?"

I approach from behind, shoving a needle into his neck, and he collapses unceremoniously to the ground.

Eli steps out of the shadows, his sniper rifle slung over his shoulder. He's my backup in case anyone unexpected shows up.

Gabriel is also nearby, keeping watch for any suspicious activity. He's here for security, but that's it, as I don't want to drag him any deeper into this.

We check Hunt for weapons, trackers, or anything else that could be traced. The dumb fuck actually listened to us. He's clean. We search the car, but there's nothing—no phone, no devices.

Eli and I haul him to the sectioned-off area that will soon be a gym. For now, it's just a hole for the footer. We chain him to an old wooden cross buried in the ground, barbed wire wound into the chains securing his arms. His head hangs, still unconscious, despite the wire digging into his skin. He's been stripped of all clothing.

I pull out a special contraption designed just for William. As I set it up, I glance at Eli. He looks a little green, realizing what's about to go down. I suppose any man would, given the device's purpose. They're fiercely protective of their... packages.

And once everything's set, I look at the man who created the person I am today. Little did he know he touched the wrong girl. And now I'm no longer a helpless victim. No remorse fills me as I walk over and slap him across the face.

He barely moves. Hmm, maybe I overestimated the dose. I might need to amp things up.

I reach into my bag of tricks, unable to hide the grin spreading across my face as I pull out the yellow gun. I press the trigger, and electricity shoots through his chest. He jolts awake, yelping as the current courses through his body. He looks down at his chest, then at his shackled arms, and finally at the spiked contraption around his shaft. Genuine fear fills his eyes as they dart between Eli and me.

"You," he gasps. "Who are you? Why are you doing this?"

"Oh, Willie boy. You had to know this was coming at some point," I mock, my voice laced with disdain.

"I don't know what you're talking about."

"Sure you do. Don't you remember me?"

I trail my fingers down his side. He jerks, but he can't move more than an inch.

"Ah, ah. Where are you going? I thought you'd enjoy this. Me touching you for a change?"

He shakes his head, nostrils flaring in defiance.

"I don't know what you mean. I've never met you before tonight," he insists.

"Perhaps I could help refresh your memory."

I turn away and remove my contacts. As I spin back around, I pull off the red wig, shaking out my blonde hair. Eli turns on his flashlight, illuminating my face as I turn back to William.

Blood drains from his face as recognition sets in.

"Tessa?"

CHAPTER 47

Tessa

"Tessa," Hunt repeats, his voice full of disbelief as his eyes rake over me. "Tessa Sparks?

I curl my lips in disdain. "The one and only."

"I don't understand. Your parents said you moved away. They haven't heard from you in years."

"All of that is accurate."

His eyes dart over to Eli. "Who are you?"

"The man who loves the woman you stole innocence from," Eli snarls.

"I don't know what she told you, but that's a damn lie."

"You want to try that again, asshole?" Eli grabs William by the throat, squeezing tightly until his face turns purple before releasing him.

"I'm innocent!" he stammers, his gaze dropping to the ground. Poor William is a terrible liar.

"Tsk tsk, come on, William, you know that's not true. You may as well admit what you've done. It isn't going to change the outcome here. It just determines how much pain I choose to put you in before you die. And honestly, what you say doesn't matter because I was there. I've had to live with those nightmares ever since," I add coldly.

I glance down at my fingernails, admiring the glossy red polish, before meeting his gaze once more. "But you know what makes them go away?" I taunt. "Ridding the world of vermin like you."

"I'm not a bad man. I help children." His voice trembles and he looks as though he's on the verge of tears.

"Help them?" I sneer. "Or help yourself to them?"

He looks away.

"So, it's like this: tell us everything you know, and I'll make your death less painful."

"Why would I tell you anything if you're going to kill me anyway?"

"Because isn't it time you redeem yourself?" I ask, my tone laced with contempt. "And this isn't just about you. It's about saving children before they're placed in the hands of pedophiles like you. It's for girls like Paisley."

He looks at me blankly. "Paisley?"

"My fucking sister, asshole!" Eli's patience is wearing thin. Before I can say another word, he's holding a drill, screwing William's left pinky finger into the cross.

Hunt screams in agony. "I don't know a Paisley," he insists.

I grin, savoring every moment of this. Few girls can say their man would torture someone else for them. Kill for them. And at this moment, I know Eli would do anything for me. He's only holding back now because he knows I need to finish this.

As Hunt continues to scream, disgust rolls off me in waves.

"Tick tock. This would be a good time to come clean. How many children have you hurt, just like you hurt me?" I pull out my phone and open the pictures of the evidence we found at Dalton's. Maybe he needs a reminder of what brought him here. I hold the phone in front of his face and scroll through each photo, watching his color drain away.

"How did you get those documents?" he forces out between ragged breaths.

"I have my ways. Did you think your minions wouldn't protect themselves?" I raise an eyebrow. "I guess you should have paid them more."

"Fuck!" he shouts.

"It's quite interesting, this trafficking scheme you seem to be involved in. At first, we thought it was just two girls a year taken from Lake Lucia. But based on the information we've collected, it goes much further than that. It turns out there are two girls in multiple areas of the south that go missing every year, never to be heard from again. Nearly 200 girls in the southeast of the United States, spanning from Miami to Richmond."

"Blondes, brunettes, redheads... I guess everyone has a preference for their own depraved desires," Eli cuts in, his voice sharp and cold, a hint of bitterness lacing his tone.

"Unsurprisingly, it seems to be the blondes that you seek out. What happens to these girls once you're finished playing with them?" I ask, with disgust dripping from every syllable.

Hunt stays silent, just staring at me. The drill churns to life as Eli screws the pinky finger of William's right hand to the cross, and another round of screams fill the air.

"You really should stop fucking around, William."

"You don't want to get involved in this, Tessa," he pants, and I nod at Eli to give him a short reprieve. "There are many important people in play—people far more dangerous than I am. You should quit and walk away now. If you let me go, I can protect you, and it will be like this never happened."

"Walk away?" I snort. "Do you think I can walk away now?"

"You need to. If you mess with the top of this organization, they'll take you and everyone you love down." He nods at Eli.

"Let me worry about that. Now, spill it."

"No, they'll kill my family."

"*I* will kill your family. Or have you forgotten what you came here for? The antidote. So quit dicking around if you want to be sure they live a long life." I press a knife to his throat. He gulps.

"We sell them to the highest bidder when we're finished with them," he spits out, his voice cracking with desperation. "To men and women all over the country—billionaires, cartel leaders, and whoever has the money. They fund my campaign."

I pull the knife away, keeping my fingers firmly gripped on the handle.

"Who all is involved?"

He levels me with a stare. "Maybe the question you should ask is who's not involved?" "I'm getting a little tired of all this back and forth, aren't you, Eli?"

"Yeah, it seems we're getting nowhere."

A look of surprise flashes across Hunt's face. "Wait. Paisley...Elijah... you're a Huntington?"

Eli tilts his head slightly, his expression hardening. "Yes."

William laughs maniacally.

"What the fuck is so funny?" Eli hisses, venom in his tone.

"You're interrogating the wrong person. You should look closer to home, young man."

Eli narrows his eyes. "What's that supposed to mean?"

"I have said all I'm saying." He spits on the ground. "Let's get on with this."

"Well, okay then." It's time to take this to the next level. Shrugging, I reach into my duffel and pull out another syringe, one with the largest gauge needle I have. Slipping on a pair of gloves, I prepare for what comes next. "I don't know if you've noticed this little gadget I have here. It's quite interesting."

Hunt's eyes go wide as he takes in the contraption positioned around his penis. He struggles to escape, but he knows there's nowhere to go. He's visibly shaking as I walk toward him.

Wasting no time, I reach for his microscopic penis, and I insert the needle directly into the shaft.

"Motherfucker! What did you do?" he hisses, sweat running down his face as his dick shrinks even further.

"Have you ever used the little blue pill, William? I mean, I'm sure you have to these days if you're going to get it up for the wife. Since I imagine that you can only get a hard-on from little girls."

"The medication I just administered is nearly three times as potent as that little pill, and it works quickly," I inform him nonchalantly. "I gave you far more than the recommended dose, old man."

"What?" he screams as a look of horror spreads across his face. "No!"

"Tape, love?" I ask Eli. He pulls off two strips and hands them to me.

I attach each piece to his right upper and lower eyelids, and Eli matches my movements with William's left eyelid.

"We can't have you missing out on anything, Governor Hunt. Enjoy the show."

Backing away, I curve my body into Eli's. He grabs my chin, and I see the flash of hunger in his eyes before he slams his lips down onto mine. There are no slow or languid movements; his tongue possesses mine. He kisses down my cheek, his hands slowly moving to my lower back to cup my rear, pulling me against his hardening shaft. The kiss goes on for several seconds. Breathlessly, we pull apart, and his eyes lock onto mine intently.

"Are you watching this, William?" Eli drawls, never breaking eye contact with me. "Notice how responsive she is to me. Do you see how she wants me to put my hands on her? This is what it looks like when a woman wants you." Jesus. It's all I can do not to jump him right here. My panties are soaked.

A painful grunt sounds out, pulling my eyes in Hunt's direction.

Eli smiles sinisterly. "You're pitching a tent over there, I see."

As William's erection grows, spikes of the torture device begin to dig into his shaft, and a slow stream of blood splatters onto the ground.

Drip. Drip. I'm transfixed. Eli turns me to face William, and I lean my head back against his chest as one hand finds a pebbled nipple. A moan escapes me as he pinches it. His other hand slides down my belly and into my jeans. He slides a finger into my wet folds as his thumb rubs circles around my clit. I clasp my arm around his neck and arch into him, shamelessly grinding my cunt against his fingers.

"Oh, oh yes." My knees weaken as I feel the orgasm rapidly building, much faster than I expected given the situation, but that's what Eli does to me. Even in the presence of the man I despise the most, a mere touch from Eli has my body humming in response.

Hunt is unable to avert his gaze from the show we're giving him.

Eli bites down on my earlobe. "Are you going to come on my fingers, Tess?"

"Yes, yes... I'm coming, I'm coming, Eli," I shout as waves of pleasure shoot through my body. He allows me to come back down from the high before he slows his movements, and I feel him smiling against my neck.

"Such a good fucking girl." He pulls his fingers out of me and rubs my juices across my lower lip before sucking them into his mouth.

With a popping sound, he pulls his fingers back out.

"No! Please no!" William stares down in horror as his fully erect penis is shredded, blood squirting down his groin and legs. He lets out a series of bone-chilling screams.

"For fuck's sake, will you man up already?" Eli shoves a ball gag into William's mouth.

"Damn, that was hot, E."

"If that was impressive, you should see what I have in mind next." He winks.

He pulls out a container of clear liquid.

I let him take over, intrigued to see what my man has planned next. He uses a plunger to draw up the liquid before dropping several ounces of fluid over William's shredded and bleeding shaft. His body convulses violently as tears stream down his face.

I walk over for a closer inspection.

"Sulfuric acid?" I ask. "Nice."

"This is for putting your filthy hands where they never belonged." Eli lifts the container and pours the acid over each of William's arms strapped to the cross. He then uses the plunger to squirt the acid into his eyes. William's body shudders violently, any screams he might have uttered are restricted by the gag in his mouth. "And that was for looking at what's mine to begin with."

CHAPTER 48

Tessa

I sit on the edge of the truck, watching as Eli backs the concrete truck toward the edge of the footer.

After William lost consciousness, I started an intravenous line, administering a full liter of normal saline to keep him hydrated longer. He's also receiving oxygen through a nasal cannula connected to a small portable tank.

We can't have him leaving this earth just yet.

Eli climbs out of the truck and turns the machine on, the rumble of the cement mixer humming steadily. I still find myself in awe of him as I watch him work. No wonder he has the honed body he does. He lifts hundred-pound bags of concrete mix as if they weigh nothing. I offered to help, but he wouldn't allow it—such a gentleman. With a contented sigh, I hop down, start cleaning up our mess, and toss the duffle into the passenger side of the truck.

We meet at the cross. I pull the ball gag from William's mouth, and he stirs, groaning. After removing the IV line, I toss the used medical equipment into the dirt behind him, no longer needing any of it.

"Any final words, Governor? Speak now if you want your wife and children to live."

He mumbles under his breath and coughs.

"What? What was that?" I yank the cock torture device, effectively castrating his penis and slap him across the face with what's left of his mutilated dick.

"Uncle!" he screams, his voice hoarse and broken.

"Yeah, yeah, you're crying uncle. Are you going to spit it out or not?"

"H—h—his uncle," Hunt finally spits out. "Walker. Alvin Walker."

Eli stills and then curses under his breath. "Motherfucker."

I reach for him, but he pulls away. Anguish etched deeply across his face. "I need a minute," he says, as he steps toward his truck and tightly grips the tailgate.

I pause and give him the space he needs. Having met none of my extended family, I can only imagine what he must be feeling—the hurt, the betrayal. The more we discover, the more questions we have. And Allie.

Oh God. Allie is going to be destroyed, and the timing couldn't be worse. She's so close to her dad. Alvin always seemed like a good guy, a good husband, and a good father. But looks can definitely be deceiving. I would know—I had to learn that the hard way.

Eli walks back over, and I lay a hand on his arm. He gives me a tight nod, signaling he's okay for the moment. Standing on my tiptoes, I kiss his cheek before releasing his arm.

We have one last task to complete.

Eli starts digging into the dirt at the base of the cross with a shovel, loosening the ground until the wood is free enough for us to lift it—and William—out of the ground. We lay the cross flat in the dirt, with him looking upwards. I smirk.

He could make a snow angel—or a dirt angel—if he could move his legs. I grab the shovel and toss dirt across his torso and extremities, saving his head for last.

"I hope you're ready for hell, you sick bastard. Let Lucifer know I'll see him when I get there." I don't bother to restrain the venom in my tone. I've never meant anything more in my life.

Burying him alive seems like the perfect endgame for a monster like Hunt. The concrete starts running out of the truck, inching closer to him. I climb out before it can reach my feet.

It doesn't take as long as I thought it would for the concrete to engulf his body and fill the footer. Eli smooths the mixture as I watch in silence. I welcome the peacefulness already seeping into my body. It's a beautiful night—clear skies, stars shining brightly. Everything feels more alive, more vivid. Lighter. The air is cleaner, as if a huge weight had been lifted off my shoulders. A burden I knew I carried, but hadn't realized how heavy it was.

Eli turns the machine off and parks the truck where it previously sat before heading my way. I give a final look back before climbing in with Gabriel. He's waiting for us at the exit, and we follow him back to the hotel, where we return the Jeep we stole. I'm careful to ensure we've left nothing behind. Heading to the hotel on foot, I leave Gabriel and Eli to dispose of William's vehicle.

Throwing my hoodie back on to cover my face—and possibly any blood splatters on my shirt—I sneak up the backstairs to the third floor before taking the elevator up to the suite. I slide the key card over the door scanner and enter the foyer.

"Bryce?" I get no answer. It's strange. It's oddly quiet in a room that would usually be boisterous. I enter the living area and freeze.

Standing beside Bryce, who is sitting on the couch with a solemn look on his face, is a handsome dark-haired man with deep, amber-colored eyes.

Instantly, my pocketknife is in my hands. Just as quickly, the man has a gun out, pointed in my direction.

"Who is this?" I aim my question at Bryce.

"He's with the FBI."

"You're going to want to put that away," the man says, turning his weapon toward Bryce.

Caught off guard, I'm not sure I could take him.

"Okay, don't hurt him." I slide the switchblade into my back pocket. "He's done nothing wrong."

"That's yet to be determined. Take a seat on the couch with your friend."

"You can take your gun off us. I'm not going to do anything."

The agent eyes me suspiciously before lowering the gun. "We have some things to talk about."

"Okay." I side-eye Bryce, trying to glean anything I can from him.

Eli and Gabriel should be back any moment now and Bryce's phone is on the end table to the right. I discreetly try to inch my hand toward it. If I could warn them, we could keep them out of whatever this is, but I have to find a way to distract him.

"Did he show you his badge?" Bryce shakes his head. "How can we be sure he's really a fed?" I ask Bryce.

The man raises an eyebrow before flashing his badge at me.

Fuck. He's actually who he says he is. I take a deep breath, thinking of a way to get us out of this. But first, I need to know what he knows.

"What do you want to kn—" I break off as I hear the suite door opening. My stomach drops, dread creeping up and tightening inside me. The guys are joking about something, and Eli carries a fast-food bag in his hand.

Seeing us, he pauses and sets the bag on a side table. "Jonah?" His eyes widen with recognition, and a broad smile spreads across his face. Eli walks toward the agent and wraps him in a bear hug.

I'm pretty sure my jaw is touching the floor. What's happening right now? Am I in an episode of *Black Mirror*? Bryce is also eyeing Gabriel and Eli in confusion.

"Elijah, man, it's been too long," the agent says, returning the embrace wholeheartedly.

"Elijah." My voice is tight with tension. "What's going on?"

"This is Jonah Miles. My old Navy buddy." Eli gestures toward me, before turning to the man who apparently is his 'friend'. "Jonah, this is Tess."

"Did you know he was coming?" I grit out as my eyes narrow.

"Yeah, I called him."

"I didn't realize he'd get here this quickly, though," Eli adds, looking at me apologetically.

"You knew who I was? And you still put on that show?" I growl. Jonah shrugs, unfazed by my anger. Which pisses me off more.

"I'm sorry I sprung this on you, Tess, but hear him out," Eli says, reaching for my hand and squeezing it tightly.

Jonah follows the movement, looking back at me with renewed interest, something unreadable in his eyes.

"My unit was called in after the murder of Wilson Randall. We have reason to believe Dalton Jones is responsible, as he's disappeared after your cousin's attack."

"And you think he came here? To Atlanta?" I ask.

"Not exactly. This is just one of several locations we're looking into. To be honest, I need your help. I know you've all been investigating this, and from what Eli shared with me, you found evidence at Dalton's that ties in with a case I've been working on for the last couple of years."

"What case is that?" My heart is racing, my hands feel tingly, and my face is surely draining of color. I try to slow my breathing and keep my expression neutral.

"Most of this is classified, but since I'm in the room with all of you involved in nefarious activity, I assume I can trust your silence. If not for me, then for Eli." Jonah takes a breath. "We've been working on locating the missing girls, and most recently, I've reopened Paisley's case."

Surprise furrows my brow, and I look at Jonah with renewed interest. "The case has been reopened?"

He nods his head in response, his eyes lingering for a moment on each of us. "Yes. I don't know why any of you are here or what you're doing, but I need to see those photos and the zip drive."

"Bryce, show him what you have," I respond.

"Sure thing." He releases a breath I know he's been holding, starting to look more like himself.

"We've got this, love. Go grab that shower you mentioned earlier." Eli looks at me intently, silently urging me to leave the room. His eyes dart to my arm, where my hoodie has rolled up. I spot a speck of blood on my wrist and quickly pull the sleeve back down.

"Okay... but I'll be back soon."

Freshly showered, I dress in comfortable clothes, and head back into the living room when I hear the hushed voices of Eli and Jonah. I peer out, noting both Bryce and Gabriel have retired to their room. Relief floods me, but it lasts only momentarily as I hear Jonah bring up William's name.

"So, the governor is involved. That likely means multiple other powerful people have their hands in this. I need to have him brought in for questioning."

"No," Eli says sternly.

"No?" Jonah says incredulously. "Eli, he could be the key to everything."

"This was the part I told you that you have to trust me about. You won't find answers with him."

Yeah, it's hard to interrogate a dead man.

Eli and Jonah face off for a moment until it's Jonah who relents. "Okay. Is there anything else I need to know?"

"I need you to look into the warehouse in these photos."

Jonah glances through the pictures before looking up at him.

"That warehouse belongs to my Uncle Alvin." I go over to wrap my arm around Eli. He squeezes me back and presses a kiss to my forehead.

"Speaking of showers, it's my turn. Excuse me for a moment, J?"

"Of course, man. I'll just get acquainted with your girlfriend."
Jonah smirks at his friend in jest.

"If you weren't my friend, you'd be a dead man right now," Eli
replies.

Jonah throws up his hands in mock-surrender as Eli leaves the
room.

"I was about to make some coffee. Would you like some?" I ask,
heading toward the small kitchenette.

"Coffee sounds wonderful."

We both sit in silence, waiting for the brew to finish. When it's
ready, I pour us each a cup.

"Cream? Sugar?"

"I'm good, thanks."

I add both cream and sugar to mine. It's not my favorite brand,
but at this moment, coffee is coffee. I'm not sure how much longer
I can keep my eyes open.

I take a sip and feel Jonah's eyes on me. Unfazed, I meet his gaze.
Something akin to respect flashes in his eyes.

"I've known Eli for a long time and never seen him like he is with
you. He loves you."

"Is this the 'if you hurt him, you'll have to answer to me' talk?"
I say with a light laugh. "You have nothing to worry about. I never
thought I'd find someone to spend my life with, but I did. He's
the one. He can't get rid of me if he tries." I smile, knowing my
emotions are written all over my face. I can hide many things, but
my feelings for Eli are not one of them.

Jonah nods and raises his mug in toast, and I clink mine against
his. It seems we've come to some sort of understanding. I know
in my bones he has his suspicions, but I also feel he has the same

mindset I do—he just follows closer to the black lines, whereas I'm clearly in the gray.

Three days later, Eli and I are back in Lake Falls after bidding Bryce and Gabriel farewell. As much as I hated to see Bryce go, I didn't want to keep dragging him into my madness. He and his partner deserve a nice, happy life, free from worry that the FBI will come knocking at their door—something Eli and Jonah have assured me won't happen. Eli admitted on the ride back Jonah is very aware of Bryce's hacking skills and is choosing to look the other way which makes my respect for him grow even deeper.

As for the investigation, Jonah and his team have opened a task force, welcomed by the sheriff's department, who willingly agreed to their help. Sheriff Randall wants closure for his son's death, and I feel a small amount of regret for that. But Wilson was crooked, and his demise was a long time coming.

William Hunt was reported missing yesterday. Shortly after, the Atlanta PD received an anonymous document with evidence of his involvement in the missing girls. His car was found in a rental lot near Atlanta-Hartsfield airport and a man matching his description was seen on camera. A last hurrah from my dear friend, I suppose, before he goes back to being a law-abiding citizen. It's believed Hunt fled to his private home in Morocco. The press has a variety of conspiracy theories floating around on all media platforms. Some have speculated that William had Dalton killed.

Alvin Walker has also been arrested and is being arraigned for his involvement in the kidnappings as well as the murder of Paisley

Huntington. The police showed up at his home with a search warrant and took him into custody. Allie called me in distress and shortly after had to be taken to the emergency department to treat her panic attack. I've been checking in with her multiple times a day; sometimes, I get a response, and other times, I don't. She's retreating further into herself. They discharged her back to her parent's house with lorazepam and a sleep aid. I'll be there for her, and I can't fail her again. As much as I hate watching from afar, I feel I need to let Jonah and his partners complete the investigation so we can find all the answers.

The man who broke into my house remains an enigma, his identity still a mystery that haunts me. The case has gone unsolved. A flicker of uncertainty remains, yet I hold onto the hope one day the truth will surface, and the pieces will finally fall into place.

Despite all the heaviness, Eli and I continue to grow closer—soulmates—we were destined to be, even when we didn't believe in it ourselves. We're leaving soon to go to the local home department store. I have a few more white rose bushes that need to be planted.

Epilogue

Three Months Later

Rolling onto my back, I let the sun's warmth soak into my skin, the soft cushions of the lounge chair molding perfectly to my body. A gentle breeze plays with my hair. Utter bliss washes over me as I listen to the waves, their soft hiss and powerful roar weaving a symphony along the sandy shore.

A shadow falls across me, and I squint up to see Eli's silhouette against the bright light. Saltwater drips from his hair, trailing down his tanned chest and defined abs. My gaze traces the sharp v-line that vanishes beneath his swim trunks.

Eli smirks, a self-satisfied glint in his eyes as I lick my lips nervously. "See something you like, baby?"

"Maybe."

He feigns a wounded look before a wicked grin stretches across his face. In the next instant, he hauls me up and over his shoulders.

Squealing as he tilted me upside down, I gasp, "Eli!" I playfully punch his ribs as he strides toward the water, undeterred, and then—without warning—tosses me in. I sputter as I surface, cool water dripping from my soaked hair.

Laughing, he pulls me close and presses his lips to mine before moving to nip at my earlobe. "Have I told you how amazing you look in this bikini?"

"No, I don't think you have," I tease, slipping from his grasp. "Race you to the sandbar!"

Before he can respond, I dive into the waves. With strong, smooth strokes, I swim as fast as I can, but I sense Eli gaining on me—then, effortlessly, he slips past.

Emerging from the water, I shoot him a glare, and he just grins. I'm competitive, and I hate losing.

Moving closer, he murmurs, "Don't pout, baby. It's okay for me to be better than you at something."

Nestling into him, I wrap my arms around his neck and my legs around his waist. "I know a lot of things you excel at."

I lean in, tracing the outline of his lower lip before biting down gently. His tongue flicks out to meet mine, and they tangle together in a slow, intoxicating dance until we're both gasping for air.

"We'd better stop," he says, voice husky, "or I'm going to take you right here, right now, in front of all these guests."

His expression burns with longing, a deeper emotion flickering beneath it. I feel the hardness of his arousal pressing against me, and though I ache to let him make good on his promise, I'd rather not traumatize the other patrons scattered along the pristine white sand.

Surveying our surroundings, I sigh. "I suppose you're right." I rest my forehead against his, willing my racing heart—and the insistent throbbing in my core—to settle.

He rubs slow circles over the small of my back, then meets my gaze with intensity. "I love you, Tessa. Forever and always."

"I love you, too, Eli." And I do. More than I ever thought I could love someone. He is a part of my soul now. Without him, I'd be a broken mess.

We head back to shore, and once the water becomes shallow enough, I reach for his hand. Fingers intertwined, we make our way to the lounge chairs.

Settling back, I catch sight of a young family nearby. A little girl and her toddler brother are playing in the sand, giggling as they build a lopsided castle.

"Mommy, look!" the girl calls as their mother, watching with a soft smile, praises their work.

The boy squeals with excitement. "Daddy, Daddy!" He is covered in sand from head to toe as he runs to his father, who is glued to his phone. The child launches himself into the man's lap.

"John! Look what you did," the man barks, roughly shoving the boy into his wife's arms as he scrambles to save his phone, cursing like a sailor. The child's eyes well with tears as he clings to his mother.

"Henry, you scared him," she says, her voice wavering. "He's just a child."

The man's face twists with anger and disgust as he leans in close to her. "I've told you to handle the kids. Now look at me. I'm covered in sand, and so is my phone. Fuck. I'm going back to the room. Be ready for dinner in an hour. I have a client to meet."

"I—I'm sorry," she stammers out. "Of course. We'll be up soon." She quickly averts her gaze as he stomps away, heading toward the hotel.

A slow rage boils inside me, and I'm halfway out of the lounger when Eli's hand clamps around my arm, pulling me back. I shoot him an exasperated look, but he leans in, whispering, "We don't know the full situation yet. Don't jump to conclusions, Tess. There are witnesses."

Fuck. He's right. But after everything with Allie, I'm a little more easily triggered. Drawing in a deep breath, I give a reluctant nod.

Glancing back at the family, I see the woman usher her children toward the water, gently rinsing the sand from the toddler's limbs while the girl splashes nearby.

Her things are left unattended on the beach, and when my eyes meet Eli's, we exchange a silent conversation. I rise from the lounger and walk toward them, stepping into the shallows, letting the waves swirl around my ankles.

"Oh my gosh," I say, beaming. "Your son is adorable."

The woman startles slightly before offering me a weary but polite smile. "Thank you."

I wave at the little boy. "Hi."

He hides behind his mother's leg before offering me a shy grin.

That's when I see it—the dark purple bruise beneath her right eye. She'd tried to cover it with makeup, but the heat and saltwater betrayed her.

That bastard.

I've seen all I need to see. I'll make him pay.

Pasting on a bright smile, I bid farewell and stroll back to where Eli's packing up our things. Leaning down to grab my beach bag, I whisper, "Did you get it?"

A smug smile spreads across his face as he flashes the key card at me. "Did you doubt me?"

"Never, Stalker."

An hour later, we sit on the patio of the resort's restaurant and bar. I take a slow sip of wine, eyes locked on my prey.

Henry and his family are at a nearby table. The kids color while their parents entertain an older couple. The men laugh loudly, drinking as though the island might run dry.

Any moment now, Henry is going to have a very bad time.

It wasn't hard to find out his food preferences—he ordered the same meal every night. The resort had to special-order his favorite brand of caviar. It hadn't been difficult to spike it with a potent laxative.

I savor my filet, cooked medium, with a twice-baked potato, while Eli polishes off his shrimp and grits. The food here is excellent—my compliments to the chef.

Eli takes a sip of his beer, watching as their food arrives. "Shouldn't be long now."

Grinning, I sit back, waiting for the show.

Within minutes, Henry's face turns green. He clutches his stomach, looking around desperately. Mumbling something about being right back, he bolts toward the hotel. His tablemates watch him go with mild concern before shrugging and returning to their conversation.

Finishing my wine, I place the glass down as Eli drops several bills on the table. As we leave, we follow Henry's staggering retreat toward the resort.

"Are you ready to play, Little Killer?" Eli asks.

A wicked grin spreads across my face. "It's game time, motherfucker."

ACKNOWLEDGEMENTS

Honestly, I can't believe I actually did this. As a longtime reader, I've always wanted to write a novel of my own. There are so many people I have to thank for helping me turn this dream into a reality.

First and foremost, I have to thank my husband. He didn't even blink when I told him I wanted to write a book, and he's patiently put up with the hundreds of hours I've spent in front of my laptop. He's been my biggest supporter and put up with a lot during this process, including answering my endless random questions about 'guy stuff.' Not once did he let me give up. I love you, babe.

Secondly, I have to thank my author mama, Lori. I would have never made it this far without you guiding and mentoring me. You've read this manuscript almost as many times as I have. Without the encouragement, constructive criticism, and kindness you offered me during this process, I may have never brought these characters to life. I'll be forever grateful that fate led our paths to intertwine, and I'm blessed to call you my friend.

To my son Cole, you are my whole world and the best thing I ever did. Though you never asked what Mama was writing about, that is probably for the best. I love you to the moon and back.

To my alphas, I'm so thankful to each one of you. Jennifer, you've been there with me from the beginning to the end. Emily, my dear cousin, you gave me many good suggestions and listened to my endless ideas. Chloe, I don't even know how to thank you enough.

To my betas, Lori, Angelica, and Briana, you three are amazing humans. You all tore into my manuscript and helped shape it into what it is today. Lori, I'll forever support you in anything and everything you do. Angelica, I can't wait to see what story you bring to life. You've got this girl.

To Jess and Jenny D, thank you for inspiring me to pursue this author thing. Everything in life happens for a reason, and I wish you both nothing but the best.

To my editor, Samantha, thank you for investing your time in my manuscript and guiding me through the editing process. I know it was a lot of work.

To my proofreader, Jan, I'm so grateful to have connected with you; your support has been invaluable.

Thank you to anyone not explicitly mentioned above who helped me bring Depraved Truths to life.

Last but certainly not least, thank you to my readers—to each of you who gave this new author a chance. All I've ever wanted was to put something into the universe that people would enjoy. I hope you have loved this story and the characters as much as I adored writing them.

About The Author

Emmy Wade, making her writing debut, lives in Georgia with her husband and their three energetic golden retrievers. After her only child left for college, she faced the challenge of empty nest syndrome and focused that energy on pursuing her dream of writing a novel. A lover of many genres, Emmy is particularly drawn to dark romance, which influences her writing style. For information on future projects and to get sneak peeks of Allie's upcoming story, be sure to sign up for her newsletter at www.emmywadebooks.com and follow Emmy on social media accounts:

Instagram: @emmywade_author
Facebook: Emmy Wade, Author
TikTok: @emmywade-author
Email: Emmywadeauthor@gmail.com

www.ingramcontent.com/pod-product-compliance
Lightning Source LLC
Chambersburg PA
CBHW050017120726
47903CB00006B/1800